"The truth," she repeated.

Stephi's life was at stake, and Zoe would not be made to run away.

"Swear to me that you are not my husband, that you have never seen me, that you know nothing of our life or our babies or—"

"I swear it."

She shook her head, still unable to take her eyes off him.

It was true, then. He knew nothing of who he really was or what they had shared. Or else her memories had betrayed her, and she was only seeing in the face of a stranger what she wanted to see. Tears pricked at her eyelids and clogged her throat, and she lashed out at him for not being who she needed most.

"It seems I owe you an apology, signor doctor. I thought your voice was the one I hear in my dreams. Was I so wrong?"

His eyes fixed on hers. The weight of the world seemed to rest on his shoulders, and they slumped. He shook his head slowly. "You have the power to make me wish it were all true, signora."

Dear Reader,

Do you remember Florence Nightingale? The mystique, the drama, the romance of a woman in the trenches, fighting overwhelming odds to save the lives of real flesh-and-blood men? In my heart, a certain fascination about men and women in medicine lingers. For in medicine, the aura of boldness and sensuality, of dark secrets of life and death and the power to control them, abides. The excitement takes hold, as fresh and vivid now as for the medicine men and women of our ancestors.

Doctors have always been my heroes. Having spent twenty years in laboratory medicine, living the real-life, day-to-day drama of it all, I wanted to write about these heroes and heroines, our modern-day healers, caught up in their passion for saving lives, wrapped up in mystery and in danger and intrigue, and of course, falling in love.

So, welcome to my PULSE trilogy! *Breathless* is the second medical thriller in the series and *Heart Throb* will be available in May, 1995. I hope you love the stories.

Sincerely,

Carly Bishop

Breathless
Carly Bishop

Harlequin Books

TORONTO • NEW YORK • LONDON
AMSTERDAM • PARIS • SYDNEY • HAMBURG
STOCKHOLM • ATHENS • TOKYO • MILAN
MADRID • WARSAW • BUDAPEST • AUCKLAND

To Charlie, who demanded a Sicilian hero

With special thanks to Ronald Foglietti
for his kind assistance with the language and culture

ISBN 0-373-22319-6

BREATHLESS

Copyright © 1995 by Cheryl McGonigle

Printed in U.S.A.

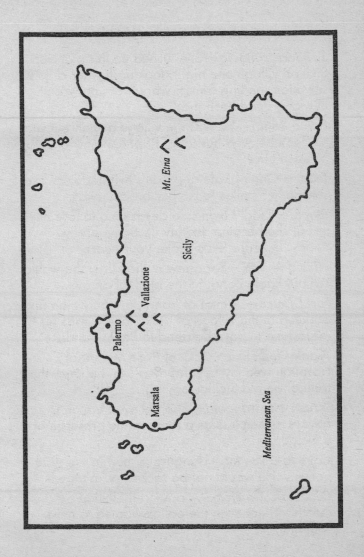

CAST OF CHARACTERS

Zoe Mastrangelo—She turned up in an ancient Sicilian village one night, looking for her child's salvation, finding a man who swore he wasn't her long-dead husband.

Paolo Bondi—He was the village doctor, but was he Zoe's beloved husband, Raphael Mastrangelo, or wasn't he?

Teddi—One of Rafe and Zoe's twin toddlers...so solemn her smiles took your breath away.

Stephi—Teddi's twin...so devastated to lose her papa, she became deathly ill. So naturally happy, her rare tears broke your heart.

Nicola Peretti—For a few million lira, she would sell out Paolo Bondi in the blink of an eye.

Turi Difalco—A man of honor, a family man and barkeep in the village of Vallazione, it was his misfortune to have befriended Paolo Bondi.

Frank Clemenza—CEO of Rose Memorial Hospital, wealthy beyond measure, he *knew* the truth of an old Sicilian saying...

Teresa Mastrangelo—She believed a man is always as helpless as a lamb in the presence of a woman.

Cavallo—The most dangerous man in the state police... He would not be tricked or escaped.

Giancarlo De Sica—A powerful Sicilian merchant, not even the police wanted to mess with him.

Chapter One

The *Persephone* bobbed gently at anchor, far enough from the southeastern coast of Sicily to make Mount Etna seem a hazy, purple cone, not so far that Zoe Mastrangelo could not make out the smoke writhing from its mouth. The seas were still and blue as sapphires, idyllic. Restful. Romantic.

But the smoke seemed a constant threat, and Zoe couldn't seem to shake the vague uneasiness such a threat stirred in her.

She stood alone at the railing on the upper deck of the yacht, clad in a white linen sarong, feeling the intense, unrelenting heat of the late afternoon Mediterranean sun. Rafe was napping with their two-year-old twins, Stephi and Teddi.

Zoe knew Rafe would laugh at her premonitions, teasing that his native Sicilian tendency to melodrama had begun to overtake her naive American optimism.

Raphael Mastrangelo—surgeon, husband, father of her beautiful babies. Even his name whispered romance in her heart. His magnificent, powerful body kindled fires in her hotter than Mount Etna had ever spilled.

Zoe closed her eyes and turned her face to the burning sun. Her love for Rafe felt like that. Maybe it was particularly Sicilian to be suspicious of pleasure this keen. How could it last? Even the spewing, red-hot lava of the fearsome volcano eventually cooled.

"Zoe, my dear. Have you enjoyed your vacation aboard the *Persephone* so far?"

Zoe's eyes snapped open. Arriving soundlessly in his expensive deck shoes and pristine white shorts and shirt, Frank Clemenza startled her, setting her nerves on edge.

"Very much, Frank," she murmured, taking a deep breath to calm her irrational feelings. She and Rafe and the twins were the guests of Clemenza and his cousin, His Eminence, Bishop Vincenti Rosario, "Centi" to all who knew him, whose family fortune was reflected in the opulence of this yacht. "We all love it, but you are too generous."

"To the contrary, my dear. I am a selfish man, and superstitious in the extreme. Debts of family and honor must be paid."

He rested his thick, hairy forearms on the railing beside her and focused his eyes far out to sea. Zoe found herself searching his face for traces of the damage Rafe had surgically repaired—the debt to which he referred.

No hint remained that Frank Clemenza had ever been mugged and beaten only three blocks from Sacred Heart Medical Center, half a world away, in Chicago.

Clemenza's gratitude knew no bounds. Rafe was not only the surgeon who had performed this miracle, he was a fellow Sicilian, respected, even liked, by mainland Italians. Zoe was not only Rafe's wife, but the niece of Sister Mary Bernadette Reilly, administrator of Sacred Heart and one of Bishop Vincenti Rosario's oldest friends.

Centi had dipped into his family fortune on more than one occasion to save the hospital from a buyout by the public sector, and Frank managed all the hospital's investments, trusts and pension funds on Centi's behalf.

Zoe had never completely trusted Clemenza, but she knew this feeling followed Mary Bernadette's sentiment. When she retired at the end of the year, Frank Clemenza would assume the helm of Sacred Heart. The hospital would cease to be an institution run by Mary Bernadette's order of nuns.

"Anyway. I came to tell you that I have been summoned to an important meeting in New York. There is a flight leaving Catania tonight."

"Centi is able to stay?" Zoe asked.

"Yes. I represent all his business interests, you know, not only those of Sacred Heart."

She had come to know the extent of Frank's involvement in the bishop's affairs only in the past few days. "Can we return to Catania by the time—"

"No. There's no need, in any case. I've called ship-to-shore for a helicopter. Your family and Centi must stay and return in three days' time as planned."

A hot breeze wafted over Zoe. "That's very generous of you, Frank."

He smiled briefly. "I've a feeling your twins would be brokenhearted if Centi left as well . . . as would Centi himself, for that matter. Zoe . . . I hope you have not been unduly upset by the tension between the bishop and me in the past several hours."

Zoe shaded her eyes to look at Frank. "Tension" hardly described the argument or its aftermath. It had to do with Bishop Rosario's estate, but she knew nothing of the particulars. Harsh words had erupted at the breakfast table, but Frank and the bishop had continued their disagreement behind closed doors.

"Don't give it another thought," she answered, smiling. "I've lived with Rafe long enough to know a day isn't complete in a Sicilian household without one really good shouting match."

Frank laughed. "True enough."

"Centi has seemed ... not quite himself since this morning, though."

Frank angled his head. The harsh sunlight was not kind to his coarse complexion. "This shouting match, as you say, is one that leaves him disturbed. However, I cannot allow him to kiss off an eighty-million-dollar fortune. Properly handled, the interest alone could fund his charities for the next several centuries."

Zoe wondered if that meant Clemenza could only inherit what he managed to keep Centi from giving away. "Isn't it his money to do with as he pleases?"

"Of course." His brow creased. "But with every passing year, Centi's judgment becomes more clouded with sentiment than even he knows is wise. This past week has been especially hard on him."

"With us, you mean?" Zoe asked, surprised. "In the time we have all been together?"

"Yes," Clemenza answered. "Centi is growing old. His options in life are closing off at a terrible rate. The twins, and you and Rafe, have made him regret again all that he has sacrificed to his vocation."

His features softened, and he smiled, though pleasure never seemed to reach his eyes. "A wife, children, grandchildren. Surely you've noticed how he watches you and Rafe together ... and your little daughters."

Zoe smiled. The bishop did take enormous pleasure in the twins. Only this morning his eyes lit with pleasure as he watched them playing in the wading pool with Rafe before breakfast, their dark hair plastered in wet ringlets to their sun-kissed cheeks and delicate little necks. Chubby knees and baby-flat feet and little bodies garbed in bathing suits with row upon row of tiny colorful ruffles.

He'd watched one of the twins paddling crazily, round and round the pool. "What is Teddi doing?"

"Making herself dizzy," Zoe had answered, smiling.

Centi had laughed until he cried, applauding Teddi's antics until Stephi was induced to compete with even sillier things. Teddi was the one, Centi had said, who was so solemn that her rare, dazzling smile took your breath away, while Stephi was so naturally ebullient that her still-rarer tears were certain to break your heart.

Zoe stared at small waves slapping gently at the pristine white hull of the yacht. A few scattered clouds passed in front of the sun, and the sky reflected the incredible blue of the sea.

"The bishop must have known many bittersweet moments of sacrifice in his life," she replied at last. "But I can't imagine that he truly regrets the way his life has been spent."

Frank shook his head at her, not bothering to hide his sardonic smile. "You are only what? Thirty?"

"Twenty-seven."

"Twenty-seven," he echoed, as if he had been reminded of what he already knew. "Forgive me for saying so, Zoe, but you have not lived long enough to know that every life is filled with such bitter regret. I am twice your age and Centi three times."

She shrugged. Mary Bernadette, who was her aunt and had raised Zoe from the age of seven when her mother had died, suffered no such regrets from a life in her religious order. But Frank certainly knew Centi far better than Zoe did. Perhaps he was right, even in this.

"I hope that Rafe and I and the babies give Centi more joy than cause for regrets."

"Overall, I'm certain you do, Zoe," Frank said in a voice that struck her as vaguely patronizing. "Still, he would give up the family fortune for the chance to have lived another life. It can't be done, and yet that's what he wants to do. Do you see my quandary?''

Zoe nodded. "I do, Frank. But—"

He wiped the sweat from his forehead with the heel of his hand and went on as if she had never spoken. "No amount of money can buy back what he refused for himself, Zoe." His lips thinned. "If you knew the choices he has made, you would find yourself somewhat less—" he broke off, gesturing as if it were pointless to speculate further. He covered her hands on the railing with one of his. "Forgive me. I can see that I have only succeeded in troubling you more. I should not have burdened you."

Zoe looked at him for a minute. The size of his squared head. The bulk that blotted out the sun. The dark, unreadable eyes...the way he looked at her sometimes. Rafe would kill him. His touch made her uncomfortable.

Beyond all that, she was bewildered by a troubling sense that there was more at stake than his words seemed to imply. She shrugged. "This is all between you and the bishop, Frank. There is no need to explain. Certainly nothing to forgive."

Frank's eyes narrowed. "Thank you for saying so, Zoe. I..." He broke off again, then continued. "I am a hard man. Unlike Centi, I will never be beloved. I know that. It is a curse.... Have you ever heard from Rafe the old Sicilian expression, *Chi gioca solo gioca bene?*"

Zoe shook her head. "No. What does it mean?"

Clemenza stared at his hands. "Roughly, *The one who plays alone always wins.*"

"Your motto, Frank?"

"Yes." He gave a self-mocking smile. "Selfish, I know. Centi has tried for many decades to broaden my horizons. Both of us have failed, time and again. My fear is that the patterns are too deeply ingrained ever to be erased."

ZOE WENT BELOW to find Rafe. Hopefully the girls would nap for a little longer without their daddy cuddling up with them. Rafe would want to thank Clemenza himself for their time aboard the yacht.

She turned the curved brass handle and pushed open the teak door to the stateroom they occupied. The suite was as elegant as any Zoe had ever seen, with forest green carpet so thick her feet left prints, furniture carved of teak, mirrors framed in gilt, and an enormous round bed covered in a mauve silk spread.

Both her babies lay on a white coverlet, sound asleep in the curve of Rafe's right arm. He was reading a foreign language surgical journal, but put it down.

To Zoe, "tall, dark and handsome" was an inadequate description of Rafe Mastrangelo. Dressed only in swimming trunks, long and lean, powerfully built, dangerous and harmless and mesmerizing at once... His commanding patrician features were as impossible to ignore as those of Michelangelo's David.

And he belonged to her.

She closed the door and leaned against it. Rafe looked at her and blinked, slowly. Invariably, whenever he did that, her heart began to pound and her mouth to water.

Zoe swallowed. "Frank is leaving."

Rafe rose on one arm. "Today? Now?"

"Yes. By dark, anyway, he said."

"But not Centi?" A smile. Rafe admired Centi. The two of them had enjoyed a few long, intimate conversations. But his smile said Rafe would not mind being left alone aboard the *Persephone* with her.

Zoe blushed. Rafe could still do that to her. "No. Centi is staying."

"Ah, well," he sighed, lying back in the mound of pillows once again, speaking low. "Does this sudden departure have anything to do with his argument with the bishop?"

"I don't think so, although Frank just spent twenty minutes explaining how he must save Centi from himself."

"From the poorhouse?" Rafe asked.

"Yes." She left the door and went to sit on the bench at the elaborately mirrored vanity. She began to brush her thick, naturally curly dark hair, and looked at her husband in the mirror. "Frank gives me the creeps sometimes, Rafe."

He frowned. "Clemenza is not a man to underestimate, Zoe. What did he say?"

She let her arms fall and clutched the brush in her lap. By Rafe's mild reaction, she knew he must never have seen Frank look at her in that way. But he was Sicilian—he *would* have noticed. Was it possible that she had misinterpreted the looks?

"Zoe?"

She struggled for an instant to remember Rafe had asked her what Frank had said to give her the creeps.

"Chi gioca solo gioca bene," she repeated softly. "It's almost as if he can't wait for Centi to die so he can have the eighty million all to himself. But apparently he controls it all anyway, so that doesn't make sense. Does it?"

"Controlling and possessing are two very different things, Zoe," Rafe answered softly, his eyes meeting hers in the mirror. "Clemenza is an ambitious man. But he would never hurt Centi."

"I know that, but—"

Rafe raised his brow. "No, Zoe. *You* don't know that."

She glared at him, at what seemed an obvious contradiction. She believed that people were at heart honest and good and honorable. Rafe never suffered such illusions, and her naïveté always amused him. If it was true that Frank would never hurt his cousin the bishop, it was not out of the goodness of his heart. She waited for Rafe to reveal the mysterious, distinctive Sicilian thinking that made Centi and his fortune safe from Frank.

After a moment Rafe's amusement faded. His arm curled more protectively around their sleeping babies. Then he looked at Zoe again. "Centi's business interests in Sicily are extensive. He's an empire to himself, but he chooses to leave it all in Frank's control, which makes Frank very, very powerful."

Rafe paused, and for a time stroked Teddi's and Stephi's backs. "It's been many years since Frank lived in Sicily, but he knows the name of every man and woman in Centi's employ, he knows their children, and if he wanted to know what brand of diapers you bought before we came aboard the *Persephone,* he would have the information inside of an hour."

Zoe shuddered, thinking about whether even she knew what brand of babies' diapers she had bought, and about the power of one man to know that. "I'm lost. What does that have to do with whether or not he would knock off the bishop for his fortune?"

"Frank Clemenza is capable of rolling his own grandmother for a nickel, Zoe."

"Then, if Centi is worth eighty million dollars—"

"Frank doesn't *need* a nickel. Don't you see?"

Zoe considered the maze of dark logic. "If a man has nothing, it's okay to roll his grandmother, but if he is wealthy, then it's not?"

Rafe nodded. "I know the logic seems foreign to you, but remember, this is what is in Frank's mind. Especially with so much money at stake, he believes the fate of his own immortal soul depends absolutely upon safeguarding Centi's life."

"So Centi is safe."

"Absolutely."

"And we're safe?"

Rafe made joking bedroom eyes at her. "You, Mrs. Mastrangelo, are never...safe."

Zoe put down the brush. "You're making this all up."

The slow blink again, the one that wasn't a joke.

Zoe swallowed.

"Come here, Zoe. I'll show you making up."

On principle, she rose and walked away from him, toward the bathroom, letting her hips sway. She sensed him coming after her, curling effortlessly off the massive bed. She darted inside the bathroom door and locked it.

She stood with her back to the door, her hands behind her on the gold-plated handle, her heart thundering. She had only made it to safety because he'd allowed her.

He knocked gently. "Open the door, my heart, or the sound of splintering teak will dismay Bishop Vincenti...and wake the twins."

"Don't you dare!" She whirled around and opened the door instantly because waking sleeping babies was the ultimate threat. He stood leaning against the doorjamb, more than half naked, close enough for her to smell, to feel the heat of his breath, to bury her face in the thick, curly black hair on his torso.

He let his hand fall to her breast and brushed a thumb negligently over her nipple, planted a quick kiss on her nose and walked away laughing softly.

Zoe caught her lower lip between her teeth. God, how she loved him. "You'll pay for that, Raphael," she threatened softly, secretly smiling, grateful that Stephi and Teddi were so soundly asleep.

"Name the price, Zoe," he answered, shucking his now-dry swimming trunks. Baring his muscled, lean flanks. Looking back at her over his bronzed shoulder.

Her breath caught.

He reached for more suitable clothing and smiled. "Get dressed, woman. Our host is leaving."

BY THE TIME the helicopter arrived and tied up next to the yacht on its pontoons, the twins were long since awake and the weather had changed. For four days it had been absolutely clear. Now, in the first minutes after the sun went down, a late-summer squall had arisen and the rain was heavy enough to keep them all inside.

The wind wasn't enough to affect the *Persephone* at anchor, but the pilot was putting in a call to make sure that conditions to the eastern coast of Sicily were a "go" for the chopper.

Zoe and Rafe sat on tall barstools in the yacht's pilot-house talking with Frank while the call was being made. The enclosed area was no larger than a good-size walk-in closet, and the darkness outside the surrounding windows made it seem even smaller. Stephi sat contentedly in Rafe's lap, playing with a doll that had buttons and snaps and zippers to open and close.

Centi had taken Teddi below deck. Of all the toys Zoe had brought along, Teddi wanted none but Centi's miniature Latin Bible, which was very old, bound in Italian leather now worn thin. Teddi loved it for the wonderful little secret compartments and fitted tabs that opened and closed the covers.

Zoe hated for Centi to let Teddi play with such an irreplaceable treasure, but he would not be convinced. He said that Teddi had an instinctive reverence for it, and insisted they go get it and play together.

The chopper pilot ended his ship-to-shore call, stood and spoke in rapid Italian to Frank, who turned to Zoe and gave her a kiss on the cheek. He shook hands with Rafe and patted Stephi's head. "I can't thank the both of you enough for making this trip with me—and for staying on with Centi."

Rafe socked him on the shoulder. "Next time, see if you can scrounge up something we could actually be comfortable on."

"*QE2* next time?" Frank joked. "I'll work on it. Meanwhile, *ciao,* my good friends." He picked up two soft-sided leather suitcases, pulled the hood of a rain slicker up over his head and disappeared into the downpour toward the aft deck next to where the chopper had tied up.

Lightning bolted from the sky, and the thunder followed so suddenly that Zoe knew it couldn't have been half a mile away. Thankfully Stephi was in a fearless stage, and the loud crack of thunder didn't bother her at all. Watching after Frank through the panel of windows in the pilothouse, Zoe shivered. It was as if the night and the rain had swallowed him up.

"I don't think I'd want to be getting on a helicopter right now."

"Mama, hel...a...ter?" Stephi repeated brightly.

Rafe kissed her on the top of her head and Zoe encouraged her, repeating the word. "Heli*cop*ter."

"Hel...i*cop*ter," Stephi shouted.

"That's my baby," Rafe praised lavishly. "How's Mama's Italian?" he asked Zoe. "Did you follow what the pilot was saying to Frank?"

"Something about going below, to speak with the captain?"

"Very good. What else?"

But Stephi wouldn't be ignored and ordered Rafe, "Mama kiss."

"Yeah," Zoe pouted prettily. "Mama kiss."

Rafe obliged, leaning over to kiss Zoe, but Stephi was equally industrious about breaking it up. "All done!"

Rafe nipped at Zoe's lip and rubbed her nose with his. "All done? Later, alligator?"

"Yeah, later, alligator," Zoe teased. "You—" The *Persephone* took a wild dive and bounce, slamming Zoe off the stool. Rafe caught Stephi and managed to stay on his feet.

"What the hell?" he snapped, holding a hand out to Zoe.

"I . . ." She took Rafe's hand and stood while the yacht bounced with the aftereffects. "What was that?"

"It felt like the runabout slipping off." Rafe whipped around. Throwing the switch of the rear searchlight, he jerked it to port, aiming its beam where the small motor launch would be if it had slipped its moorings.

"Rafe, look." Zoe pointed just outside the beam and further from the *Persephone*. "Isn't that it?"

He eased the handle right, and the beam caught the motor launch. The pouring rain made it almost impossible to see. Rafe handed Stephi, who was crying now, to Zoe. The small motorboat was turning, nose away from the yacht. "Look close. Isn't that Raoul, our captain, aboard?"

Murmuring to Stephi, Zoe peered hard and nodded. Dread filled her. Why would the yacht's captain be taking the motor launch anywhere in the midst of a storm? "Rafe, what's going on?"

He bit off another curse. "He's got to be out of his mind. Come on." He grabbed her hand and ducked through the door and down the stairs down to relative safety.

The rain drenched them instantly.

They heard the helicopter blades beating the air, fading, and the engine of the small runabout growing fainter and fainter.

Barefooted, Zoe slipped on the rain-slick deck and grabbed at the railing to catch herself from falling, but in the same instant a huge booming explosion reverberated from below deck, and ripped her out of Rafe's grasp.

She fell and screamed, and when she hit, she slid farther away. Curled around Stephi to protect her from banging into anything, Zoe slammed into the lifeboat housing and pain splintered through her upper arm and shoulder. Stephi shrieked, over and over again.

"Zoe!" Rafe shouted, crouching, running to her.

Clenching her teeth, almost paralyzed in pain, Zoe cried, "Teddi and Centi! They're below!"

Rafe nodded and touched her to see how badly she'd been hurt. The pain she'd forgotten in her fear for Teddi ripped through her again as another explosion went off. The searchlight and every running light went out, and flames from the lower decks began to reflect crazily on the turbulent sea.

Panic tore through Zoe. "Teddi," she screamed. "Rafe, get Teddi!"

"I will," he answered fiercely. But he climbed up to haul out life jackets and hoist the life raft over the edge of the yacht. The wind fought him every inch of the way, but he jammed his shoulder against the release mechanism. The life raft dropped like rock down to the churning sea, and he hurled the rope ladder after it.

She knew the precious moments were wisely spent. She knew he had to get them all to safety, and she knew the life raft was their only chance with the yacht in flames, but Stephi was shrieking and clinging, drenched and cold and terrified, and Zoe couldn't stand knowing that even with Centi, Teddi would be screaming for her. "Teddi, Rafe," she begged him, fighting him. "She'll be trapped!"

"I know! Zoe, dammit, I know!" He grabbed a life jacket and headed toward her, slipping, soaked to the bone, his hair hanging and dripping in his eyes, a fierce anger on his face.

He steeled himself against the cry of agony it was going to rip from her and threaded Zoe's broken arm through the life jacket.

He knew it was only her fear for Teddi that kept her from passing out. She jammed her own arm through the other hole, then took Stephi and held her facing away, and Rafe closed the life jacket over them both.

The yacht pitched and bucked, and the rain came down in sheets. Rafe swung himself up to check the life raft moorings, then leapt down, skidded in the puddling rain and gashed his head. Zoe bit off her scream, but Stephi wailed at the blood pouring down the side of his face. "Papa! Papa!"

He touched her cheek, and Zoe's, and then dragged them to the side. Lightning flashed through the storm-blackened sky. Breathing raggedly, stunned, bleeding and in pain himself, Rafe held Zoe by both shoulders, looking at her, afraid for her, feeling a terrible, brutal fear that he would never see her again if he let her go.

She cried out at his expression. He clenched his chattering teeth. His resolve gathered. He kissed Zoe hard. "Go. Over the side." His voice was gritty and loud, nearly lost in the wind. "It's our only chance.... Loosen the ropes so when I get Centi and Teddi in we can cast off."

She nodded and dragged in one breath and then another to keep focused and do as Rafe instructed, but when he turned away to go after Teddi, Stephi cried out, over and over again for him, her arms and little body trapped against Zoe, twisting in the life jacket.

"Papa's coming. Don't cry. Papa's coming," Zoe promised, as much to herself as to Stephi. She forced herself to think, to reason and plan every move so that she wouldn't fall back, or into the sea. Her arm was broken, and she couldn't afford even one tiny mistake.

Instinctively chanting, murmuring, soothing Stephi, talking to herself, Zoe fought to climb over the railing, to do exactly what Rafe had told her.

The sea roiled and foamed, rocking the yacht. Somehow she managed to crawl over, to make it onto the unstable rain-slick rope ladder. Her right arm was useless. The pain shot up her shoulder and through her body and

made her nauseous and unable to think, much less concentrate in the stinging downpour.

Every time she worked up her resolve to try another
slippery rung, the yacht seemed to pitch one way or another, and she was slammed against the hull. Chilled and
terrified for Rafe and Teddi and Centi, the pain rico-
cheted through her and then she couldn't feel anymore.

She forced herself to find and take the next rung down,
and the next and the next, every nerve, every cell in her
body, attuned to surviving.

The rain made it impossible to see; the fires on the lower
decks provided the only light, but by some fluke she could
hear Rafe's desperate calls on the wind.

She steeled herself against thinking for even one second
that Teddi and Centi were already trapped in the fires.
That Rafe couldn't reach her baby...

She reached the bottom step.

Now, compared to jumping into the life raft, the steps
seemed so easy. Cradling Stephi tight, Zoe fought off her
fear of hurtling down into the sea and missing the raft altogether.

Somehow, she would never remember how, she made it
to the side of the life raft. It tilted, threatening to capsize,
but she clambered inside.

She took a second to breathe, to will her shaking to stop,
to comfort her sweet, frightened baby, and shove hand-
fuls of her sodden hair out of her face. She felt no pain.

She thought she must be in shock, but she imagined that
she could make it now. That Rafe would get out, with
Teddi and Centi. Tugging at the knot on the safety line, she
grasped the rope and began to unwind it, leaving a couple
of loops around the cleat so she could hold on till the last
possible moment.

At last, shivering, shaking so hard that it seemed she
would never stop, she clung to her end of the safety line

and sank to the floor of the raft, which was already inches deep in water, and turned so that she could watch for Rafe.

Her voice cracked and trembled, but she was singing to Stephi...*hush little baby...don't you cry...*when she saw Rafe emerge from below deck, hollering for Centi, holding Teddi to his chest. Flames shot up behind him as he climbed to the railing beside the pilothouse more than a hundred feet forward from the life raft. So far away...

Fear seized Zoe's throat. She couldn't sing to comfort Stephi, or scream or even breathe.

Rafe reached the railing to leap from the *Persephone*, but one explosion set off another...and another...and a wall of fire and flaming debris erupted as the bow of the yacht burst into flames, consuming everything, vaporizing the silhouette of Rafe's body.

Numbed by disbelief and horror and shock and grief too savage to express, Zoe's mind shut down, but though the blasts had temporarily deafened her, her baby Stephi's anguished cries sliced through to her very soul.

"Papa-a-a-a!"

Chapter Two

September 1995

Zoe Mastrangelo didn't believe in sages or portents or omens, but looking back, she could point to the time, the day, the *hour* when Stephi had started to get sick.

They lived in a wonderful old brownstone given to Zoe by Frank Clemenza after Rafe died three years ago, across the street from the hospital. Born, baptized and beloved in the hospital's old halls, Stephi sprinkled joy like stardust everywhere she went. Everyone knew her. Everyone loved her.

Her pediatrician, Emma Harding, had advised Zoe from the beginning to tell Stephi the truth—that her daddy and Teddi had gone to heaven and wouldn't ever come home. The assumption was that Stephi's memories would fade, and she would forget.

Emma was only partially right. Stephi never truly forgot. Her memories may have faded—she thought of Teddi in the way another child might think of a doll. But every day for the past forty-three months, she had asked about her baby sister Teddi.

The child psychologist, Peter Lewiston, believed it to be a "twin" phenomenon. A certainty that her other half was alive. No matter what.

And so her papa must be alive, too.

Zoe always cringed inwardly, because if Stephi believed Rafe and Teddi were alive, she must believe that Zoe was lying to her.

Three months ago, on the Friday before Father's Day, the children in the hospital's day-care center had created cards of construction paper and glue, crayons and colored sparkles.

Not all of them—not even half—had daddies living at home, but every one of them had at least an address, somewhere to send a Father's Day card. Everyone but Stephi. So when her teacher had addressed the card to Dr. Raphael Mastrangelo, Heaven, something had broken inside her little heart, and from that hour, the spirit and joy, the *sparkle,* had gone out of Stephi.

What should a mother feel, Zoe wondered, when her child took seriously ill? Why *my* child? Why me? Outrage or guilt? Or shame?

She had run the gamut of them all already. It felt now, as she stood by the windows of the conference room looking out onto the courtyard gardens in the midst of Rose Memorial Medical Center, as if she might never feel anything but cold again. A chill had overtaken her that no sweater or blanket could dispel.

All of the trees had begun to turn color, the maples and ash and oak. Autumn had always been her favorite time of year. The wealth of scarlet and orange and golden hues appealed to her senses, and falling leaves tugged at her heart.

Life was so tenuous. No one knew better than Zoe Mastrangelo what it was to lose lives so precious to her. If it weren't for Stephi, she might have died herself of a broken heart.

Rafe. *Dear God. What if I lose Stephi, too?*

This autumn, because Stephi was so desperately sick, the turning leaves mocked Zoe. Stephi was unable to fight off even the slightest infection. According to the specialists, her immune system had simply shut down, but they hadn't even a name for what was wrong with Stephi. Zoe couldn't believe they were going to walk in this morning with some miracle cure that would let her take Stephi out of here.

"Zoe, sweetness," Mary Bernadette interrupted her reverie, letting herself into the conference room. Garbed in her traditional nun's habit and clinging to her rosary beads with aging, crooked fingers, she looked at Zoe with an expression so filled with enduring compassion that tears prickled at Zoe's eyelids.

"Don't even start, Auntie," Zoe warned her fiercely, afraid that the beloved old woman's sympathy would poke a hole in the dam of her tears.

Sister Mary Bernadette put her beads away in some hidden pocket and sat down at the conference table. "I was just going to suggest that you go sit in the sun. I'll call you when—"

But she was interrupted by a knock on the conference room door, followed by Stephi's doctors entering the room. Zoe felt a sudden panic, an uncertainty. Unable to cope with this. Her hands clenched at her sides in the pleats of her beige linen skirt. Her shoulders went rigid.

Emma Harding was accompanied by Joel Sebern, a widely renowned childhood oncology physician, and Peter Lewiston, the child psychologist. Emma took the lead.

"Sister Mary Bernadette. Thank you for being here." She turned to the men at her side. "Joel, Peter, you remember Sister, the hospital's immediate past administrator?"

Both men nodded, and Sebern murmured something complimentary about the good old days of Sister's velvet-gloved iron hand. They knew Zoe as well, both in her official capacity as head of the medical records department and as Stephi's mother.

Emma put a hand on Zoe's upper arm. Just over six feet tall, a slender, pretty brunette, she was one of the smartest, most compassionate women Zoe had ever known.

"Shall we sit down?" she asked.

Zoe took a deep breath and pulled back the plaid-covered chair at the conference table beside Mary Bernadette. "Emma, please. Whatever it is, just get it out."

Emma nodded her agreement. "The results of the bone marrow biopsy are back, but they only confirm what we already knew. Stephi's marrow isn't producing any immune-competent white blood cells. That's why she keeps coming down with infections she's unable to fight off."

Zoe swallowed. Her glance passed between the oncologist, Peter and Emma. "So, do we know why?"

Emma deferred to Joel Sebern, who shook his head. "We're not sure, Zoe—"

"Even after all the testing the poor child's been through?" Mary Bernadette demanded.

Zoe reached out to hold her aunt's fragile, bony hand. She knew what her aunt was thinking. *How dare they not know?* How could they come to her after everything they had put Stephi through and say, *We're not sure...?*

Mary Bernadette had always held her staff and physicians to the highest standards of accountability, long before it became a managerial buzzword, but Joel Sebern was the best, and if he didn't know, no one knew.

"We hate the uncertainty as much as you do," Emma replied gently, taking both Zoe and Mary Bernadette into her gaze. "What we believe is that some molecular signal that orders Stephi's marrow to produce the correct cells has been somehow... switched off."

"And no one knows what to do to switch it back on again. Is that right, Joel?" Zoe asked.

"Yes." Sebern was the classic egghead. No taller than Zoe's own five-four stature, first in his medical school class, bespectacled, half bald though he hadn't reached forty. "That's the hell of it. Which leaves us with only one viable option—to transplant Stephi with immune-competent white blood cells that will repopulate her own bone marrow. The tricky part, of course, is to match Stephi's HLA type."

"In layman's terms," Mary Bernadette asked, "what does that mean?"

"These kinds of cells are very specific, Sister," Sebern explained. "It's their job to identify and destroy anything that they don't recognize as 'self.' So when they recognize foreign invaders like a cold virus or a cancer cell, they destroy them."

He pulled a pen from his pocket and drew a picture, putting an *X* over the squiggles he'd used to represent diseases. "But if the HLA type isn't a match, the transfused cells could see Stephi's own cells as the enemy—creating a whole new set of problems."

He drew circles with an *S* inside to represent Stephi's own cells, and then *X*'ed them as well. *End of Stephi...*

Zoe covered her trembling lips with stiffened fingers. Her thumb curled under her fingers and twisted her wedding rings. "Are you saying you haven't found a match for Stephi?"

Sensing the depth of Zoe's dread, Emma Harding reached out to cover her hand. "We've searched every national registry and all the international data banks. A few come close, but there is no perfect match."

Sebern let the chair fall forward and placed both forearms on the table. "Close does count, Zoe. A near match is a better alternative than doing nothing."

Zoe felt her throat swell. Doing nothing meant that Stephi must keep living in an isolation room where the air was filtered and pets were prohibited and flowers were screened and kisses only happened behind paper masks.

But a frown had crossed Emma's face. "You don't agree?" Zoe asked.

Emma exchanged glances with Sebern and Lewiston. "It's not that I don't agree, Zoe. Stephi is in constant danger. Every infection is life-threatening. But I'm not satisfied that we've exhausted all the possibilities. Until we do, I can't support going ahead with less than a perfect match."

Though sunlight streamed into the conference room and touched her own shoulders, Zoe's constant chill grew worse. "What possibilities, Emma?"

"Rafe's family."

"In Sicily?" she asked, startled by Emma's blunt reply.

"Yes."

"Mother of God," Mary Bernadette whispered, ashenfaced, her fragile hands trembling. "That's not possible!"

Alarmed, Zoe clung to Mary Bernadette's hand. "Auntie, are you all right?"

"It—" Mary Bernadette shook as if she were palsied. "It can't have come to this!"

Zoe breathed deeply and straightened, murmuring comforting words. Mary Bernadette was old, and more frail with every passing day. Stephi's illnesses had exacted a shocking toll on Mary Bernadette's own health. She could be forgiven for faltering.

Zoe couldn't afford the luxury.

She turned back to Stephi's doctors. "I don't even know my husband's family.... Rafe's mother called when the babies were born, but—" Zoe broke off. She and Rafe had planned to take the twins to meet his family after they left the *Persephone*.... "I—we never—I didn't meet anyone else."

Sebern leaned across the table on his forearms. "The HLA types do follow ethnic lines, Zoe. There's a very strong genetic basis for Emma's suggestion. You, of course, have no family to speak of. We have no guarantees, certainly, but Stephi's white blood cell antigens are statistically much more prevalent in her father's ethnic population, anyway.

"I didn't know Rafe," he went on. "I'm sorry we never met. I understand he was a fine man. Our purpose here is to find a cure for Stephi, so I hope you'll forgive what may seem insensitive questions. Stephi's twin—"

"Teddi's dead," Zoe interrupted bitterly.

"I know." His Adam's apple bobbed with his own awkwardness, and he had a hard time meeting her eyes. "I only meant that as a twin, Teddi would have been the ideal donor. The question now is this—is it possible that your husband had other children—by a previous marriage or even out of wedlock?"

"No." Rafe had always been painfully honest with her about his past. There had been many women before her, but no marriages and no children. "He would have told me." She shut her eyes, wondering why it had taken her so long to see where Emma and Sebern had been going with this all along. "Siblings are always the best possibility for a match, aren't they?"

Agreeing, Emma's own eyes watered with emotion, for she *had* known Rafe, and taken care of Teddi and Stephi from the first moments after their birth. But Teddi was dead, and Emma knew Stephi was all Zoe had left. Another child of Rafe's would be the next best choice.

"Then we're back to Rafe's family," Peter Lewiston said, entering into the discussion for the first time.

Mary Bernadette's old chin raised. "Are you leading up to the suggestion that Zoe fly off to Sicily herself? With Stephi so desperately ill?"

"Yes," Emma Harding answered. "We think it is that important. Sister, Stephi is sleeping more than twenty hours a day now. You would still be there for her—and all of us, for that matter. It should take Zoe less than a week. Wouldn't you agree, Peter, that Stephi would be all right with Zoe leaving for that short a time?"

"It's a trade-off, but yes.... Zoe—" he hesitated, searching her eyes "—there's another reason to be thinking along these lines. Maybe if Stephi knew the cells that were going to make her get better had come from her father's family, she will finally be able to grieve losing him."

Zoe broke off her eye contact with Peter Lewiston and bit her lip. She knew he believed it was her inability to get over losing Rafe that fed Stephi's persistent fantasies that her father was still alive. That at some deeply subconscious level, Stephi's sickness was her last valiant stand to make her papa come home.

Sebern began to shift in his chair. "Time is not on our side, Zoe. We either need to proceed with the best match among the available donors, or we need Rafe's family tested. They don't know you or Stephi. They're likely to be suspicious as hell and they'll need—"

"Who wouldn't be?" Mary Bernadette asked, anxious to seize upon any alternative that would allow Zoe to stay with Stephi. "Joel, you must have colleagues in Italy to turn to. Someone who could orchestrate this search. UNICEF or the Red Cross or—"

"Most people don't have any idea what we're even asking for, Sister," Sebern responded impatiently. "I understand your concern—believe me, I do. But the treatment we're recommending isn't exactly well-known or understood even in the medical community."

"But all you need is a blood test to find a match to Stephi's type. Surely that doesn't require Zoe's presence!"

"That's only the beginning, Auntie," Zoe answered uneasily. She had never seen Mary Bernadette so pale or troubled.

"Zoe," Sebern began, his respect for Mary Bernadette barely winning out over impatience, "the point is, the donor would have to come here. We think that as Stephi's mother and Rafe's widow, you're the one who can best plead Stephi's case with people who are essentially strangers."

Zoe sat back in her chair. He was probably right. And the possibility that Stephi might be perfectly matched by someone in Rafe's family gave her hope, which was more than she'd had coming in. Still, Mary Bernadette's unnatural anxiety worried her. Her aunt was a smart woman, used to making tough decisions, and Zoe couldn't understand her opposition.

"Do you have any other questions, Zoe? Any concerns?" Emma asked.

Zoe shook her head. "Not really. But I'd like to speak privately with my aunt. Can I let you know in an hour or so?"

"Of course. But please don't worry, Zoe. We'll all be here to deal with Stephi's emotional state," Emma said, squeezing Zoe's icy fingers. "Right now, we need to be looking to any cousins Stephi might have. And after that, to Rafe's extended family."

She stood, as did Joel Sebern and Peter Lewiston. Preparing to leave. Mary Bernadette stood as well, as had been her custom at the end of countless meetings in her years of administering the hospital.

Zoe smothered the fleeting, angry feeling that Stephi was just another case to them, and this was just another meeting with an anxious mother. They could leave now, and forget for a little while.

The feeling was irrational, of course. No one could be more committed to making Stephi well than her doctors. Zoe was not really alone in all of this, either. Her own mother, who had never married—or spoken of Zoe's father, for that matter—had died when Zoe was seven. As Mary Bernadette's ward, she'd practically grown up in what had once been Sacred Heart Medical Center, endearing herself then much like Stephi had in the past three years. The staff had become like an extended family, so Zoe was never alone.

Still, without Rafe, she felt endlessly alone.

And faced with Mary Bernadette's unexpected opposition, she was torn between doing what had to be done for Stephi's sake and staying with Stephi because that's where a mother should be.

At the door, Emma paused. Concern permeated her voice. "If I were you, Zoe, I'd be on the next flight out to Sicily."

ON THE TWENTY-THIRD DAY of September, Dr. Paolo Bondi sat in a scarred wooden rocking chair with his daughter. The chair was of untold age, built of Sicilian oak. He didn't know anyone who had ever occupied the chair before him. He despised his lack of family history, more for his child's sake than his own.

Five-year-old Teddi sat curled in his lap, reading aloud from *Peter Pan,* practicing her English. Her childish voice touched him to his soul.

So like Zoe's.

September 23 was the date of his sixth wedding anniversary, and his heart ached. He hadn't touched or heard or even seen Zoe since that night more than three years ago. The night the *Persephone* had been torched and gone up in flames more horrendous than the fires of Mount Etna.

He clenched his teeth against the pain grown old but never dulled. Struggling over words so foreign to her, Teddi required his attention. "Sound it out, *coccolina,*" he urged her in English. "Like this."

To please him, she echoed the foreign sounds he made, but she was tired. She closed the book, letting the oversize volume fall into her lap. She twisted her small body and reached up to pat Rafe's cheek. "Papa, will I ever learn good enough?" she asked in the Sicilian dialect she heard every day of her life.

Rafe sighed deeply and closed his arms around Teddi's tiny shape. She had forgotten that she had begun to speak in English. But she knew—*how* she knew was something Rafe didn't question—that her mama and sister spoke English.

She was determined to learn so that when Zoe and Stephi weren't lost anymore, which was what she believed, when they found their way home, she could understand them.

There were half a dozen reasons why Teddi should learn to speak English, but the truth was that Rafe heard Zoe's own rich intonations in their daughter's childish voice when she spoke in English. He had only himself to blame for encouraging her.

Maybe he was making it all up. Maybe he heard what he wanted to hear. But sometimes the reminder of Zoe was all that kept him sane.

How could he endure a life without her? Without touching her, or hearing her husky, feminine voice wash over him, or holding her or fighting with her or sinking his rigid flesh into her soft, welcoming body, his soul into hers?

Rafe shook his head. The thought was unendurable, and so he avoided it at all costs.

He cradled Teddi closer still, treasuring her childish scent and her innocence. "A story before bedtime is just enough learning for now, little *signorina,*" he murmured, comforting her, though maybe she was too tired at night. She was already asleep.

He felt too agitated to sit rocking her, and rose from the chair to carry her up the steep, narrow staircase that obliged him to duck down. Teddi's small room, with its slanting ceiling and heavy plaster, was strewn with crude toys and dolls and hand-sewn stuffed animals.

Toys that stamped her the motherless child of a poor village doctor. Paid, when he was paid at all, in loaves of bread, or bottles of olives packed in oil. Or baskets of quinces, pomegranates and lemons layered with heaping, respectful quantities of grape leaves.

He laid Teddi in her small iron bed and turned on the heart-shaped, mechanical music box. It was exquisite, and possessing it set her apart from other village children. But Zoe loved music boxes, and it was the only thing Rafe could think of to keep her mother's memory alive in Teddi.

Silvery moonlight streamed through the window. Teddi's beautiful, childish face lay half in, half out, of the moonbeams. Her hair was thick and naturally curling, dark though not black, like Zoe's. Even in such light, the contrast made her skin pale by comparison. Her eyebrows were Zoe's as well, flaring wide to the outside of middle, narrowing dramatically at each end, and her forehead was kissed by a widow's peak. Her small, wide lips curved in her sleep as the strains of "Autumn Leaves" faded, and Rafe turned away.

He heard a knock at the door, and returned down the stairs to answer it. His mother stood on the old stone doorstep. She was wrapped in a shawl against the unseasonable bite of the night air. Surprise at seeing her delayed his greeting.

"Dr. Bondi, I must see you right away," she announced imperiously, so anyone lingering nearby would hear. She used the name Rafe had assumed, creating the illusion of a peasant woman calling on her physician.

Rafe shook his head and gave a much put-upon sigh, also for the benefit of onlookers, for there was no possibility that someone would fail to notice.

Across the street from his physician's office and home, only one street off the palazzo, was a bar where every night men sat drinking both inside and out at the café tables. The night air was thick with their lewd bantering and the scent of jasmine.

It was not unusual for Dr. Bondi to accept patients in the night. It would, however, be notable and therefore very dangerous for Paolo Bondi, whom Rafe had become, to receive Rafe Mastrangelo's mother. He addressed her by an alias as well. "Come in, Senora Vitale."

When he had closed the door, Teresa Mastrangelo unwound her wrap. Looking approvingly around her, she rubbed her hands together.

"No kiss for your mother?" she asked.

Rafe went to her and took her thin shoulders in his hands and kissed each cheek.

She stood back from him, observing. "You move as if you are in a great deal of pain."

Rafe shrugged. He was always in a great deal of pain. The explosion had left him nearly deaf and crippled for months. His hearing had mostly returned, but his lower back was a patchwork of scars and constant aching, and his right ankle had failed to heal properly at all. "What are you doing here?"

She stood back and angled her head. "I came to make sure that tonight you do not wind up stinking drunk in a jail cell, crying Zoe's name. You will get your Theodora and Stephania and Zoe herself murdered in their beds with such behavior."

Rafe clenched his jaw and looked away from the rebuke that had been a year in coming. Every man, woman and child related to him in the whole of western Sicily knew that the lives of his children depended upon *his* behavior—because every *other* man, woman and child, from the men drinking across the street to the woman who served as Rafe's assistant, could be considered *sbirri*. Spies in the service of Frank Clemenza.

Rafe must do nothing, must not say *anything* that might creep across the stark Sicilian landscape, wash across the sea, find its way to Chicago, Illinois, and reach Zoe Mastrangelo, informing her that her husband Rafe was alive.

Such was the demented power of Frank Clemenza, to devise such an apparently random—and so all the more cruel—demand, and to enforce it.

Rafe could only shake his head, and know that his mother would take the gesture for an apology. Winding up like some drunken riffraff on the cold stone floor of the local jailhouse had endangered the lives of his children, and to a Sicilian, nothing could be more abhorrent.

"You won't find so much as a carafe of wine here."

The harsh line of Teresa's mouth softened, but her thin body did not. "Do you think I don't know what you go through? That you are only half a man without your Zoe? That you ache here—" She pointed with the back of her hand to her head. "Here—" She covered her heart, then brought her hand low. "And—"

Rafe cut her off with an angry, age-old Sicilian curse. She embarrassed him. "You go too far."

"You should take another woman and be done with it."

"You should mind your own business, old woman," he warned her. "The vows I took were till death do us part."

"You are dead to Zoe! Theodora is dead to Zoe!"

Rafe turned away from his mother, pacing the confines of the room. Despite her warnings she persisted in formulating plans for the day when Clemenza might be taken by surprise and his tyranny ended. Above all, she believed Frank should never have kept Teddi from her mother, no matter what he let Zoe believe had become of Rafe.

He had ignored his mother's opinion in this, but she would not be ignored tonight. "Where is your self respect? Where is your manhood? Where is your life? Raphael, *by the blessed Madonna*, you must end this obsession with Zoe—for her sake and for the sake of your children.''

Rafe ceased his pacing and stared straight into the dark eyes of the woman who had given birth to him and kissed his scraped knees and raised him to manhood. She was an educated, intelligent woman, a science teacher, but she didn't trust him.

Despite her education, she still called out *"buon giorno"* to an empty house to appease the spirits. In the same way, she believed a man would always be helpless as a newborn lamb in the presence of a woman. And the only way to forget one woman was in the arms of another.

Only he would never, *never* forget Zoe, which in his mother's mind made him as dangerous as a wounded animal. He reached into a cabinet, withdrew his bottled water and poured bitters in it.

"Go home," he told her. "I am tired of your tongue."

He knew she understood him. He meant no disrespect and she would find none. Knowing that he had heard her, she would imagine that he needed time now to think and to take to his heart what she had put into his head.

She nodded, blew him a kiss in a classic Italian gesture and departed in the guise of Paolo Bondi's patient.

Rafe drained his water and bitters. In truth, an edginess had been growing in him. He had always had a sense of Zoe's well-being. He didn't question it. It was part of the bond forged of fire and sex and undying love between them, no matter how long ago.

But lately the edginess had increased, as had the unrelieved tension of remaining as celibate as a monk. And it was a restlessness stamped with an ill-defined feeling that all was not well with Zoe.

Perhaps his mother was right. Perhaps it was only the longing for Zoe, the need of her, that wore him raw, grinding his defenses to so much sand. But by definition, an Italian, and most especially a Sicilian, *survived* any tribulation—physical or otherwise.

Not every night was so torturous as this one. September 23 came only once a year.

Chapter Three

The Alitalia flight out of New York left at 6:42 a.m. on the morning of September 24. It wasn't until Zoe boarded that connecting flight to Palermo that she remembered.

Yesterday had been the sixth anniversary of her marriage to Rafe. She'd been consumed with Stephi, with packing and preparations and international calls to labs in Palermo to set up the HLA screenings. Too absorbed to even think what day it was. How important it was.

Or how much she missed Rafe, and how adept she had become at hiding from her pain.

But it was Mary Bernadette's strained silences that cost Zoe her peace of mind. If Stephi's recovery depended upon Zoe journeying to the moon, she would have attempted it. But it seemed Mary Bernadette would prefer any journey to this one.

She couldn't verbalize her objections. She couldn't say why this trip troubled her. She admitted it was Stephi's best chance, but Zoe's going shook her badly.

Her native Irish brogue had thickened under her strain. "I can't think that this is right. Someone else should go. That precious child needs you, Zoe—all the more *because* she's already lost her father and her twin."

Zoe's heart had seemed to fill her throat. All her own childhood losses seemed to have been repeated in Stephi's life, only far, far worse. Zoe had never known a father at all. Her mother had been fragile for as long as Zoe could remember, until she died.

"What Stephi needs, Auntie, is to be made well. What good am I to her if she dies?"

"D'y think I don't *know* that, girl?" Mary Bernadette cried, her staunch control betrayed by the quivering of her chin.

Zoe's problem was that even in her own heart, she had no idea how she could leave her child, no matter what the circumstances. The prospect of being half a world away from Stephi terrified her. So Mary Bernadette argued with Zoe's heart, and she had racked her brain for any solution but the one that would take her away.

She had come up with only one possibility. In the weeks and months following the explosion of the yacht, Frank Clemenza had spared no expense or trouble to see that she and Stephi were taken care of.

Rafe himself had taken pains to explain to her how powerful Frank was. As Bishop Vincenti Rosario's cousin, his connections and influence in Sicily were sweeping, and because the bishop had died in the explosion as well, Frank's power was absolute.

Sitting quietly with her aunt in Stephi's isolation room, both of them masked and gowned to protect the sleeping child from exposure to infections, she had brought up Frank as an alternative to going herself. "What if I asked Frank to handle this? I'm sure he'd be willing—he's done so much for Stephi and me already."

"Zoe, no!" Dread seemed to fill her aunt. Her color turned ashen again.

Zoe had had to bite her tongue. Her frustration at her aunt's inexplicable resistance grew. Frank was a real possibility. He knew Sicily, and the people. He knew how to get things done. But Mary Bernadette was reacting as if the idea were unthinkable.

Zoe took a deep breath. "Auntie, why not? Surely with his connections, if anyone could win the help of Rafe's family, it would be Frank, don't you think?"

"Has he even troubled himself to visit Stephi in her isolation room?" Mary Bernadette asked. "No."

"That doesn't mean he doesn't care about her!" Zoe had protested, her frustration shriveling into a nameless fear. She focused on Stephi, so small and vulnerable and pale, asleep in her small hospital bed. The room was filled with pinups and posters and balloons meant to brighten Stephi's surroundings, but they only made her seem more fragile and waxen by comparison.

She stood and smoothed Stephi's dark, thick hair against the pillow, thinking she should bring in a satin pillowcase. She had brushed Stephi's hair only an hour or so before, but the hospital linens seemed to catch and make it tangle, and brushing hurt.

Everything hurt Stephi now.

Zoe backhanded a tear and turned toward her aunt. "I don't understand you." She imagined Mary Bernadette's weathered old lips tightening implacably beneath her mask. "Please. Tell me what's wrong."

Mary Bernadette held Zoe's gaze for a moment, but then looked away, fussing with the edge of Stephi's comforter. "When Centi was alive, things were different. Frank held himself accountable to someone—but now..." She shook her head and lowered her eyes, then went on. "It's God's own truth he helped you after... after you lost Raphael.

"But Zoe," she went on, her tone begging to be understood, to be heard. "You have blinded yourself to his heartlessness. Ask anyone. There is no soul and no joy left here. Sacred Heart is no more." She lifted her chin. "And what he did for you and the babe he did to salve his small conscience."

Zoe stared in bewilderment at her aunt. Frank Clemenza was not a man people loved. He had admitted to that years ago—aboard the *Persephone*. But the harsh business decisions her aunt could never have made had fallen to him. Sacred Heart would never be what it had been under Mary Bernadette's control, but Frank had at least made sure that Rose Memorial could keep its doors open.

And he had always been there for Zoe with whatever she needed—time and resources. A place to go to be with Stephi, to grieve for Rafe and Teddi and heal her broken arm and shattered life. He had even asked her to consider marrying him, knowing full well that she would never love again, but for the security and comforts he would provide her. He accepted her gentle refusal even to consider such a thing, and never, after that night, mentioned his offer again.

But he would be there for her now if she asked. "I should at least tell him I'm going."

They had discussed Frank Clemenza many times before, and Mary Bernadette knew all that Zoe was thinking. She shook her head sadly.

"Whatever else he may be, Zoe, Frank is not suited to your task. You should say nothing of this to him because he will go storming in like a bull in a china closet. His brand of power inspires fear, not cooperation. He is the last person in whom you should confide, or ask this favor."

"Then who should I ask?"

Again Mary Bernadette's lips pursed, and she crossed herself. The pain in her eyes was unlike anything Zoe had ever seen, and it scared her badly.

"Forgive me, Zoe, my child," she begged. "Your friends—Stephi's doctors—were right." She drew a deep, ragged breath to compose herself. "This is something only you can do."

Something only you can do... At the last moment, as Zoe climbed into the cab to O'Hare to make the flight that would take her to New York, Mary Bernadette pressed into Zoe's hand a small piece of notepaper with the name and address of the doctor who practiced among the people in Vallazione, a mountain village southeast of Palermo where Rafe's family might be found.

Dr. Paolo Bondi.

Find him, Zoe, Mary Bernadette had insisted. *Trust him....* Frank Clemenza could do nothing for her that this man, who was a physician and understood these things and his people, could not do better.

THE FLIGHT TO PUNTA RAISI Airport lasted seven hours. Zoe dozed on and off, ate fruit and crackers, drank a few bottles of water and planned her interview with Paolo Bondi. She deplaned into the typical bureaucratic hassles. Her passport was fingered at length by an older man with ridged, unkempt nails who was far more interested in picking her up then stamping her through the line.

The clerk at the car rental, small and swarthy but graced by a quick, broad smile, took a long look at her American passport, and a longer glance around to determine that she was without an escort. He dragged his thumb across her passport photograph in a way that made her skin crawl.

"Mastrangelo," he murmured, staring hard at her photo, his Italian-accented English heavy. "A famous Sicilian doctor of that name died a few years ago. A terrible disaster aboard a yacht."

Zoe swallowed. The intense heat and ripe scents and international crowds of people in the airport were so foreign to her. The clerk's accent, strong as it was, reminded her of Rafe.

"He was my husband."

His small dark eyes darted to hers and he seemed to recoil from her. "No! You are the widow of Raphael Mastrangelo?"

She felt a frisson of warning crawl over her. "Yes. Did you know my husband?"

"No, no, no," he hurried to assure her, acting as if it would have been a dangerous thing to know Rafe. Zoe had never understood such overblown Sicilian reactions. It probably had to do with not wanting to know anyone with such terrible luck as to die in the explosion of a luxury yacht.

He avoided the subject of renting her a car, then warned her against driving, against driving alone, and most specifically, against driving into the mountainous area she proposed.

He refused to rent her a car at all, speaking English well enough to predict dire consequences if she was so foolish to disregard his advice.

He reverted to his native dialect and clacked his tongue, shrugging elaborately. She finally made him understand that she would take her half-million lire elsewhere if that's what he wanted. It was easily five times too much money.

He took her bribe. Zoe wished her mind could be as easily placated. Something indefinable in his manner reminded her how secretive Sicilians were—and that their secrets weren't anything you wanted to know.

Something too personal in his warnings and too regretful in his small, constantly moving eyes made her wish she had never come.

But as he handed her the keys and wished her *buona sera,* she reminded herself that it was for Stephi. She would do anything for Stephi. Anything at all.

THE TINY FIAT CLIMBED the narrow, winding mountain passages on the strength of her prayers. The roads were fine and then dreadful in the space of a single kilometer. Heat waves rose off the pavement under the mercilessly hot sun, then suddenly, round a bend, the little car was plunged into cool, dark shadows.

Several larger and more powerful cars, ignoring the *Vietato Il Sorpasso* signs, careered around her, a hair-breadth from hurtling over a steep precipice taken up by forests of pine. Her hands ached from gripping the wheel. She had to remind herself half a dozen times that Stephi's life depended on her now. That she could, and would, do whatever she must do.

It was dark by the time she drove into Vallazione. She parked on the cobbled street at the north end of the square behind a battered, fifties-era pickup truck. She sat there for a moment behind the steering wheel, absorbing the fetid scents of a centuries-old palazzo, and a dialect spoken too fast for her to understand. There were no women or children on the streets, just men and roaming bands of teenagers.

She took a deep breath, grateful that she had made it this far. She promised to reward herself with a hot, soothing bath, and later, a call home to talk with Stephi. First, though, she would try to see Dr. Paolo Bondi.

The villagers were as deeply hospitable as they were curious at a woman traveling alone. But their kindnesses seemed fraught with tension the moment they heard *Mastrangelo,* and to a man, every one of them denied ever having even heard so much as the name of Paolo Bondi.

RAFE LET HIMSELF into the private side entrance to his home and office, puzzled by the lights left burning. Nicola, his assistant, should have left hours ago, not long after he had gone himself to deliver the Arlacci baby. Hours before there was any necessity of turning on the gas lanterns.

For a moment he wondered if Nicola had failed to take Teddi to stay with his friends, Turi and Grazielle Difalco. Teddi stayed with them, disappearing into their family of seven children, whenever he was called away, whether they had an hour's notice or none. But Teddi would already have come running if she were home.

Rafe sighed deeply, grateful for an hour to himself, and dropped his medical bag on a chair at the kitchen table. Maria Arlacci's labor had stopped. He knew one of her older children would be on his doorstep again before the night was over.

He turned back to the sink, preparing to dunk his head and wash his face, when Nicola Clemenza Peretti turned up in the doorway leading to the rest of his house.

He didn't like her. He never had. She dressed in clothes better than anyone else in the village and was forever flaunting it. She made herself a walking advertisement to everyone in or near Vallazione of the power and expectations of Frank Clemenza.

Years ago Rafe had tried to convince himself that it wasn't her fault that she made a better living spying on him for her uncle than she could on the subsistence wages Rafe could pay her. But by and large, she had nothing to report. Her attitude and constant snooping grated on him.

He slapped the soaking cloth on the sink's edge and turned to face her. "What do you want?"

She tossed her head and smiled, which was the only thing that could make her face at all attractive. But the smile faded and her small eyes followed his every move. Her voice was thick with insolence. "There is a woman in the palazzo."

"A woman in the palazzo," he repeated. What did this have to do with him? "A sick woman? A pregnant woman? A dead woman? What woman, Nicola?" She was not so slow-witted as to miss his sarcasm.

She couldn't have cared less. "An American woman."

"Oh. An *americana*." Rafe sighed heavily and turned back to the sink, refusing to rise to the bait. It had taken years for him to convince her that Americans didn't all know one another. "Get this through your head.... No

American is ever coming to Vallazione who will recognize me."

"You're wrong."

Rafe shrugged and reached for a bottle of aspirin. His back ached like the blazes of hell. He tossed down two aspirin and chased them with a glass of lukewarm water from the pitcher by the sink. He was in no mood for this woman's nasty little drills.

"Go home, Nicola," he said tiredly.

"Not so quickly."

"Now," he snarled, pleased to notice that her eyes widened in fear for one sliver of a second.

She jutted her chin out stubbornly. Whatever she thought she knew, she wasn't going to give it up. "This one is no tourist, *padrone,*" she mocked. "This one claims to be searching for the relatives of her dead husband. She says she is the widow of Raphael Mastrangelo."

Rafe felt his throat convulse and his body tense. It took every shred of his overdeveloped self-control to keep his expressive face still. To hide the shock.

Zoe.

He forced himself to swallow. *Zoe. Dear God.* It must be a trap...but if it wasn't, if she had come here, to Vallazione, she was within a hundred paces of him and closer than that to Teddi.

And they were all in terrible danger.

"You're boring me, Nicola," he said softly, forcing himself to a show of total indifference. Clemenza's niece was like a shark. The scent of blood would invite a feeding frenzy. He took up the sopping cloth and ran it over his face, letting the excess water pour carelessly down onto his rough, sweat-stained linen shirt. "Get to the point, or get out. I'm tired."

Her features twisted in some perverted kind of satisfaction. "She's asking—no, demanding—to see Dr. Paolo Bondi."

Rafe's breath locked in his lungs. How did she know that name? He shut his eyes and clenched his teeth and brought the cloth to the back of his neck. He doubted that Nicola would be fooled by the ordinary actions, but he felt stunned senseless.

Only Zoe's aunt, Sister Mary Bernadette, could have given her the name of Paolo Bondi.

She had sent Zoe, exposed and unwitting, straight into the depraved, deadly aim of Clemenza's assassins. And if Mary Bernadette had done that, she had broken a vow at least as sacred as the one she had taken committing herself to God.

Something must have gone so terribly wrong that Clemenza's retribution no longer mattered to the old woman, but it mattered to Rafe. His wife and his children were as good as dead....

Why hadn't Clemenza's assassins already gotten to Zoe? The only possibility was that he didn't yet know she had come here.

There was no possibility that he could escape Vallazione with Zoe and Teddi. They would be followed and dead before the sun rose.

His only other option was to turn and walk away from this. From Zoe, from Nicola. If he went back to the Arlacci farm and sat with Maria until the baby was delivered, Zoe would never see him and Clemenza would have no reason to kill her.

But he couldn't walk away.

Zoe was in trouble. He knew it. He'd known it at some gut level for weeks. And the fact that Mary Bernadette had defied Clemenza by sending Zoe to Paolo Bondi, *sending her when she knew Zoe would pay with her life,* could only mean Zoe was threatened by something or someone more fearful than death.

He might have sent in someone else, pretending to be Paolo Bondi, but the only way Rafe could know what threatened Zoe was to see her himself.

He took a deep breath, then wrung out the cloth as if it were the neck of Frank Clemenza. He draped it very deliberately over the cheap, peeling aluminum towel rack above the sink, then tore a wilted bloom from a violet. He turned to face the niece of his enemy.

"Where is she?"

"At Turi's bar." But Nicola panicked at his expression and blocked the arching doorway. "Don't be a fool!" she hissed. "She doesn't know who you are. She—"

"You can't convince her to go away, Nicki. I'll have to do it, won't I? Frank should be happy with an audience to her humiliation."

"Rafe."

"Paolo," he corrected her, despising the sight of her, the smell of her. "Get out of my way before I kill you."

She raised her chin defiantly. "You wouldn't dare." But he was a man with nothing left to lose and she knew it. She stepped aside, but her eyes flew to his telephone. Besides a few primitive radios, his phone provided the only functional communication to the outside world in all of Vallazione.

He moved to the telephone, jerked the cord from the wall and turned back to her. "Now get the hell out of my house."

ZOE SAT AT A FILTHY TABLE littered with cigarette ashes and spent matches and shot glasses, effectively trapped by a pack of men. The bar was owned by his only real friend, Turi Difalco. Rafe's heart twisted and he tasted something far worse than his own bile. He wanted to take the heads off of at least those five sorry slugs.

She wore a modest white sundress buttoned up the front with tiny rose-colored dots on it. She was sitting sideways to him. Her dark, heavy hair was gathered into a banana clip, and she seemed pale. Thin. Delicate to the point of exhaustion. She was more beautiful than he had allowed himself to remember. His heart thudded heavily in his chest and his blood pulsed in his groin.

Until this moment, he hadn't ruled out the possibility that this was just another of Nicola's vicious tricks. Now he wasn't sure he could believe his own eyes.

He stood on the stone doorstep, staring in, all his senses blunted by the sight of Zoe. How fragile her wrists were. How feminine and vulnerable her neck was. Heat streaked down his belly. He was thinking of the quarter-moon-shaped birthmark on the full upper curve of her left breast. His throat went dry as chalk.

He seemed frozen, unable to feel the staggering gratitude he had imagined seeing Zoe once more in this life should evoke. He exchanged glances with Turi, who stood unhappily behind the bar wearing a hole in the glass he was polishing.

"Please," she was begging, her eyes darting between the men surrounding her. "*Non capisco. Per favore.* I must see Dr. Bondi. I know he's here. I am certain that my aunt spoke to him...."

She swallowed and shivered and turned to appeal to Vito Cavallo, whom she must instinctively have recognized as the head of the local infestation of carabinieri—the state police. Trying to make herself understood, she struggled with the language. "*Siamo venute da lontano...pro... proprio per visitare....*"

"'*Siamo,*' signora?" Cavallo asked her, mocking her in an uncanny imitation of her own voice. "You and who else?"

Her mouth clamped shut. Her expression told Rafe that these men had been acting for some time as though none of them understood or spoke English. "Not '*siamo,*'" she explained. "Not...we. I mean *I* have come a long way to see...him."

Tilting his chair on its back legs, Cavallo swallowed the dregs of his alcohol. "It seems unfortunate that you have made a very long journey for nothing." He smiled. His teeth were disgusting. He reached toward Zoe's face. Rafe froze, certain that Cavallo knew he was there.

Cavallo stroked her cheek. Cavallo, the macho bastard who bragged that even as an infant he had impregnated his wet nurse. "Come home with me, Signora Mastrangelo.... I will burn your widow's weeds and give purpose to your travels."

In the split second it took Rafe to recognize the trap—Cavallo baiting him by such obscene treatment of Zoe—she slapped Cavallo in the face.

Every man in the bar went stock-still, waiting for Cavallo to hit her back, but the brass she had displayed earned even Cavallo's grudging respect.

Tears filled Rafe's eyes.

She stared at the welt left by her hand on his face until it turned violently red. "My husband would have killed you for far less than that, *signore*," she snarled. And I am not without friends now.... You may either take me to see Dr. Bondi, or answer to Frank Clemenza."

Zoe held her breath. In the stale, smoke-filled air the name of Frank Clemenza caused a silence so complete that she could hear the bartender's towel squeaking against the glass he polished.

The insulting carabiniere began to smile and then laugh, and the others began laughing uproariously as well, exchanging barbs and one-liners that set them off again. Jokes at her expense in a dialect she couldn't comprehend.

She flushed. Using Frank's name had backfired. Her bluff had been a mistake, and she had no way of guessing why. She had somehow stepped out of the world she understood. The world in which renting a car was simple and mundane, where if you had done nothing wrong, the police were there to help.

And where, when you asked for directions to the doctor, they were given without an interrogation.

It should all have been so simple. She only had to find Paolo Bondi and explain what she needed, what Stephi needed.

Stephi.

Zoe swallowed, suddenly aware of the gathering spectators, of another drama being played out around her. Of men, waiting.

But with the thought of Stephi, she had suddenly understood that she had gone about this all wrong. Sicilians valued their children over everything else. She should start over. Tell these men who must have children of their own...make them understand that her child's life was at stake and that that was why she needed to see Dr. Bondi. They would understand that. They would sympathize. They would stop lying to her....

"Per favore," she began, determined to make them see. "Let me explain—"

"Signora Mastrangelo."

Zoe turned. She felt the blood drain from her face. The half circle of onlookers parted like the Red Sea for Moses. The laughter stopped. The silence returned, heavy as smoke hanging in the air.

Shocked, Zoe realized that the voice that had hushed the strident, confusing laughter belonged to the flesh-and-blood ghost of Raphael Mastrangelo.

Chapter Four

"Rafe."

Zoe stood. Her heart beat frantically. Hope surged in her. Rafe! He was alive, standing here before her.... Alive. But confusion stifled her instinctive joy, for he was staring blankly at her.

"Forgive the inept fumbling lies of my compatriots," he said. "I am Paolo Bondi. My assistant—" he nodded toward the woman who had followed him through the crowd "—came for me. How may I help you?"

Paolo Bondi? The men surrounding Zoe erupted in conspiring, threatening murmurs. She heard, but she didn't understand, any more than she understood why the man who spoke with Rafe's voice and looked at her through Rafe's eyes called himself Paolo Bondi.

Her body reacted, shivering violently, but her mind felt sluggish and numb. "Rafe..."

"Bondi, *signora*. Dr. Paolo Bondi."

"—You're...alive." It was him, or she was going crazy.

He gave her a sad, pitying look as he handed his doctor's bag over to the bartender's keeping. His eyes were the color of Rafe's, the shape, the depth, but they were empty. "Very much alive," he said. "You were expecting to meet a dead doctor?"

"No, I..."

"*Signora,* are you well?"

"No!" How could she be well? She swallowed. "Don't you know me? Rafe...it's...I'm...*Zoe.*"

"I have never had the pleasure, *signora—*"

"But you have. You're...we're—" She broke off. "Rafe, what..." She couldn't complete a simple thought. His expression never changed. For a moment, she imagined she saw a flash of terrible pain shuttered in his eyes, but maybe she was mistaken. "Rafe, please! Don't you see? Don't you recognize me?"

"No."

"You must..." But he only shook his head. Zoe trembled. It wasn't possible. "You must know me."

"Take a hint, *signora,*" Cavallo jeered contemptuously. "The doctor swears he's never had the pleasure. Don't you, Signore Doctor?"

"Stay out of this," Zoe warned Cavallo, using her eyes to flash the danger of crossing her. Her heart pounded. The rush of her own strangled breath roared through her ears. Her scalp and ears and neck and breasts felt feverishly hot. Inside, she felt chilled.

She stared at Rafe. "Why are you doing this?"

He blinked. "Doing what?"

"Pretending that you don't know me," Zoe cried.

"Because, Signora Mastrangelo, I don't," he answered gently, as if he were dealing with an unstable patient whose hold on reality was already slender. "Please. I must go soon to deliver a baby. Tell me why you came here. What you want."

"The truth," she whispered. What about their child? She stared at him. Couldn't stop staring at him, just like in all her days with him when, if he was near her, she couldn't stop looking. Admiring.

Her head began to ache unbearably. Stephi was dying because this man had disappeared from her life. Had he chosen to disappear? Was it possible that he had survived the explosion with no memory of his life before?

Or was it only a trick of the light that made her think this man was Rafe?

Zoe closed her eyes, but when she opened them again, he was still there, surrounded by men who were too interested and a woman who hung on his every word.

Rafe. If he knew who he was and hadn't come home to her...if Stephi didn't get well...if she lost Stephi, she would kill him.

Zoe shook her head. His actions, and his words, clashed horribly with what her eyes and ears and heart told her were true.

But her husband would have called out the carabinieri for Cavallo's vulgar treatment of her. Her husband would have moved heaven and earth to come back to her. Her husband would never have abandoned his child.

Not in this life.

He would have found a way, or died trying. This man was not her husband, but her senses told her differently. The conflicting evidence tore at her.

"The truth," she repeated. The feverishness heightened. She felt disowned and humiliated, and Rafe would never be party to that, either. But Stephi's life was at stake, and Zoe would not be made to run away.

"Swear to me that you are not my husband, that you have never seen me, that you know nothing of our life or our babies or—"

"I swear it."

She shook her head, still unable to take her eyes off him. Rafe would never have sworn to that.

It was true, then. He knew nothing of who he really was or what they had shared. Or else her memories had betrayed her, and she was only seeing in the face of a stranger what she wanted to see. Tears pricked at her eyelids and clogged her throat, and she lashed out at him for not being who she needed most.

"It seems I owe you an apology, Signore Doctor." She chose her words carefully, as if he were Rafe and she could hurt him as much as she had been hurt. To make him suffer as much as Stephi. Her breath came in stricken, odd little gasps. "Your whiskers grow in patterns I...I thought I once knew."

A muscle throbbed along his temple. She was tempted to believe she recognized that, too.

"I thought your voice was the one I hear in my dreams. I thought it was *your* babies who once crowded my heart." She hated herself for giving him one more chance to deny her, but she couldn't stop herself. "Was I so...wrong?"

His eyes fixed on hers, then on the ragged pulse at her neck. The weight of the world seemed to rest on his shoulders and they slumped.

The part of Zoe that Mary Bernadette had nourished and nurtured, the part that chose to believe God's truth would always reveal itself, that part of her held out. But he shook his head slowly. "You have the power to make me wish it were all true, *signora*."

"It is." *Please. Be Rafe. Be the father Stephi is dying for... be my beloved.*

"It's not. I'm sorry."

Zoe let out her breath and clasped her hands. "Okay. But Stephi, my daughter, Signore Doctor, is dying. And whatever you choose to call yourself, I need your help."

Rafe felt as if he'd been slammed in the chest. He couldn't breathe. Stephi was dying?

He could have tolerated Zoe's recriminations. He'd prepared himself for them. He hadn't gone through the days and weeks and *years* apart from her, or put Zoe through all of that, for nothing. Not for anything less than her life, and the life of their babies.

He bowed his head and shut his eyes. There had never been such a terrible silence in Turi Difalco's bar. His jaw clenched. His fists doubled. The pain in his chest was unimaginable. He had looked Zoe in the face and lied to her... and his tiny daughter was dying?

The realization invaded him. This was what had provoked Mary Bernadette to defy the vengeance of Frank Clemenza.

But everything he had done and suffered and made Zoe suffer would be meaningless if he gave Clemenza or his thugs reason to kill them both now. He could count on Nicola to tell Frank what she had seen here. To explain in lurid detail the extent of Zoe's humiliation, so that Frank might be mollified and find it unnecessary to kill them.

But Rafe couldn't know which of the men who drank themselves into a stupor here every night might decide to take matters into his own hands. Which of them already belonged to Clemenza. Which of them would spill his blood and Zoe's on Turi's floor—making orphans of their little girls—before Frank had a chance to appreciate Nicola's account of the emotional death he had forced on them both.

Rafe drew a deep, ragged breath and asked Zoe to sit down.

"*Signora?*" He held a chair for her. Their eyes locked. He thought she would refuse, but at last she broke off their eye contact and sat in the chair.

He couldn't stand her sitting there in the filth. He turned to Turi and asked for a rag to clean the table, then ordered Cavallo and the others to back off.

Nicola shot him a warning glance, but even she could not dismiss a dying, innocent child. She gathered all the empty glasses by the fingers of one hand and wiped the table with the rag Turi had tossed over. "Be very, very careful, *padrone*," she warned in her Italian dialect. "If this is a trick—"

"She will die," Rafe interrupted softly, in a voice she knew to fear. "And my children will die. Then, Nicola, you will die. I promise you that."

He turned away from Nicola and sat down at the table across from Zoe. His pretense would only buy him time to think, but time was all he had. "Please. Tell me why your daughter is . . . is dying."

Zoe's glance flicked toward him, then angrily away. He imagined she had hoped that the shock of hearing that Stephi was dying would make him abandon his lies. But it hadn't, and if that felt like yet another blow to her, she didn't show it.

"My daughter's immune system has shut down. Her body isn't producing the right cells to guard against infections. She's been sick off and on for months."

She brushed stray tendrils of her hair back from her face and met his eyes. He saw that nothing, not even his betrayal, mattered to her so much as finding help for Stephi.

But she was running on nothing but her willpower. The shadows beneath her eyes made them look bruised. She was small, but Rafe had never thought of Zoe as fragile. She must be exhausted from the flight here, the drive, the jet lag. But everything about her now betrayed the toll Stephi's illnesses had taken on her.

"Her doctors," she finished, "assure me that catching a cold now could kill her. She can't play or go to school. She's confined to a sterile isolation room."

Acutely aware of Cavallo's eavesdropping and Nicola chain-smoking behind him, Rafe swallowed. Zoe's brittle, unadorned account of what had befallen Stephi made it all the more terrible. But what had she believed Paolo Bondi could do? "I'm a simple country doctor, *signora.* Surely you need the help of specialists."

"Ohhh, listen to this," Cavallo jeered, slopping a glass of beer in a mocking salute. *"I am a simple country doctor,* signora. *Surely you need the help of specialists."*

Zoe swallowed. Cavallo's tone and inflection perfectly mimicked Bondi's voice. She forced herself to ignore him. She turned back to Bondi. "I have the help of specialists. What I need now is to reach your... I mean, my husband's family."

"Why?"

Zoe's eyes watered, and she let her gaze drop to her hands clutching her purse on the table. She took a breath and blew it out, then straightened, drawing on her last reserves. "Stephi's doctors sent me. They're convinced her only chance is to find a donor for cells to help her fight off infections."

"A bone marrow donor?" Rafe asked, racking his brain to remember what he had ever learned of immunity.

Zoe shook her head. Even that small movement betrayed her weariness. "Not exactly. There's a process they're using now—apheresis, they call it—for separating the cells Stephi needs from the donor's blood. The rest is returned to the donor."

"So it's like a blood donation?"

"A little more complicated, but yes."

Rafe frowned. *"Non capisco,"* he murmured softly. She had focused now on Stephi, and her composure had returned. But cheated out of the energy of being angry at him, she was struggling, and it was tearing him apart to put her through this in these surroundings. "I don't understand. Why did you need to come so far to find a blood donor?"

"A match for the cells Stephi needs is much more difficult to find than for red blood cells. Her doctors want as close a match as if it were a bone marrow transplant."

As if it were a transplant... Rafe felt a clamor in the sudden stillness in his head. "Because...?"

"They hope the donor cells will repopulate Stephi's marrow, so that her body will be able to reproduce them again by itself."

An argument erupted behind him. Rafe ignored it but moved more protectively into Zoe's space to shield her from the violence. "And in your husband's family you hope to find such a match?"

"Yes. We know Stephi's white cell type is much more common in Italian and Mediterranean people, so I came to ask Rafe's family members to be tested."

Holy hell... Suddenly he knew what the clamoring in his head was about. He'd known at some instinctive level the moment Zoe had uttered the word *transplant.*

She needed to have no one in his family tested. Teddi and Stephi were identical twins. The match would be perfect.

Waves of revulsion passed through Rafe for what he had done and what he had to do now. Tell her, *Sorry, yes, the gig's up?* Admit he'd lied? Admit that Teddi—the beloved child she had already mourned, the answer to her prayers, the one who might save Stephi's life—was also very much alive, *asleep, Zoe, in a room just over your head?*

He stared at her. She was the woman who made him powerless as a newborn lamb. He needed to touch her. To reassure her. To take her hand and kiss her wrist and beg her forgiveness. Confusion flickered in her eyes. He couldn't afford to let her see his powerlessness.

"Turi," he ordered, never taking his eyes from Zoe, "pour me an anisette."

His friend, whom he had asked never to pour him a drink again, told him to bugger off in Sicilian terms much more graphic. Nicola lit another cigarette and glared at him.

"Now, Turi," he said in a voice that brooked no compromise. *"Favore."*

Cavallo added his mocking support. *"Caro* Difalco, give the good doctor his dose of anisette."

Turi delivered the shot glass. Rafe turned it round and round on the table. "Tell me what the testing involves," he said, so she wouldn't have the time to think too much.

He listened without hearing her. He knew it couldn't be much longer before Zoe took stock of his ridiculous answers and trusted her own intuition. She was tired now, exhausted from months of sleepless nights with a sick child and hours of traveling.

But when her defenses were down she would think and a tiny flicker would ignite in her heart and she would begin to wonder. If he was alive, even if he didn't know who he was, *wasn't it possible that Teddi had survived, too?*

He tossed down the shot of anisette in one burning swallow. Staying away from her, even under Clemenza's threat of death, was one thing; keeping her child from her was another. Her fury would make all hell breaking loose seem tame.

He couldn't blame her.

But he couldn't let it happen in front of Clemenza's henchmen, either, or they would both die tonight. He knew what must happen. He had lived under the daily threat of Clemenza wiping out his family for a very long time, but he saw clearly now how in the space of an hour, all that had subtly shifted.

An infection could take Stephi in the blink of an eye, and that threat changed everything. He had to find a way to get Teddi out of Vallazione tonight while he still had the slender advantage of Clemenza's ignorance—and to keep him in the dark for as long as possible. He needed a few hours to form a plan.

No more than a minute could have passed as all this went through his head, but Zoe had finished explaining about the blood tests and sat waiting for him to respond. He knew she didn't understand why his reactions took a beat too long in coming.

"Nicola, get my bag," he ordered. She ground out her cigarette and fetched his bag from Turi. He ignored her open resentment, opened his bag, then opened a vial and spilled out a few tablets.

"I imagine you're too exhausted to rest, Signora Mastrangelo. These are very mild sleeping pills." They weren't sedatives. They were tranquilizers. Whatever plan he came up with, Zoe would have to do exactly what he told her to do. He took her hand and placed them in her palm and closed her fingers over them.

He only meant to give her the tablets. Maybe to gauge the temperature and moisture of her skin. But he had closed her fingers other times, other places, and his body remembered too well.

She loosened her fingers and stared at the tiny pills.

"They're safe, I promise you," he said. Safer by far than memories. "I'll have the names and addresses of your husband's family members by the time you wake in the morning."

Nicola lit another cigarette and blew the smoke deliberately in his face. "How will you do that, *padrone,* with your phone ripped from the wall?" she baited in rapid, scathing Italian.

He reached out and took the cigarette from her as if he were doing her a gentle favor, then crushed it out.

"I'll fix it."

He smiled at Nicola so that Zoe would not be alarmed, then turned back to her. "My assistant will put away her cigarettes and offer you a bed for the night."

Zoe looked steadily at him. "A hotel room would be fine."

"But then I would have to worry for your safety." Nicola would understand that her own life wasn't worth the price of a single pack of her precious cigarettes if anything happened to Zoe in the night.

But she would not be cheated of the last word again. "Be very careful that you don't start a bloodbath, *Signore Doctor.* Her life depends on what message I choose to give my uncle."

Cavallo sat back on his barstool, having lit a cigarette, both elbows planted behind him on the bar. "Listen to her, *amico.* You know she is always right."

THERE WERE HALF A DOZEN messages waiting to be picked up on his voice mail when Frank Clemenza returned from his weekend with the beauty queen of the local dairy industry.

The messages lodged in his voice mail would doubtlessly spirit him back into the eighty- or ninety-hour week he devoted to his investments and the affairs of Rose Memorial Medical Center. He wasn't anxious to spoil the lazy afterglow that hung on him like the dairy maiden's earthy perfume. In all likelihood, his personal assistant, Carlin Santini, would have dealt with any emergencies by now, anyway.

He ignored the half-dozen messages. Replacing the phone in its cradle instead, he handed his coat and hat to his housekeeper and turned to the hundred-gallon tank of outrageously expensive saltwater fish.

"Everything all right, Maisie?" he asked his housekeeper, seeking out the Kuhli loach undulating across the bottom of the tank. "All creatures great and small taken care of as usual?" There was a veritable menagerie of dependents on his goodwill, in which he took little interest but great pride.

A woman of few words—the essential quality that had separated her from other very fine applicants for the position of his housekeeper—Maisie nodded.

"Mr. Santini is waiting in your study."

Frank gave a sigh and checked his Rolex, noting how close the dinner hour was. "How long before you prepare the dinner trays?'' He rarely used the cavernous dining room, preferring to take his meals alone in his rooms or with company, if he chose, in his study.

"A quarter of an hour?''

"That will be fine. Make one up for Mr. Santini, will you?''

"Of course.''

He sprinkled a few treats over the top of the water in the fish tank, then made his way to the study.

An inside room, the study had none of the glorious windows overlooking the expanse of Lake Michigan or the rest of his estate. The only light in the room was given off by the exquisite marble-based library lamp on his desk.

Carlin Santini sat in an oxblood leather club chair smoking one of Frank's premium imported cigars. "Have an entertaining forty-eight hours, Frankie?''

Frank smiled sublimely in answer, but irritation began to gnaw away at his goodwill. He still wasn't in the frame of mind to have minor irritants tarnish his mood.

"Watch the ashes, my friend.''

"Do I ever fail to watch out for what is yours?''

Frank shook his head. "No. It's not in you to fail.''

Carlin glared at him. "Have I ever given you bad advice?''

"Rarely any bad advice,'' Frank conceded, sinking into the chair that matched the one Santini occupied.

"Still, advice you chose to ignore.''

Frank returned Carlin's look but said nothing. Neither would Carlin say anything more before Frank replied. He reached for his box of cigars and took one out, closing the lid soundlessly. He peeled the cellophane and sat inhaling the rich tobacco scent.

He lit the cigar and exhaled. The smooth taste lingered on his tongue. "Anything you care to expound upon in particular?'' he invited at last.

Carlin's spare features hardened, giving him the look of carved granite. "You should have killed Mastrangelo and been done with it."

Frank's mellow mood of goodwill evaporated in an instant, but it lingered like the smoke curling in the air, mocking him. He was careful, though, not to reveal even to his most trusted aide the extent to which he had been shocked.

"Is there no quality of mercy in your soul, Carlin?"

"Don't spout mercy to me," Santini snapped. "If it weren't for your morbid superstitions—"

"What has happened?"

"Nicola called last night. Collect, person-to-person, long-distance from Sicily."

"And?"

"That's all. You weren't here. She was cut off by the operator."

"I assume you have not managed to return her call?"

"Paolo Bondi's telephone is out of order at this time. Naturally, Cavallo cannot be reached, either."

Frank puffed on his cigar, waiting. Glutted with angry, unformed suspicions, he sent Maisie away when she knocked at the door with their dinner trays. His appetite had vanished along with his equanimity.

"Do you know where the little widow is?" Santini asked.

"Zoe?" Frank asked, stifling the revulsion her name elicited. "At the bedside of her sickly brat, no doubt."

"She's not."

Frank stared in disbelief at his aide as logic leaped beyond Santini's implication. No one, *no one* had ever dared defy him. "Are you saying Zoe Mastrangelo is absent from Rose Memorial?"

"For at least twenty-four hours."

"And that her absence has anything to do with the call from Sicily?"

Carlin shrugged elaborately. "The old crone Bernadette swears her niece went home last night. And that she must only be out on a few errands."

Frank sat very still for a long time. Stretched out with his head resting against the back of the club chair and his arms extending well beyond the support of the armrests, he let his cigar ashes drop silently to the antique Persian carpet.

His anger resolved to profound disappointment in Bernadette. People had only to follow his rules to be taken care of by him. To be given far more than he should ever have allowed in the first place. The lives he had spared! Where was her gratitude?

What was it in her that resisted his graciousness and benevolence at every turn? The fault lay in her if Zoe Mastrangelo had, in fact, gone to Sicily. The blame for their deaths would lie at her feet. Heaven knew, Frank prayed fervently, heaven knew *he* had tried to spare them.

He examined the various possibilities open to him for finding the truth behind Bernadette's treachery. "Get the child's doctor on the phone," he ordered Carlin at last, sitting up now. He waited until this had been accomplished, then carried the cellular with him as he paced the dark room.

"Dr. Harding. How good it is of you to take my call."

"Think nothing of it, Frank. What can I do for you?"

"I have been out of touch over the weekend, and I'm unable to locate Zoe to ask how Stephi is doing by now."

"Not well. She spiked a temperature last night, which is a very disheartening sign of a possible infection taking hold."

"Ah, God above," Frank responded heartfully. "The poor child. Zoe must be beside herself—"

"She doesn't know yet, but of course she is out of the country. You knew, didn't you, that she'd gone?"

"As I said, I've been out of touch, though I have meant to check in with her," he responded, not wanting to arouse any suspicions. "But I can't imagine anything can have induced Zoe to leave Stephi's bedside."

Emma Harding sighed. "I know. It was very hard for her, but there was really very little choice. If there's a chance of matching Stephi's HLA type, it was imperative that Zoe get her husband's family tested."

"In Sicily."

"Yes."

"Emma. You are a jewel in the crown of Rose Memorial Medical Center, and I personally thank you." He pressed the Off button on the telephone, then dropped it in Carlin's lap.

He wanted to believe this forbidden trip of Zoe's was only an errand of an international nature. That the misbegotten daughter of Bernadette's whoring sister would, in fact, result in nothing of any significance to him. Then Frank thought, let her find Mastrangelo's family. What did it matter to him? He could not have invented a better test of their sworn secrecy if he had tried.

But he was forced to admit to himself that Bernadette had betrayed him, and her misbegotten niece would stumble upon the truth. She would have to die.

Frank smiled grimly, which reassured Santini. Zoe would never again be prevailed upon to perform another of life's imperative little errands. And Bernadette would get to live with a horror even she hadn't yet begun to see.

Frank rang for his dinner. His appetite had returned.

Chapter Five

Zoe understood one thing clearly. Nicola Peretti would as soon kill her as look at her. But why?

Her eyes burned from the cigarette smoke lingering in the hot, stagnant air of Nicola's small apartment. She had taken the pills Bondi had given her, but they had not had the desired effect of allowing her to sleep.

They'd had almost the opposite effect. She felt alert, but not in the choppy, painful, anxious state that she'd been in before. Sleep seemed as impossible now as when she'd taken them. Stephi was too much on her mind. Zoe had never dreamed she would be unable to phone her.

Curiously, she felt less upset. Able to deal with things. She knew Stephi was probably sleeping now, anyway, no matter what time it was in Chicago. All her reasoning seemed clear and rational.

Right now, she thought, she would rather take her chances sleeping in her rented car on the ancient cobbled streets of Vallazione than spend the rest of the night at the mercy of Bondi's assistant. The woman was sneering and hostile one minute and ingratiating the next.

On their way to her apartment, she'd warned that Zoe would never see Paolo Bondi again. But then she'd walked deliberately by an old house where Zoe couldn't miss see-

ing his medical shingle bolted to the massive arched
wooden door.

Nicola was also getting very drunk on a bottle of expensive wine, and the more she drank, the less she managed to hide.

It seemed to Zoe that Nicola Peretti had a lot to hide.
That the strain of keeping her mouth shut was wearing her
thin, because Paolo Bondi also had too many secrets. Zoe
couldn't have said where the insights came from, or exactly what things Peretti had said that set her suspicions
into motion. But it didn't matter.

The secrets were being kept from *her*.

So Zoe planned to sit at this lovely old oak table and
pretend to get drunk herself while she kept Nicola's glass
full and lit her cigarettes for her—until Paolo Bondi's de-
ceitful assistant drank herself into a stupor. Then Zoe
would escape to the house of the man who swore he wasn't
Rafe Mastrangelo. If there were secrets to uncover, she intended to find them.

Her plan had only one flaw. It might be dawn before
Nicola Peretti had had enough to drink to make her fall
asleep.

She wanted desperately to take the near-empty bottle of
wine by the neck and break it over Nicola's head like any
decent movie heroine would do in such desperate straits.
The image made her smile, which didn't improve the mood
of her drunken hostess at all.

Nicola planted an elbow on the edge of the table and
held the glass close to her face. Inhaling the scent of the
wine, she peered darkly at Zoe over the lip of the wine-
glass.

"Something funny?" she demanded, slurring her words.

"Sorry," Zoe apologized. "It must be that I'm tired."

Nicola's eyes narrowed and grew dark with suspicion.
She began to mutter shrilly, forgetting her English. Wary
of Nicola's unpredictable behavior, Zoe didn't under-

stand her until she waved angrily at the sofa bed she had pulled out and made up hours ago.

Zoe's skin crawled with fear. Nicola knew she had been tricked into drinking too much. She slammed her glass down onto the table and started to stand and grab Zoe by her hair.

Zoe jerked her head and backed away, knocking her chair over as she went. But Nicola had moved too quickly and the blood must have rushed from her head. By the time Zoe realized Nicola was incapable of coming after her, the woman had already crumpled to the floor with an awful thud.

Zoe clamped her mouth shut to keep from crying out. Relief washed over her. She backed away as carefully and quietly as she could. The apartment building seemed eerily silent, as if daring her to move.

Think, Zoe. Be smart about this.

Maybe if she looked like Nicola, even a little, she would attract less attention.

She took a deep breath, and pulled her hair up and clipped it high on her head. She picked up Nicola's hat, a dark plaid felt fedora, and anchored it over her hair clip. She took a black, loosely knit shawl from the hooks by the door and threw it over her shoulders. Nicola's keys lay on the end table where she had carelessly tossed them.

Goose bumps swept over Zoe's flesh. She picked up the keys and put them into her purse. She would leave her clothing bag. The less she had to carry, the better. She would be back before Nicola woke up.

She took one last glance at the woman who lay crumpled and snoring on the kitchen floor, then let herself out. The stairwell was dark, lit by a low-wattage bulb hanging from a cord. She stood there for another few seconds, collecting her thoughts. Fending off ridiculous fears of crazed and dangerous carabinieri standing guard with Uzis hanging from their shoulders.

No one but Nicola Peretti really cares where I go, she thought. *The men in the bar, maybe, but they're probably all either still drinking or passed out cold as well.*

What was there to be scared of? That someone would knock her off and dump her body in some dark alley? "You're losing it, Zoe," she scolded herself softly. She straightened her shoulders, took a deep breath and started down the narrow stairs.

She encountered no one. Not in the stairs where she might have been trapped. Not on the dark, unlit street. Houses were stacked against one another, tight enough that there were no shortcuts, not so tight that someone couldn't be hiding in nooks and crannies everywhere along the way.

The centuries-old village gave her the creeps. It felt like a rabbit warren, dark and full of unexpected twists and turns made more unsafe by the uneven cobbled streets. The night air was still hot and smelled ripe with the scent of citrus and olives and jasmine. But if there was anyone watching her, Zoe couldn't detect him.

Covering the distance between Nicola's apartment and the arched doorway where Paolo Bondi's name was engraved on a shingle took her no more than a few minutes.

It must have been nearly three in the morning, and even the bar across the street was dark and silent.

Zoe shrank into the deep shadow of the awning above the door. She'd made it this far. Now was the time. She had no way of knowing whether Paolo Bondi lay sleeping within, or if he had gone to deliver the baby he'd spoken of.

Or even if he was who he said he was . . .

She had no idea what she hoped to find. *No,* she thought. That wasn't true. She did know. But her mind refused to go beyond the moment or to consider what knowing what she suspected was true would mean to her life. Or Stephi's.

Secrets were kept here. Things no one in Vallazione wanted her to know. Things that weren't true... Lies a man would disown his wife and child to protect.

Zoe felt more threatened than if someone were holding a gun to her head. But Stephi's life depended as much on uncovering the lies of Vallazione as it did on a transfusion of any cells.

Leaning against the door, Zoe opened her purse. Nicola's ring held only four keys. Two for a car. One to her apartment. One to this house. The lock turned easily. The door creaked open at her shove, and Zoe slipped inside.

She stood briefly in the darkness, absorbing the cramped feel. No one was here. She would swear to it. Relief poured through her. She would not be caught. Her eyes adjusted, and she shouldered her purse, clinging to it like a lifeline.

There was a fireplace, and next to it a brass tray on a claw-footed tripod. Sicilians used the trays to carry hot coals to bed, to make their covers warm as toast. There was one in her town house in Chicago, because Rafe had had such strong sentimental feelings about them.

Zoe swallowed. In her and Stephi's home there were many things that had been precious to Rafe.

To her left was a small foyer that she imagined was Bondi's waiting room, and to her right was the kitchen. Ahead, a narrow set of stairs ascended. Zoe stared at them. Her heart began to thud uneasily.

She could make out to the left of the stairs the shape of an immense old rocking chair, and behind it a hutch where she would have displayed photographs in brass and ceramic and wooden frames.

There were none, but a child's oversize book lay in the rocking chair.

Zoe moved nearer and looked down at the book resting askew on the cushion. She could make out nothing more than vague shapes in the cover art on the book jacket, but the shapes seemed familiar to her. She picked up the book.

Peter Pan.

Surely it belonged to the office of Paolo Bondi. Surely it was for children waiting to see the doctor for a sore throat or a scraped knee.

But what use was an English version of *Peter Pan* to a child in Vallazione?

The instinct to turn and run from this place swelled in Zoe. Distantly she heard her own strangled cry fade in the silence. The truth she had set out to uncover was likely to tear her apart and she knew it. Numbed, she let the book fall from her hands and turned away.

She went to the stairs and climbed them. At the top was a small bathroom. She turned left and went a few steps to the doorway of a bedroom filled with a massive, heavy wooden bedstead and an equally immense old armoire.

The furniture filled the room. The curtains were drawn, but hung limply. The bedcovers were carefully made up.

Rafe never cared if a bed was made or not. Ridiculous or not, the thought comforted her. Rafe would never make a bed. This wasn't his.

She could find out for sure. All she had to do was uncover a pillow and inhale the scent, but she couldn't even bring herself to cross the threshold.

Like a puppet pulled along under someone else's control she turned away and went in the other direction. The room was a child's, a girl's. Toys were strewn about, roughly made dolls unlike Barbie or baby dolls made in the States, stuffed animals and piles of paperback coloring books.

A tiny iron bed, also made up but a little rumpled, sat beneath the window. A night-light plugged into the wall, a little lighted seashell, glowed in the dark. Some of its light glinted off a small glass box on the windowsill, drawing Zoe's attention.

Her throat closed off. Her heart told her it was a music box and she knew even before she turned it upside down and turned the key to start the mechanism what it would play.

"Autumn Leaves."

The truth hit Zoe as if she had never begun to suspect from the moment she saw the English edition of *Peter Pan.* This was Teddi's room and this was Teddi's music box. The dolls were Teddi's, and the animals and the coloring books and the seashell night-light.

Rafe had done more than stand in a bar in Vallazione surrounded by mountains and lie to her. He had kept Teddi from her.

He might as well have carved her heart out with a butcher knife.

Her senses shut down. She heard nothing but the melancholy tune tinkling from the brass mechanism in the music box and the rush of blood past her ears. But one moment she was standing there holding the fragile music box, and the next a powerful masculine body engulfed her from behind. One hand clapped over her mouth and the other held a knife beneath her left breast, poised to drive upward into her heart.

He whispered harshly in her ear. Though he spoke in the Sicilian dialect, she understood the threat of instant death if she so much as breathed. *"Capisce?"*

Zoe whimpered and nodded and slumped against him. One or another of her actions broke through his consciousness and he reacted as if her slackened body had scalded him.

"Zoe!" The doctor swore and took hold of her shoulder, swinging her around. She lost her balance and fell awkwardly to Teddi's bed. He knew her. He *knew* her. Anger and confusion spilled into her blood. Tears sprang to her eyes as she pushed herself upright, eyeing the stiletto gripped in his hands. In that moment she would have turned it on him.

"Zoe, *Mio Dio.* How could you be so foolish!" He stared at her in disbelief, shaken to his core at what he had nearly done. "Why are you wearing that hat? That shawl?"

Zoe snapped. "I thought it would be safer!"

"I could have *killed* you. Where is Nicola?"

"Drunk on her kitchen floor." Zoe clamped her mouth shut and breathed raggedly. Rafe. Dear God. Her throat ached. She felt a trickle of sweat run down her midriff. Or was it blood? A hundred questions clamored inside her. Only one mattered. "Where is she, Rafe? Where is Teddi?"

He sank to his haunches, breathing out fast to blow off the effects of the adrenaline surging through him. Seconds passed like hours. "I could have killed you."

"Where is my daughter?"

Nothing else mattered. Nothing. But even in the dark the slope of his shoulders, the power and size of his arms, the profile of his face, even the strained quality of his voice—everything once familiar and beloved to her—dredged up emotions and needs left unfulfilled too long.

But she would die before she ran to him, or clung to him, or begged him to take her back. Nothing mattered but her little girls.

Rafe put the knife carefully aside and sat on a little wooden chair. His head fell forward. "She's not here."

"I can see that she's not here," Zoe hissed, tears threatening in her eyes, her throat tight. "I asked you where she is."

"With Turi."

"In the *bar?*"

"No! For God's sake, Zoe, he has a family—"

"Oh." Her lips trembled. Her jaw ached. She couldn't take her eyes off the shape of Raphael Mastrangelo. "Imagine that. He has a *family.*" He turned his head away from her. She had struck at his heart and hit her mark. "I want to go to her."

"You can't."

"Try to stop me." She sprang from the bed and rushed toward the door. He was faster. His hand darted out and grabbed her wrist. "Let me go," she cried, fighting his grip. "I swear to you I'll scream!" Even then her voice rose.

"Stop it, Zoe," he whispered fiercely. His grip on her wrist tightened. He stood, and in one lightning-fast move he jerked her tight against him by the leverage he had on her arm. She struggled, but she had no chance against his superior size and strength. He held her head cradled hard against his chest, then bowed his head low to speak into her ear.

His whiskers scraped her ear, caught in her hair. Zoe shuddered. She tried once more to twist away, but he only held her tighter to him. His voice was low, barely more than a warm, moist whisper against her ear. "Stop it, Zoe. Don't scream. Don't fight me. Please, don't fight me."

Again her body slackened against his. He let go of her wrist, but it was trapped between their bodies. His forearm scraped over her breast, and Zoe cried out softly against the sharp pang of pleasure streaking from her breast down her belly, into her womb.

She felt his body reacting violently, swelling, engorging, and he covered her breast with his hand and her mouth with his own to muffle her cry.

She couldn't breathe but it didn't matter.

Couldn't pull away, but she no longer tried.

She felt engulfed in him, in the sudden heat, in the power and craving of his body. Her own body struggled now to get even closer to his. The smoldering coals of every physical and sexual and emotional response he had ever aroused in her broke into flames. Stephi's fate, and Teddi's, consumed her, but in that one instant, she couldn't contain herself or the neediness of her body.

Or think or reason or remember that she should hate him.

"Zoe," he croaked. "Zoe." His lips parted again and he kissed her parted lips at one corner and at the other and at the center.

He wanted to plunge his tongue into her starved mouth. He wanted to grind his sex against the cradle of her. But she whimpered half in pleasure and half in agony. The tiny high-pitched vibrations broke through his mindlessness and he knew she would hate him more for making her feel again.

For reminding her of her needs and making her forget everything else when it was their precious little girls whose needs and lives were in such grave danger.

Danger Zoe didn't yet even understand.

She pulled back. It broke his heart but he let her go. Her lips pursed and she swallowed and looked up at him, then away. She returned to Teddi's small bed, sank down onto it and hid her hands beneath Nicola Peretti's shawl.

She shook her head slowly, and a tear fell as she stared at him. "I don't understand what's happening."

Rafe bent to pick up the tiny child's chair. He set it down backward and closer to Teddi's bed and sat before Zoe. "There isn't time—"

"Tell me about her."

Rafe hung his head. "Zoe, there isn't time—"

"Please."

Rafe shook his head. He should get her out of Vallazione now. But what would it hurt? A few minutes to reassure her. If she knew Teddi was all right maybe she would go along with him without fighting him every step of the way.

"Teddi's fine, Zoe. Growing like a weed. She's happy. And smart. Still quiet. She feels things pretty deeply."

Zoe nodded. Quiet, solemn, precious child. "Does she smile?"

"When she thinks you and Stephi won't be lost anymore."

"She thinks we're lost?"

He nodded. "But she tells me almost every day that soon you'll...find your way home. Zoe, about Stephi..."

She swallowed the sudden lump of guilt and shame in her throat. Teddi had flourished with Rafe. Stephi was dying. "She's very sick, Rafe. Please," she begged, "take me to Teddi."

"Zoe, I can't."

"I have to see her. I have to hold her. I have to see my baby! I can't...please. You have to let me see her."

"Zoe, listen to me—"

"I can't! Don't you see? Don't you know? I don't know who you *are!* How can I listen to you? All I want is..." She broke off, unable to finish.

All she had ever wanted included everything they had once had. But Rafe wasn't hers anymore or he could never have lived this lie, apart from her. Or apart from Stephi, who missed him so desperately that she'd made herself sick and defenseless against so much as a common cold.

"Rafe, listen to me." All she could see of his eyes were dark holes, but she could tell that he was listening. "When I came here I didn't know Teddi was alive, but now... I have to take her back with me. There is no time. Stephi will die without her."

"Zoe. You don't understand—"

She shook her head. "It doesn't matter! I don't care!"

Rafe sat back, straightening to reach a lighter in his pants pocket. He twisted and leaned over to the table where Teddi's chair had been and lifted the globe from a lantern. He lighted the wick and replaced the glass, then turned the flame low.

He leaned forward again. He wanted to touch Zoe, to hold her hands, but she sat huddled tight. He had to make her understand the dangers, and it wouldn't matter in the end whether he held her hands or not. He couldn't cushion the blows.

"I've already sent Teddi down the mountain with Turi—"

"No!"

"Yes." He watched the color drain from her face. "To Palermo."

She shook her head. "You're lying! I don't believe you."

"It's the truth, Zoe. I promise you—"

"Don't you promise me anything! You have no right."

Rafe's whole face darkened. Even on the child-size chair he towered over her. "Don't judge what you don't understand, Zoe. Now, listen to me. It doesn't matter whether you believe me or not. Turi left to take Teddi to my mother. She will take Teddi to Chicago because I believe you. I understand how sick Stephi is. How much she needs the transfusion."

"Then—"

"No. Listen. Unless we do this my way, Teddi won't live long enough to get out of Sicily. And neither will you."

Chapter Six

Zoe stared at him. The light of the small lantern flickered on half his face and left the other half deep in shadows, and the image suddenly terrified her. She was afraid of him, of a dark half she had never seen before.

"You must be mad."

"I wish to God it were that simple." He rose and kicked the small chair aside. Zoe jumped. "It's not. *I'm* not."

"Rafe, please. Just let me go, let me take Teddi—"

"No."

Zoe swallowed hard. "I could pick her up at your mother's ... or she could come with us if that's what you want ... if you think it would be easier for Teddi—"

Rafe turned and slammed the butt of his hand against the doorjamb and spoke away from her. "You just don't get it, do you?"

Zoe took a breath and squared her shoulders. "Get what, Rafe? That you—"

He cursed and swung around. His hands hung unnaturally at his sides, like a fighter, loosening up, poised to deliver a sucker punch. "Zoe, do you think it was an accident that the yacht went up like some freaking inferno?"

"Rafe ..." Her throat locked. Had he imagined—believed all this time—that someone had caused the explosion on purpose? "The yacht was struck by lightning, there was an official investigation. Centi died. Frank explained it all to me—''

Rafe laughed bitterly, cutting her off. ''And did Frank explain to you that Teddi and I were dead as well?''

Zoe swallowed. ''That was the finding of the investigation— ''

''Which Frank invented.'' He dragged a hand across the back of his neck. ''It was a lie from start to finish.''

''No.'' Zoe shook her head. It wasn't possible. ''Frank would never lie to me.''

''But I would.'' Her naive certainty, her faith in the likes of Clemenza over him, felt like lead shot pelting his chest, powder burning his flesh.

''You *have* lied to me.'' Her voice broke. Her teeth chattered as if she were chilled to the bone in the midst of the sweltering, breathless night. She stared at him. ''Something must have happened to you.'' How else could she reconcile the fact that he and Teddi were alive when Frank had told her they were dead? ''You must have lost your memory. Maybe you washed up on shore somewhere without knowing your name or what had happened or—''

He swore.

She flinched.

''There was never a moment when I didn't know who I was.''

Her chin ached. ''Then you are even less a man than I thought!'' she railed, seeing in his dangerous expression that she had already gone too far. ''You knew! You've known all this time and let me go on believing you and Teddi were dead.''

His eyes narrowed and for a moment he turned his head away, refusing to look at her. He turned back to her, and his eyes burned into her. ''That is the difference between us, *carissima,*'' he said, turning the endearment into a curse. ''I would not have taken the word of the Madonna that you were dead.''

Her face and neck and breasts felt suddenly inflamed. "That's not fair—"

"But it is the truth. We were supposed to die on that yacht. And Frank made sure I would wish that I had."

Zoe bit her lip to keep from protesting. Frank had never meant any of them to die, or even come to harm. She didn't know what Rafe meant or what he was talking about, and not knowing scared her more than his fierce, angry posture.

She had to get away from him. She couldn't. She had no hope of finding Teddi without him. She had no choice but to reason with him. "Rafe, please—"

She was cut short by a sound of someone breaking in the door, racing up the stairs. She shrank back on the bed, and Rafe flattened himself against the wall by the door to Teddi's room.

"Signore Doctor!" a strained, hysterical voice called out on a harsh whisper. "*Signore,* it's me, Carlo."

Rafe let out a breath. "Carlito." He grabbed the shadowed figure by the front of his shirt. "What is it?"

Zoe saw that he was no more than a boy. His body was immature, strong but gangly. His arms and legs were thin. His hair hung in his face, and he scraped it back and began rambling incoherently.

Rafe answered him in Italian. Zoe understood little of it except that he was trying to calm the boy down. Gesturing wildly, Carlo took a few deep breaths and plunged into his story. Something about an *americano,* about the radio and the carabinieri coming. He was terrified. And the way he looked at Zoe and crossed himself over and over again kindled stark, nameless fears in her.

Rafe subjected him to one harsh question after another. Zoe understood nothing but a few names. *Clemenza*... "Si." Carlo's head bobbed. *Cavallo*... "Si."

The fear began to writhe in her and Zoe shuddered. Rafe stroked the boy's head in praise, kissed him on both cheeks, then sent Carlito away. Rafe moved across the floor toward her, and for the first time Zoe noticed that he limped, but she had no time to ask why. He grabbed her by the wrist and pulled her near to the edge of the bed and knelt down beside her, holding both her hands.

"Zoe, listen to me now, because I only have time to say this once. Clemenza knows you're here, and he's just given that boy a message to take to Cavallo." He paused and wiped the sweat from his brow with the back of his hand. "He's ordered you dead, Zoe, before dawn, and Cavallo will kill you without a second thought."

She could barely breathe in the stifling heat. "That's not possible. Carlo must have misunderstood the message—"

"Zoe, stop it!" He dropped her hands and took her by the shoulders and shook her. "Stop thinking there must be some sane, logical, harmless reason for what's happening around you. There isn't. No one is harmless. No one! The sooner you get that through your head—"

"Why?" Her lips began to tremble. "Why would this boy warn you? How does he know? Why was it him and not Cavallo coming here if what you say is true?"

"Because Cavallo pays Carlo a measly few hundred lire to listen to the police radio every night." He reached beyond Zoe, stripped the pillowcase from Teddi's pillow and began filling it with her treasures. The music box. A doll. A crocheted lamb.

"Carlito's leg got mangled up in a cycling accident over a year ago. I saved his leg. He figured he owed me. He came here first, Zoe, but he's going to Cavallo now because if he doesn't, he's dead meat and he knows it." Rafe twisted the end of the pillowcase and knotted it. His eyes fixed ruthlessly on her. "Believe me or don't. Unless you come with me now, it won't matter what you believe. You won't live to see Stephi or Teddi again."

Zoe gave a small cry. Even if everything Rafe said and believed was the produce of paranoid delusions, the wild-eyed fear in that boy's face was real. Too real to disregard. "Are you sure Teddi is . . . is away from here?"

"Turi left with her hours ago. No one saw him go. But—"

"Won't he be in terrible danger if Cavallo finds out Turi took her away? And your mother?"

"Yes." Rafe grimaced. "The only way Turi's family will be safe is if Cavallo believes *we* took Teddi and made a run for it. They won't be watching every international flight out, either." He stood and looked down at her. "Decide, Zoe. And do it now. There's no time left."

Her children's lives hung in the balance. If their only chance of getting Teddi to Chicago was to create a diversion, to make themselves the target, then that was what she must do.

She had no choice but to trust the man who had first loved and then betrayed and finally denied her. She understood none of that, but it didn't matter. "Just tell me what to do."

He let his head fall forward, savoring an instant of relief, then caught her by the back of her neck and kissed her, hard. "We'll make it, Zoe, *cara*. I swear it."

HE LED HER OUT the kitchen door into a narrow, dark alley where his old, battered Fiat was parked. The scent of jasmine and garbage mingled in the hot, stifling night. Rafe's hand cupped her cheek and he spoke almost imperceptibly into her ear.

"Get in on the driver's side. I'm going to push. As soon as you feel any momentum, pop the clutch. Keep it in first gear. Turn left onto the street. I'll get in then. Drive slowly, as quietly as you can."

He wanted her to drive? She shook her head and began to say "I can't," but his thumb covered her lips.

"You can, Zoe. You must. The ignition would wake the dead. Until we get to Turi's we need to go unnoticed. Now do it. Go."

He handed her the pillowcase filled with Teddi's things and gave her a small shove toward the car. She felt herself shaking all over, trembling inside and out. She couldn't work the door handle at first, and then the latch gave, sounding to her like a gunshot echoing in the forbidding silence.

Do it, she told herself. *Get in. Just get in.* She glanced back once at Rafe, then pulled the door open and slid into the car. She didn't see him, but it was Rafe who closed the door.

She tossed the pillowcase behind her. Swallowing hard, she took two deep breaths, then grasped the steering wheel. She put her foot on the clutch and plunged it to the floor.

The small car began to move, slowly at first, inch by inch, then a little faster. She concentrated hard. Rafe had taught her this trick years ago, when she'd left her lights on and killed the battery, but it had been so long. She waited. A little more. A little more.

Her hands gripped the steering wheel so tightly they hurt. The car rolled almost silently into the narrow street. Rafe banged on the bumper. *Now.* She let out the clutch and stepped on the gas and turned the wheel hard to the left. The engine rolled over, took hold. She peeled out, then braked and almost killed the engine.

She swore at herself, thinking she would have done better to have turned on the ignition. But Rafe jumped in and touched her cheek. "You're doing fine, Zoe. That way. Take it slow, easy."

He guided her around three blocks. It seemed to her that they were going in a circle, inviting trouble. But they must drive slowly around the piazza so that Zoe could pull up to the door where Turi unloaded the cases of liquor and casks of beer and wine.

Even in the darkest part of the night before dawn the shadows of buildings loomed darker, threatening, concealing a thousand eyes watching. Waiting.

Rafe rolled down a window so that he could listen. Cavallo lived in a farmhouse miles from town, but Carlo had almost certainly reached him by now, and he would be coming after them with every intention of fulfilling Clemenza's execution order. He had Zoe back up a bit, to pull deeper into the shadows, then touched her cheek again.

"Will you drive?" she asked.

Rafe nodded quickly. "Move over when I get out. Leave the car running. Be ready. I have to make a big, public show of taking Teddi. Grazi will give me a sack of flour or something bundled in blankets. I'll put it in your lap. As far as you're concerned, it's Teddi. Can you do that?"

"Yes." She covered her lips with her fingers. It wasn't going to be Teddi.

"Remember this. Teddi is already safe, but people are watching even now. Can you feel it?" She nodded, not trusting herself to speak. "You have to be convincing, or it is Turi's family who will suffer."

She gave a brave, brief smile. She must do her part to create the illusion that together they had stolen Teddi away.

He didn't use the back entrance. He disappeared around a corner, and she could hear him banging loudly on a door. "Grazielle, let me in. Grazi!"

More pounding.

Zoe shivered and climbed over the stick shift to the opposite seat. She listened intently. She saw candles flicker and silhouettes of people turning up at windows in their morbid curiosity. What if one of them...? But no. None of them would act. Cavallo was coming. They would all know that.

A part of her wanted to make a break for it. She could see her rented Fiat across the way. She could follow Turi down the mountain, find Rafe's mother and steal Teddi away herself.

Whatever Rafe believed, Frank could have nothing to do with the explosion on the yacht. He would never hurt her.

Rafe swore the explosion was deliberate, but he had sworn he was not her husband, too. She couldn't trust him.

Frank Clemenza would not have done those things. He would never have ordered her death. But in this place, in this town, Cavallo ruled. Nicola watched. And Rafe believed.

Anything could happen in Vallazione.

Despite Mary Bernadette's fears, Zoe thought, despite her beloved aunt sending her to Paolo Bondi saying *trust him,* Zoe knew she should have gone to Frank in the first place. She should go now. Frank could still help her. Especially now, knowing Teddi was alive. He would find her, no matter what. He would bring her home, and then Stephi would be all right, too....

Rafe's pounding ceased. A woman hushed him. The door closed firmly behind him. Zoe felt alone. Vulnerable. A breeze caught up a piece of crumpled newsprint and it skittered across the cobbled, crumbling piazza. Zoe couldn't move.

No one is harmless, Zoe. No one.

Not even Rafe, she thought. But the terror in Carlito's frenzied eyes convinced her that the lives of other people were at stake now for reasons she could barely grasp. So it didn't matter what Rafe had done, or what lies he told or what delusions he clung to. Right now she had to believe he had done what he must. And that he would find some way out of this hellish nightmare for all of them.

A door latch opened. The woman's voice scolded. Rafe apologized loudly, almost drunkenly, then rounded the corner. Zoe opened her door, and Rafe lowered the sack of grain wrapped in blankets that was supposed to be Teddi in Zoe's lap.

"*Now,* Zoe. This is your long-lost child. Make them believe it."

She closed her arms around the sack of grain and gave a keening cry. "Oh, my God. Teddi. Teddi."

"Louder." He shut the car door.

Zoe cried out again. "Teddi. Teddi." It wasn't hard. It wasn't a pretense. The sack of grain wasn't Teddi, and it broke her heart. No matter how certain Rafe was that Teddi was safe with Turi Difalco, Zoe wouldn't believe it until she could hold her child. She noticed again the limp as Rafe slung his body into the car, but it didn't seem to hinder him.

He rammed in the clutch and peeled out of the alley, laying rubber, intending that everyone watching should know. Everyone asleep should wake and take notice. His actions were a slap in the face of Frank Clemenza himself.

Vallazione's Paolo Bondi, the doctor, the tragic hero, the pitiable village doctor destroyed by grief and unnatural celibacy, Paolo Bondi was no more.

Instead it was Rafe Mastrangelo who dared to take the *americana* and their child and run for it. He'd broken Clemenza's rule, defied Clemenza's edict, and he would pay.

Every man, woman and child in Vallazione knew how dearly. Cavallo would not be thwarted; Clemenza would not be so insulted.

But Rafe had already paid too dearly.

Chapter Seven

Carved from the side of a volcanic mountain, only one road led into and out of Vallazione, back to Palermo or higher up the mountain. Rafe took the route that climbed higher, and less than a mile out of town, he shut off the headlights.

Zoe had no idea how he could see the winding, twisted, treacherous road. Several times his steering adjustments to stay with the road flung her toward him or against the door. "Shouldn't you—"

"No," he answered, anticipating her question. "Cavallo will be coming right at us."

"Why didn't we go the other way, then?"

"You came in on that road. It's long and lonely and there is no way to get off it. One call from Cavallo and we'd be facing roadblocks. Up here, he's the only law around." He grimaced. "If we're lucky, we'll get beyond his cutoff before he sees us."

"Why would he conclude it was us, anyway?"

"Who else in a village the size of Vallazione?" Pressing the accelerator to the floor, Rafe rounded another broad curve and nodded in the direction of a valley. "That's the farm Cavallo lives on. His road intersects with this one—and it is the only place to turn around."

"What if we're not lucky?"

"Then—" he shrugged "—we improvise." In another second he spotted the sweep of headlights coming from the farm up the hill to the road they were on, confirming his fears.

He swore. They would never make it beyond the intersection in the road without being caught in the path of Cavallo's headlights. To the left, the road gave way to the impossibly steep mountainside. Braking, he steered the little Fiat off the road to the right—on the downhill side. Zoe saw his dilemma. Too far off the edge of the road, the car would roll. Not far enough, Cavallo would spot them, anyway.

Tilted at a sickening angle, she knew the ground could only be a few feet from her head. The little Fiat jolted and bucked, barely scraping by a thick patch of scrub before Rafe brought it to a stop.

The silence after the terrible scraping noises seemed deadly. She clung to the sack of flour. Rafe reached over and cupped the back of her head with his hand. "I take it we're improvising?" she asked softly.

"Are you all right?"

She could only glance at him and nod.

"Shh, now."

They watched the headlights Rafe was certain belonged to Cavallo's car fishtail onto the main road, coming in their direction. The winding road took the car out of their line of vision. But when the car rounded the next corner heading downhill, for a split second the beam of headlights glinted off the top of their windshield.

Rafe swore again and bounced his fist off the steering wheel.

"Cavallo was terribly drunk tonight, Rafe," Zoe offered. "As fast as he's driving, maybe he wasn't in any shape to notice the light reflecting off us."

"I wouldn't want to trust him to be so accommodatingly blind."

"Still, maybe it will take him a little while to connect the reflection to us. And he'll have to go all the way into town before he can turn around. Won't he?"

Rafe nodded. "Unless he catches on faster than that, and just backs up." He rolled down the window and listened, but the sound of Cavallo's powerful engine was gone. "Unless he's stopped, he must be out of earshot of us."

"Would he just stop?"

"Let's hope not." Rafe gave it another agonizing minute, but heard nothing more. He turned on the engine, wincing at the grinding ignition. "He's smart, Zoe. I wouldn't underestimate him, but he's never been what you'd call subtle." Rafe pressed down the accelerator and babied the Fiat, inching, sidling back up onto the road. When he reached the pavement, he switched on the headlights and pushed the old Fiat to its limits, hard and fast.

Zoe held her breath. "So. How long before he catches up with us?"

"If he caught the reflection, ten minutes. Fifteen, at most. If not, half an hour. But he will be back, and we can't outrun him in this heap."

"Great." Beyond exhaustion, her most practical fear being that Rafe's driving would get them killed before Cavallo could do it, she let go of the breath she'd been holding. "What are we going to do?"

His eyes were trained hard on the road. "There's a grotto up ahead where my great-uncle used to hide out from the carabinieri. We're going there, but we're going to have to go separately."

"Separately? Why? I'm not going—"

"Listen to me," he interrupted. "In another mile or so, I'll let you out. Head straight uphill. Don't stop until you hear Cavallo's car, then drop down. I'll take that for a cue. You'll be hidden and I'll know when he's coming. I'll catch up to you."

She felt afraid to ask. "What are you going to do?"

"Give Cavallo one spectacular crash."

Zoe swallowed. Here was a real fear to cling to. "You're crazy! How, Rafe? Wait for him to catch up and then drive yourself off a cliff?"

Steering hard, he took his eyes off the road and gave her a harder look. "That's exactly what I'm going to do."

"And I'm supposed to believe you'll survive it?"

His eyes went back to watching the road, just in time to react, to dodge a goat grazing on the uphill side of the road. His jaw clenched. "I have no intention of going over with the car, *carissima,* but if I die, there's always Frank Clemenza to take care of you."

His answer knocked the breath out of her. His glance flicked toward her, but if he saw her shock at his pitiless gibe he didn't apologize.

"Zoe, there is no other way." He rounded a bend and just before the next curve, maybe only half a mile, slammed on the brakes.

She braced herself against the dashboard. The back of the car skidded off the pavement onto the dirt.

He closed his eyes for a minute. "This is it," he said. "Take my medical bag and Teddi's pillowcase. Please. Do what I told you." Again he reached for her and stroked her hair. "Please."

Zoe stared at him, much as she had always caught herself staring because his looks compelled her. Would he put them through all this if they weren't in real danger? By the scant light of the dashboard she saw his intense determination and it struck her—what monumental willpower it must have taken him to survive the explosion. To save Teddi.

"Were you burned badly, Raphael?" she whispered, tears clogging her throat.

Rafe's eyes searched hers. He gave a brief smile. His voice was choked, too. "Not so badly, *carissima.*"

Strong emotion made her heart tighten. Her chin began to quiver. She lowered her eyes and nodded. Rafe clenched his hand in her hair, holding to her fiercely, then let go and reached across her to open the door.

"Listen. If I don't make it—"

"I don't want to hear this."

"If I don't, *cara*," he insisted, "you are all Teddi and Stephi have left." He saw that he had her reluctant attention. "Keep going over the mountain. Pick landmarks. Always head east, and you will finally come to a farmhouse where if you say you are the widow of Raphael Mastrangelo, they will help you."

Zoe nodded, but she wasn't going to think about how she would survive this without him.

"Hurry now," he urged. She let the bag of flour tumble to the floor and got out. He grabbed his medical bag and Teddi's bundle and handed them to her. "Straight up. I'll be there, Zoe. On my honor, I'll be there soon."

He pulled the door shut, then waved her on. He would wait here, both to mark her progress and allow Cavallo to catch up to him.

Zoe gave herself one brief moment to feel the panic of setting off alone, then shook it off. Shouldering her purse, she took his doctor's bag in one hand and Teddi's parcel of treasures in the other, crossed the road to the uphill slope and began the climb.

The incline wouldn't have been too extreme or difficult except that it was so dark and she was wearing sandals. She thought about stripping off her panty hose so that her feet wouldn't constantly slip in the sandals, but knew Rafe was watching her and wouldn't know what to make of her stopping. Besides, she needed him to see strength and determination on her part equal to his own.

She continued to climb, choosing her footing carefully. It was just luck that when she stumbled and went down hard on one knee, which Rafe would take for his cue, that was when she heard the engine of Cavallo's car roaring up the mountain road.

Prickly pear stabbed at her arms and ankles. The dry, exposed roots of the scrub oak had tripped her, and she had dropped her bags to catch herself. Tiny spines from some other smaller cactus stuck in the palms of both her hands.

"Damn!" She bit off her cry of pain and swiped angrily at her tears with the backs of her hands, then crawled behind the clump of scrub to watch and wait.

Fear for Rafe bit into her. From the sound of the low, purring engine, Cavallo's car was powerful. Rafe's was barely more than a heap of spare parts. She could still see the dark shape of the little Fiat huddled at the side of the road. Go! she thought. *Why doesn't he go?*

Still, when the Fiat lurched onto the road and careered out of sight, she wasn't prepared for the icy sensation of dread at being left so alone.

Cavallo's car roared around the curve, maybe only a minute behind Rafe. He'd been right. Cavallo was not stupid, or even drunk or hung over enough to miss the glint of light reflecting from a car that shouldn't have been there.

Her head filled with self-recriminations. If she'd listened to her own instincts and gone to Frank...but Rafe believed it was Frank who had ordered her death. And what of Mary Bernadette?

Zoe stopped cold. How had her aunt known? What did she know? How could she possibly have sent Zoe to Paolo Bondi and not known he was Rafe?

Staring at a dead, shriveled stump of a tree, clinging to Rafe's bag and Teddi's dearest possessions, Zoe shivered. Mary Bernadette had to have known. The certainty made her heart knock painfully. They had all lied to her. All of them.

She still couldn't believe it was Frank Clemenza orchestrating this nightmare. But even if he was, even if everything Rafe said was true, his lies were the worst. The most unforgivable.

If he had loved her, if he had ever cared for her, he would have found a way, no matter what the obstacles, to let her know he was alive.

A bird, startled out of its nest on the ground a few feet away, spooked Zoe from her thoughts. She couldn't think of any of that now. Couldn't afford the luxury of all her righteous anger at Rafe.

The danger now was that she had argued with him one moment too many in the dark of Teddi's tiny room. If she hadn't, they might have made it past the junction in the road before Cavallo could have caught sight of them. Dear God.

"Stop it, Zoe," she chided herself angrily. There was more than enough blame to go around, and right now, here in the dark and the cold and the harsh, forbidding landscape, none of it mattered.

Ignoring the smattering of cactus spines in her hands, she grabbed up everything again and began to climb, aware every second of the sounds of both engines, Rafe's and Cavallo's, whining, echoing eerily against the stark landscape.

The road wended round the mountain. She had no hope of keeping watch. She couldn't see for herself whether Rafe had managed to escape from the car he intended to send over a cliff. Even if Cavallo was convinced that all three of them, Rafe, Zoe and Teddi, had plunged to a certain fiery death, it was only a temporary diversion.

She had progressed no more than another fifty feet when the sounds reverberating around her changed.

She stopped, straining to listen. Afraid to listen. By the absence of its whine and friction, she knew the Fiat had hurtled off the road into space. She began to measure time in heartbeats, but maybe her heart had stopped. The second car, Cavallo's, squealed and skidded, shrieked horribly to a stop.

Silence.

Listening intently, Zoe matched the sounds to events she pictured in her mind. The Fiat falling silently through the air, crashing, rolling, crumpling, exploding.

And bursting into flames.

Zoe collapsed. Weeds and cactus tore at her but she hardly noticed. How many times had she suffered the nightmarish explosion she *had* witnessed with her own arm horribly broken and Stephi screaming for her papa? This one seemed to Zoe far, far worse. At least then she had seen the fiery blast consuming him. She had *known* Rafe's fate.

But she'd been mistaken.

Fear coursed jaggedly down every nerve in her body. This time she knew he had somehow jumped clear.

But what if she was mistaken this time, too?

Her energy flagged. The exhaustion she had been holding at bay for so many hours caught up with her. Whatever adrenaline she had left was spent when the glow of flames seemed to frame the echoes of Cavallo swearing, shouting rapid-fire orders in a language she had no hope of understanding. Were there others with him, or was he radioing for help?

The sky lightened by slow degrees. The sun would rise in another hour. She felt herself going numb. She had to keep moving, now while she had the cover of darkness, but she tried too hard and slipped and stumbled and sent a spray of rocks and dirt spilling back down the mountain.

In her mind the sound of sliding rock was magnified a hundred times. Cavallo wasn't stupid. She knew he would not fail to notice.

She was on her own. Cavallo would find her. All he had to do was track the path of the slide. She had to find a place to hide. There was an enormous boulder, embedded in the landscape several feet to her left. Or the clump of trees. Or the side of the cliff. *I have no intention of going over with the car,* carissima, *but if I die, there's always Frank Clemenza to take care of you.*

She wasn't rational anymore. Thinking was out; decisions, impossible. She pulled herself up from sheer grit and clawed her way behind the boulder. In other seasons, other years, the rains had eroded the stone smooth. She sank into a small cavelike hole where the earth had long since been washed away from the roots of an ancient olive tree growing almost out of the stone itself.

The sounds of her own tortured breathing taunted her. Cavallo would hear that, too. *Let him,* she thought. Let him find her. She would scratch his eyes out if it was the last thing she ever did.

She had been gone from Stephi less than thirty-six hours. It seemed years. She understood next to nothing of what had happened, even that Rafe and Teddi had survived. But Teddi was alive and healthy and no matter what happened now, surely to God Rafe's mother would get her to Chicago. Stephi would be safe.

Saved.

Something, some creature, a field mouse or lizard, scurried over her foot. Zoe shivered violently and clamped her teeth tight, fighting to keep from giving herself away.

Then she heard the telltale snap of a footstep and the whispering. "Zoe? Zoe, where are you?" She almost cried out, almost, but Cavallo mocking her in her own voice flashed in her mind.

It might be Rafe, but she had heard Cavallo perfectly mime his voice in Turi's bar, as well. She held her breath and pressed a fist to her lips. Cavallo or Rafe? How could she know?

"Zoe, answer me now, *cara*. Where are you?"

Cavallo. She knew it. He had followed the trail of newly fallen rock, and then he had heard her breathing. He was trying to trick her. Would he call her by name or *"signora"* if he was trying to trick her? The sun would reach the horizon very soon now. The darkness was beginning to fade to light more and more.

But then she heard the approach of more cars, the screech of tires, the jumble of anxious men, and distantly, Cavallo's voice shouting frenzied angry orders through a bullhorn. Through her muddled mind, she understood that if it was Cavallo's voice below, it must be Rafe who was so near to her.

"Zoe? Zoe! Are you here?"

He was so much closer now. He was almost upon her. "Here," she managed to say.

He was at her side in a heartbeat, gathering her into his arms in another. A sob of relief tore out of her, muffled against his chest.

"How did you get out?" Such a stupid question. What did it matter how he had escaped? Disappearing was his forte. Another sob caught in her throat.

"I told you I would." He held her and stroked her hair and crooned, over and over again, "Zoe. Zoe. Shh, my heart. Be still. Look, you found the grotto by yourself."

Still holding her, he leaned to her right and eased one dry brittle root aside, exposing a finger hold, and pulled hard. It took several sharp tugs, but finally a circle of old wood like the lid of a cask clattered loose. A rush of cool, clean air streamed through the circular opening. Clumps of dirt rained down.

Zoe recoiled. "He'll hear," she warned, mouthing the words.

"Cavallo?" Rafe shook his head, answering in a low voice. "He won't. It's deceptive, I know. We can hear him, but he can't hear us up here." The sun was within moments of rising. "Come on."

He let her go and went ahead. Crawling on all fours, he was forced to angle his shoulders to get through the narrow opening. The movement cost him, and he growled fiercely in pain. For an instant Zoe thought he might pass out. And then she saw the reason. His shirt was ripped at the back shoulder and soaked through with blood.

"Oh, my God. Rafe, your shoulder!"

"Zoe," he ground out. "Hand me my bag and Teddi's."

"But your shoulder—"

"Will wait another few minutes! Zoe, for the love of God, hand me the stuff and get in here!"

"I'm never, ever going anywhere with you again," she whispered at him. "Stupid, stupid man!" Admittedly, he was about as responsible for the gaping wound in his shoulder as she was for the cactus spines in her hands, but she was too angry to care. "Do you hear me? Never!"

He stared at her for a moment, and an ache began deep inside him. "Never is a very long time, my heart," he retorted at last.

"Not nearly long enough!"

"Foolish woman." Tears filled his eyes. It was true that his shoulder hurt like the blazes of hell, but Zoe picking a fight made his chest tighten.

They had always picked foolish, frivolous fights to put their real tensions into perspective, and such arguments had the added advantage of leading inevitably to bed.

This tiff would not. Still, it began to ease the agony of the years without her.

"Does that mean, Zoe, that you're going back down the mountain to deal with the carabinieri?"

She wanted to laugh, but it was still real anger fueling her emotions. "I hate you."

She hurled his medical bag through, and Teddi's filthy and ragged pillowcase, then crawled through the hole herself, using the heels of her hands to keep from driving the cactus splinters even deeper. Two feet inside the opening, he showed her how to turn around and jump down to stand up. He dug through his bag for a penlight and handed it to her.

She held the ridiculously thin beam while Rafe eased the wooden circle past the root that guarded it and jerked hard to position it back in as tightly as he could.

But when he finished, the beam of the penlight she held passed over his shoulder and Zoe saw the spread of fresh blood flowing from his wound, soaking through his shirt. He turned, instinctively protecting the wound, but he slumped against the dirt wall.

"Get the smelling salts, Zoe."

He would pass out in another minute. Either he had lost too much blood, or his brain had checked out as his only defense against the pain. She stuck the penlight in her mouth, aimed inside the bag and raked desperately through his medical supplies for an ampoule of ammonia to crack under his nose.

He coughed and batted at her hand and coughed again coming out of it. "Better," he croaked. "Much better."

She shook her head and wiped away a tear from her cheek. He was only slightly better. She started to hand him the penlight so she could pick up his and Teddi's bags, but he shook his head. "There should be a flare somewhere in my stuff—shaped like a baton."

Again Zoe rifled through his supplies and came up with the flare. "Do you have something to light it with?"

He reached across his body to dig the lighter from his right front pocket with his left hand. He grimaced, and it was all Zoe could do to keep her mouth shut and let him do what he had to. Seeing the pain it cost him, she didn't manage to keep quiet, anyway. "I could have done that."

He lit the flare. "Why didn't I think of that?"

Her eyes locked with his over the white glow of light. "Must be modesty."

"Must be."

He swallowed. "It's been three years. Nearly four."

Zoe bit her lip and nodded. She had counted days until it was easier to count weeks, then months became easier, and years. She knew as well as he did exactly how long it had been since they had been together.

He put his good left arm around her shoulders. "C'mon," he said, rising. "There's springwater and bedrolls about a hundred feet down the shaft."

His willpower—it sure as hell wasn't energy—was nearly spent by the time they reached the natural cavern. For thousands of years, springwater, filtered and forced up through the earth, had carved the grotto from volcanic rock. Now it collected in a bottomless pool, then ran its course back into the earth several hundred feet down into the mountain.

"It's beautiful," Zoe said softly, helping Rafe to ease his arm from her shoulder. "But if you know about it, won't Cavallo?"

"No." He kicked his shoes off and sat on the ledge of the pool, dangling his bare feet. "I haven't been here since I was a kid. My grandmother lived in Vallazione as a girl. Her brother was the local version of Robin Hood. This is where he hung out when the carabinieri were on his trail. Even Turi doesn't know this place." With that he shoved off, slipping into the pool, sinking until even his head was submerged.

"Rafe!" Crouching over the fathomless pool, unable to see even his shape, Zoe bit her lip. "Rafe, *damn* you, come up!"

He emerged, every muscle in his face tautly drawn against the shock of the icy water. His teeth chattered. "You've learned to sw-swear, *caris-sima*."

"Yes, and *damn you* is the least of it!" She spouted off every name she could think of to call him to prove her newfound skill. "And if the cold doesn't kill you, I will. Dear Lord, Rafe, what are you doing?"

"Next best thing to a cold shower." *Mio Dio*. He loved her more now than he ever had. Still, he hadn't the strength left to tease with her. He swallowed. There was nothing left in his tone but grit. "The blood has stuck my shirt to the wound."

"Please." She could see that he was in trouble, shivering, spending heat he couldn't spare. "Can you get out?"

"First, go beyond that ledge over there." He described where she would find the trunk his *bandito* great-uncle had stashed with the blankets and bedrolls.

Zoe took the flare. Though the trunk had not been opened in more than thirty years, in the cool dark climate of the cavern, protected from moths and weather, the bedding had survived intact. She loaded her arms with blankets and carried them to the side of the pool.

Treading water, Rafe worked his way to the edge. "There's a toehold here, but if you could give me a hand—"

"Of course." Together they accomplished pulling him from the pool.

He sat, soaked to the bone and dripping. Zoe threw one of the old army-issue blankets over him. Shivering hard, he clung to her shoulder.

The cold had sufficiently numbed the pain. He couldn't afford to zone out on the morphine in his bag because it was up to him to get Zoe through the next nasty little bit of business.

"Now, my heart," he told her, "you are going to have to sew the edges of my shoulder back together."

Chapter Eight

Zoe blinked. He couldn't be serious. "Me and what surgical team, Rafe?"

"Me," he snapped. "It's what I do best. Or what I used to do. It's what I *am.*"

"Yes, and I'm a *librarian—*"

"Look." His teeth clenched. "If I can't talk you through this, I'll take down my shingle and use it for scrap wood, okay?"

"Too late," she shot back. "Clemenza has already done that and you weren't around to stop it!"

"Wouldn't it be more fulfilling to beat up on me another time?" he asked her, his voice ominously low. "Never mind. You can either stitch up my shoulder and save your insults for another day, or let me bleed to death now. Take your choice, but in either case, *cara,* be quiet. I am done with listening today."

Zoe blew out the breath she'd held. Their eyes locked. She would not blink first.

He'd been handing her impossible choices, do-or-die choices since the first, and she was tired of it. Of him. Of caring what the hell became of him. But she could no more sit there in that cave in the middle of cursed Sicily and watch him bleed to death than she could get out of this mess on her own.

"So talk."

He let his gaze fall, and his head. Praying again, Zoe thought, for small mercies. He should save them up for whenever it was going to be that he saw fit to explain all of his lies.

"Give me some gauze."

She ripped open a package and handed the squares to him. He took them and covered the gaping, bleeding hole in his shoulder. Her stomach heaved.

"There's catgut in sterile packages. It's primitive and expired, but it'll have to do. I have half a dozen needles in the smaller zipper case. Sterilize whichever one matches the catgut with the flare." He paused. She turned to find the supplies he described. "And Zoe." She glanced back at him, afraid of the quaver in his voice. "*Pronto,* eh?"

More frightened, she nodded. The light from the slow-burning flare glinted off his whiskers, which only underscored how ashen his complexion had become. His eyes, dark and filled with pain, seemed to loom in his face.

She forced herself to sort through his supplies, picking out a needle, sterilizing it, threading the catgut. He watched all her jerky, unpracticed, frightening movements. She was shaking like mad, but he murmured his approval as each task was accomplished.

At some point his attention snagged on the mass of tiny eruptions on the palm of her left hand. "Zoe, what is that?"

"I fell into some cactus." She shook her head at the concern in his eyes. "They aren't bothering me."

He cradled her hand. "*Cara mia,* I'm sorry."

"It's nothing. Really. They'll slough off." She pulled her hand away from him. "Tell me what to do next."

His eyes closed. He forced them open again. Her hands worried him, but waves of nausea swept over him when he let his eyes fall closed. He took a deep, steadying breath. "Get the iodine. Pour the whole thing over the gauze."

Holding the suture in one hand, she unscrewed the lid from the small plastic bottle of iodine and squeezed it all out as fast as she could to soak through the gauze. Rafe flinched, close to passing out again. "Hurry, Raphael. What next?"

Through the wrenching pain and gritted teeth he instructed her. "The wound is really only superficial, Zoe. Just go for the skin, but go as deep as you need to pull it together. Hold the gash closed from the narrow end first. I can't keep talking. Just do it. Go. Pull one stitch tight and go on to the next."

He flexed the muscle beneath the wound as much as he could stand so later her stitches would not be too tight. But when the needle pierced his skin for the first time, he lost all ability to think and just endured.

Years ago, before the twins, Zoe knew she would never have been able to do this. But motherhood had changed her. The things she had already gone through, even before Stephi's diagnosis, gave her the strength to look at his wound and gauge her stitches, to pierce his skin repeatedly and draw together the jagged edges.

She finished with a coating of balm. When he was at last able to think again, to look into her eyes and thank her, she wiped away the tears of exhaustion and relief. "Raphael, I have to see Teddi. Please. I'm begging you."

He looked into her eyes for an eternity, and then, on the crest of the last wave of his consciousness, he promised, "If they have not already gone, Zoe, you will see her."

SHE MANAGED TO GET a bedroll beneath Rafe before he fell too heavily asleep, and put another next to him for herself. At least they could share and conserve body heat in the deep chill of the cavern. Lying down, she fitted herself against him. Even in his profound sleep he accommodated her, taking her head onto his good shoulder. Zoe knew then that she'd purposely placed the second bedroll on his good side for a reason other than that she might accidentally bump into her handiwork.

She wanted, even expected, that he would hold her.

She hadn't the energy left to upbraid herself for thinking something so foolish. There was no worry left in her.

The flare burned out as she pulled the last of the blankets over her shoulder. She would worry about that later as well.

They slept for more than ten hours according to the lighted dial of the watch on Rafe's wrist. That small circle was the extent of light in the cavern. Although Rafe was still soundly sleeping when she woke, her slightest movements stirred him.

As if the missing years between them had never happened at all, he curled his arm and brought her closer. Tucking her head next to his neck, he rolled to face her.

"Zoe." Her name mixed with the groan of pain the movement of his shoulder exacted from him.

"Rafe, you'll hurt yourself!"

"Please, Zoe, don't move." The soreness gave his voice a strained quality.

Her warning had come too late. "I won't. I won't. Just let it settle."

He barely nodded. She felt the slight movement of his chin against her head. His fingers caught up in her hair and clenched tight and she knew his pain hadn't eased at all.

She reached to touch his cheek, to stroke him and give him some reassurance that the spasm would pass. But it was pitch-black in the cavern and she misjudged. Her touch happened upon his lips.

His breath warmed her fingers. She started to jerk away, but he moved again, catching her hand, staying her fingers with his. "Don't," he commanded harshly. "The touch of your fingers heals me, heals my soul. Don't take that away from me."

Stroking her palm, he kissed her fingers, each tip in turn, until he reached her thumb, and then he kissed that and took it into his mouth and held her with his teeth.

It didn't hurt, or it hurt too much. She didn't know, couldn't tell beyond sensations that his mouth against any part of her caused. Pleasure and pain ripped through them both, one feeding on the other. Her nipples tightened. Her stomach clenched, and she had no hope of regaining her better judgment.

It had been too long. The stark, boundless black of the cave made what was happening between them easier, somehow more necessary. More powerful.

Inevitable.

She cried out in her own urgent need. With his good arm already holding her close, he rolled onto his back and brought her on top of him.

"Ah, Zoe. Feel what you have done."

"Yes. Yes." He had always made her feel, made her *know* that what became of him when they made love was in her power. "Yes." She straddled him, and climbed him, bringing the hard ridge of his need between her thighs. She had gone beyond thought, unable to think of anything but the hollow need in her, more dark and consuming than the cavern where he had brought her.

His hand had never let go of her hair. He pulled and she came to him. Her lips touched his neck, his chin. She whimpered for the lost pleasure of the scrape of his whiskers on her lips, the taste of his skin and the heat.

He raised his head to catch her lips. She turned away but only for the pleasure of his love bite, his teeth scraping her neck, his tongue laving the curve of her ear. When that pleasure peaked, then she turned back fiercely to him and gave him her lips.

Arching his body, grinding upward, one-armed, he held her. His tongue entered her mouth. The slick, sliding sensations curled in her, curled down, low in her body. But even after he had tasted and stroked and drunk from her lips, drawing her need still higher, even that was not enough.

He pulled her higher still and she went to him. His mouth closed over her breast and his teeth on her nipple. The growl of fierce masculine pleasure reverberated through his chest, resounding again in her.

She cradled his head in her hands. His tongue traced the modest neckline of her sundress, one side to the other, and then he stroked and suckled her other breast, dampening, biting, tugging with the skill of a babe grown well into a man. The flow of her first climax pulled a groan of pleasure from deep within him, inflaming her senses.

She thought of fireworks going off in the dark, shooting into the night sky, breaking into dazzling clusters, into a thousand pinpoints of light. She longed to be filled again with a child of his. As he entered her and she felt the warm flood of his long-denied passion, she willed it to happen. And then, she collapsed on his chest, and for a long time she thought of nothing.

He lay still for long moments as well, but lovemaking was never over with Rafe. Never done. Never quite complete. He could always make her feel more, and need more, and he had never fallen asleep before her.

He nuzzled her neck, tasted her. "I needed you, *cara mia....* So many nights. So damned many godforsaken nights without you."

Zoe froze. It was exactly the wrong thing to say. He was the one who had known where to find her and had still left her alone in her bed for those thousand merciless nights. More than a thousand.

And it was Rafe who stayed away from a child who so loved him that she was sick, even dying. How could she have thought to conceive another child with him?

Her tears fell on his neck.

He begged her not to cry.

She shook her head and lifted her body and pulled away from him, clamoring to put distance between them. "The tears are not for you. I don't even know you. I don't want to remember what just happened here, and I don't want it to happen ever again."

The breath rushed out of Rafe, and the pain in his shoulder returned in full force. But even that seemed inconsequential. The pain in Zoe's voice was enough to kill him. In all his experience, a moment so precious and poignant as making love with Zoe had never ended so badly.

He gave a bitter laugh. He knew from her sharp gasp that she would have slapped him had she known where to find his face. He was tempted to remind her that she had taken the truth of his death on the word of the lying, depraved bastard Clemenza.

But no matter what she thought, he would drain his own life's blood before he would hurt her.

He swore to himself that there would come a time, a chance to hold a knife to the throat of Frank Clemenza. In the end, Frank would reveal himself for the weak, spineless, inhuman creature that he was. He would confess to the offenses he had inflicted on them all because he would know Rafe meant to send him to meet his Maker. In truth, if Zoe didn't truly believe him until that moment, Rafe couldn't blame her.

She sat there in stone-cold silence.

He cleared his throat. He reached into the pocket of his pants for the lighter. Grace of God, though his pants had not completely dried, the flint was dry. The flame burst forth, hurting his eyes.

He let the lid fall down on the brief flicker. "Zoe, we have to call a...what do you say...a, um, cease-fire?"

"Truce." She had never known him to fail to find the word in English that he wanted. The pitch black surrounding them protected her from seeing exactly how upset he was, that Raphael Mastrangelo could fail to remember such a word.

"Yes," he said. "A truce—between us. Nothing is what it seems, except what Stephi needs. For her sake, can we just get on with this?"

She lifted the weight of her hair back from her face. "For Stephi, yes. And you promised—"

"I know. I promised you might see Teddi. If it's possible, Zoe, you shall see her."

She turned back toward him. "How will we get there? What arrangements do you think your mother will have made?"

He checked his watch. "It's nearly 5:00 p.m. At best, Turi could have gotten Teddi to my mother no more than ten or twelve hours ago. She would almost certainly plan to take a flight out of Athens."

Zoe frowned. "From Greece?"

"Yes. Damn it, Zoe, I can't talk to you in the dark." He had done so, of course, many times, long ago. Holding her. Touching her. But it was unnatural for him not to do those things, and just as unnatural to speak with her at all without doing them. "Was there any lighter fluid or pitch in the trunk?"

She tried to remember. "There might have been. I just grabbed the blankets."

He opened his lighter again and flicked the wheel, then rose from the floor of the cavern and made his way, barefooted, subtly limping to the trunk.

"What happened to you," she asked, "that you limp?"

He straightened. "It's nothing." He had always been vain and would willingly admit to it, even brag about it. The explosion aboard the *Persephone* had left him less than whole. A good deal less than physically perfect. But circumstances had taught him bitter lessons, and he had come to know how little his physical image of himself really mattered. "Nothing. Only a break that didn't heal properly."

She didn't think it was nothing. "Why? In this day and age? There's no excuse—"

"They were fighting to save my life, Zoe." He shrugged. He'd lived with things as they truly were for so long that it was difficult to remember how little Zoe knew. How much there was to tell her. "A fractured ankle was the least of their concerns." He bent down, lifted the lid of the trunk and swore softly. "There's nothing here."

"Rafe, I'm sorry about your ankle. I had no idea...."

He shut the trunk and looked at her. "I'm sorry your arm was broken, too."

"At least it was properly treated."

Rafe shook his head.

"What?"

"Nothing." She would never guess how meaningless it all was. If he'd been given the choice, he would have traded both ankles to have back the years with her.

He hadn't been given such a chance. He had to make her understand, and it would have to be soon. He had to explain the hellish choices he'd had to choose from. But his lighter would soon run out. They needed some other light sources to make their way out of the cave or be trapped inside it without hope of escape.

"Any ideas?"

"I saw a small canister in your medical bag last night. It reminded me of candles where they pour the wax into tin boxes.... Is that what it is?"

"Of course!" Rafe rose. That would do. He should have thought of it himself. "Actually it's pretty awful. It's meant to give off a noxious smoke to keep away mosquitoes. It won't give much light, but maybe enough to get us out of here."

Zoe took advantage of the meager light from his lighter to locate and wrap herself in the shawl. "Won't Cavallo have men crawling all over the place?"

He shook his head at her naïveté. "Of course, *cara*. But no self-respecting bandit would hide out in some hole he couldn't get out of. There's an opening at the end of the underground spring that's probably three miles down."

"But farther over land?"

"Ten miles, or fifteen." He went to his medical bag and held the lighter so she could find the tin of wax, then lit the wick and shut off his lighter. "Cavallo is persistent, but he won't think to search that far afield until he's exhausted every other possibility. And by the time we make it out of here, it will be nearly dark."

She gave a sigh. As he'd said, the tin of wax wasn't putting out much light. "Is there no hope that Cavallo will stop coming after us?"

"No, Zoe." Cavallo was what he was. In debt or loyalty to Frank Clemenza, Cavallo would do as the message Carlo had delivered instructed him. Soon, Rafe swore to himself, soon she would know. "There's no such chance."

She broke eye contact with him and stared at her fingers twisting knots in the fringe of a shawl that didn't belong to her. "I don't want to miss Teddi, either."

Her body still hummed. His voice still made her quiver inside. The disparity between what her body told her of Rafe's actions and feelings toward her, and what her head and heart insisted must be true, was making her crazy.

But no matter how impossible all of this seemed, she couldn't imagine Rafe putting her through this nightmare to shore up his own defenses. And she needed to see Teddi. To be with her, if only for a few moments.

"We'd better pack up and go. You'll have to be careful not to tear open your stitches. What can I do to help you?"

"Could you cover the stitches with more salve?"

"Of course." He let her cut away the ragged, bloodied edges of his shirt, then put the shirt back on. Zoe scooped more of the healing balm from its tin and soothed it over the stitches. "There. Will that do?"

"Yeah." He dumped things randomly back into his bag, but Zoe reorganized them so that she could fit her purse back in and fit Teddi's pillowcase of belongings in as well.

She caught him examining her stitches through the hole in his shirt. He turned back to her and looked steadily into her eyes. "You did a fine job, Zoe."

"ALLOW ME TO COMPLIMENT you on a fine job. A fine job," Frank Clemenza mocked Cavallo. "*Cretino!* What do you mean you've lost them? Twelve hours ago you assured me the happy little family had gone up in a funeral pyre of their own making. Now, you've *lost* them?"

Cavallo was sweating despite the electric fan in his tidy office. He missed the good old days, such as the ones before some fool invented cellular telephones. He liked remote, backward little Vallazione because no one paid him enough to take crap from *anybody*.

In Vallazione there was no one he ever need answer to. And if his superiors in the province had to wait until he could be summoned before upbraiding him for some petty infraction or other, then their disposition would be cooled by the time he got there.

Cellular telephones ended all that. From thousands of miles away, Clemenza could curse him for as many minutes as he cared to pay the outrageous charges.

Cavallo had been in hot water even before having to report that there were no bodies found in the burned-out shell of Mastrangelo's Fiat. Clemenza had tried repeatedly to call him personally on the cellular but was finally forced to convey his orders through the boy Carlo.

Cavallo snorted. He was expected to carry the thing around every waking moment? Well he hadn't. And now he hadn't any idea where the fugitives were, either.

He'd tried to explain. Mastrangelo had taken his child and the woman and lost control of his car while he, Cavallo, had been in hot pursuit of them. The metal wreckage was still smoldering when he'd finally been able to get close enough to pry the remains open and see inside. There were no bodies. No skeletal remains. Nothing.

He had been tricked, and his anger was a far worse thing to behold than even Clemenza's.

Nevertheless, he brought up the name of Nicola Peretti to spread the heat around a little. "The woman escaped your niece because she had passed out drunk on the floor of her apartment."

"I will deal with my inept niece," Clemenza said. "You find Mastrangelo and his wife—and the child."

"I will catch up to them. They have only temporarily escaped their fate. Only temporarily," Cavallo swore. Unless he found Mastrangelo, his woman and child, he could kiss off the amenities being in the employ of Frank Clemenza brought him.

"It had better be, *paesano*," Clemenza warned softly. "Or you will find yourself suddenly unemployable."

Cavallo blanched. He didn't know exactly what Clemenza would do to him, but his imagination provided him with any number of possibilities, each more gruesome and degrading than the last.

He reached for the cursed cellular telephone. Time to make a few calls of his own. He must find and eliminate the fugitives who had only temporarily escaped him.

It would be one thing to lose the luxuries Clemenza's money afforded him. It would be quite another to lose any livelihood at all.

It took them nearly two hours to wend their way through the grottoes and passageways cut by the underground spring over the centuries. Rafe led, carrying the tin can of burning wax, and as he picked his way along, he told her what he thought his mother would do to get Teddi out of the country.

Her choices, to avoid the *sbirri* of Frank Clemenza, would be to drive Teddi across Sicily, take a ferry or private boat to the mainland, get to Rome and seek a flight from there—or Athens.

The drive would be a foolish risk. Too many hours, too many ways to be spotted and detained. On the other hand, Teresa Mastrangelo had a paramour in Marsala at the westernmost tip of Sicily. A moderately wealthy man who would look the other way, not bothering about a child with her, who would fly her in his private helicopter out of Italy.

But she would still need a passport for Teddi to enter the States. For that she would have to take one belonging to one of her other grandchildren—one of the small daughters of Rafe's sister in the city of Trapani, also to the west of Palermo. All of this might take a couple of days. If there was a chance of Zoe seeing Teddi, it would be in Marsala.

Zoe tried to concentrate on what Rafe was telling her while watching her footing as well. He was keeping an eye out for her, too, angled as he went so that he could help her with his good arm if need be. But she didn't understand the need for such secrecy, such extraordinary plans, and she stopped.

Rafe turned back. "Are you tired?"

"No. I want to know why we're doing all this. I want to know why I'm in danger, why anyone needs to make up such schemes. The plans you're describing, Rafe..." she paused, gesturing her sense of futility. She breathed to steady her emotions and clarify her thoughts. "I want to know why Teddi is in such danger."

Rafe leaned back against the cold wall of the underground passage. "I don't know why, *cara*. I only know that she is."

"From Frank."

"Yes. Or Frank's minions."

Zoe bit at her lip in frustration. "It always comes back to this, doesn't it?"

He stared back at her, the light of the noxious candle reflecting in his eyes like fire off obsidian. "If you mean, whether to place your precious trust in me or Clemenza—" he shrugged "—then, yes. It will always come back to this." He paused again. "I have survived for the sake of what we once had together, but if you will not believe that or trust me, then very soon, *cara mia,* it will be easier for me to let go of all that was between us than to give a damn. Perhaps you should take the time to make your decision now."

Chapter Nine

She refused to be intimidated.

"Make a decision or what? You'll leave me here to fend for myself in the dark? Forgive me if that consequence doesn't seem so very different from what you've already done!"

Her anger felt to him like a scavenger returning time and again to pluck out his heart. Sooner or later, it would succeed.

"Don't misunderstand me, Zoe." He sank to his haunches against the wall and put the tin of wax beside him. "Everything I have done has been to spare your life and the lives of my children. Only my death will change that."

Zoe's whole face ached from the constant effort to control her emotions. "If you could just tell me why—"

"It's a mystery," he snapped, gesturing so broadly that the rush of air nearly extinguished the flame. "Clemenza knows, I am certain. And maybe his twisted slug assistant, Carlin Santini. But I don't know why. And so now you have before you the question I have asked myself ten thousand times."

Zoe sank down as well. "What does Frank know, Rafe?"

"He knows why. He knows all of us but Centi survived the explosion. He learned by his network of *sbirri* when Teddi and I were taken from a rock off the mainland coast to the hospital in Messina."

Zoe felt the intensity of his eyes boring into her. These were things she needed to know, but some instinct, some inner voice, warned her. If she could have the tens of thousands of years it had taken the wellspring to sculpt this cavern, she would still not be prepared to hear what he would tell her.

"Maybe your aunt could explain it all to you."

Zoe swallowed hard. The voice inside her stilled. Too late. She had lost all track of time, but it hadn't been that many hours ago that she had realized her aunt must have known Paolo Bondi and Rafe were the same man. "Mary Bernadette? What could she explain?"

"She is the one Frank sent to deliver his condolences."

"What condolences?"

"On the death of my wife and child, Stephi. Her own beloved nieces."

Zoe shook her head in disbelief. "That's impossible. Mary Bernadette arranged for the private clinic where I was taken. She stayed with us, with Stephi and me for weeks!"

"Who paid for it?"

"Frank, I suppose."

"He paid for a spa in Trapani where I was taken, as well. Frank was a very generous patron, after he arranged the phony death certificate. After he put out the tragic news of my death to the Italian press. *Corriere della Sera* printed an article that my mother saved."

He held up a hand with his fingers spaced to indicate the size of the headlines. "In English the title would be roughly, World-Renowned Surgeon Dies." Woodenly, he translated the rest of the text from memory.

"'Raphael Mastrangelo, noted Italian plastic surgeon, died today at the age of thirty-five in a hospital
in the port city of Messina. Mastrangelo's valiant
seven-week struggle to overcome massive injuries
suffered in the explosion of the yacht *Persephone*
ended tragically this afternoon. Cause of death is
given as pneumonia. *Requiescat in pace.*'"

The cavern seemed suddenly airless. Zoe's stomach
turned. "I never saw anything like that."

"It was hardly international news but necessary to put
to rest the concerns and inquiries of my friends and colleagues here in Italy. I wasn't expected to survive, so the
reports of my death must have come as no great surprise."

"How did you survive?"

Rafe shook his head. "I don't know. I have no memory
at all of immediately after the explosion. The blast, the
burns." He stared at his hands. "All that mattered was
keeping Teddi safe."

"Where was Teddi in all of this?"

"She was treated for exposure and released to the care
of my mother."

Zoe felt confused. "Who was around to let your mother
know where you were?"

Rafe shifted his weight. "I was recognized immediately, Zoe. I was in the hospital, remember. Burn specialists were called in. In Italy I am...I was well known. At
least in the medical community. My mother knew and
came within a few days of our rescue."

Zoe's throat felt swollen. "Didn't she think of trying to
reach me? Of letting me know? Or that Teddi needed
me?"

"Most certainly she did. But you were whisked off to a
private clinic as well. Frank took her calls. She under-

stood that you were seriously injured as well, unable even to care for Stephi.''

Rafe hesitated and shook his head, knowing, *feeling,* the betrayal Zoe felt. ''After, of course, it would have been impossible to return Teddi to you without arousing your suspicions that I had survived as well.''

''Still—''

Rafe cut her off. ''There was never a time when my mother did not believe that Teddi should be with her mother. But I was glad she was not, *cara.*'' His voice was gravelly with emotion. ''She was all that I had left.''

A tear seeped out of Zoe's eye. She brushed it away and cleared her throat. She could not blame him for that. Stephi had been Zoe's emotional lifeline. Without Teddi, Rafe would have had none. But there were so many things she didn't understand, or believe.

''If Frank wanted us dead, if he is so all-powerful, surely it would have been easier to let you die, or even administer some fatal injection, than to fake your death. Wouldn't it?''

Rafe nodded. ''Infinitely easier.''

''Then *why?*''

''Only he knows that, Zoe. I think it became a game with him. I think he's insane. Most certainly he tried to kill us. I think when we didn't die, he got concerned for his miserable immortal soul. So he did a complete turnaround. He is superstitious to the extreme. Remember?''

She nodded. ''About Centi. And about repaying his debt to you for the surgery you performed on him.''

''Exactly.'' Clenching his teeth, Rafe rubbed his wrecked shoulder for a moment. ''So, Frank had to believe maybe it was the hand of God that spared us all.''

He seemed to be staring out into the endless inky black of the cavern passage. ''Somehow,'' he went on, ''it didn't matter. Perhaps, in the end, he was even pleased. He'd found a way to spare our lives, and condemn us to living hell in the same stroke.'' Rafe gave a bitter laugh. ''I suppose I should at least be grateful that he left me with my profession. But *I* ceased to exist. *We* . . . '' He looked toward her, focusing possessively on her and then into her eyes. ''We also ceased to exist.''

Zoe looked away and covered her lips for long moments with her knuckles. He was telling her the truth. Or at least, what he believed was the truth. There was no part of what he'd said that she could point to and say, *No. It didn't happen like that.* The chill of the cavern was nothing to the cold in her heart. ''What role did Mary Bernadette play in all of this?''

''Frank sent her to convince me that you and Stephi had not survived.'' Rafe remembered that moment with terrible clarity. Mary Bernadette in her nun's frock, hovering around, displaying stoic grief. ''I refused to believe it. She came to my bedside and begged me to accept the truth. She reminded me what an enormous task lay before me, just to recover. And there was Teddi, who needed me. For Teddi's sake—'' He broke off, scowling darkly.

''She came too close,'' he went on. ''I grabbed the crucifix that hung around her neck. *Swear on this,* I told her, and I will believe it.''

It is so, Raphael. Believe it.

Swear it.

I swear it!

''She swore to it, but—'' He shrugged one shoulder. The physical agony he'd been in was linked inextricably to Mary Bernadette's earnest, desperate lies. ''I did not believe it. I would not promise never to come searching for you. Naturally Frank had an alternative that Mary Bernadette relayed to me.''

''Which was?''

''That our lives would all be spared so long as you never had contact with me again in Frank's lifetime. So long as you never learned the truth. That's why he created Dr.

Paolo Bondi. I could live my life but not anywhere or under any name you might stumble upon."

"Are you telling me it was Mary Bernadette who gave you this ultimatum?" Zoe cried.

"Zoe, think about it." He let his head hang for a moment. "You're the one who told Cavallo your aunt had sent you to Bondi. How could she do that unless she knew? Unless she had been party to the lies? Yes, Mary Bernadette delivered the ultimatum."

Zoe began to shake. She got to her feet and started to pace, her mind reeling, rebelling against what must be true if anything Rafe had claimed was fact.

"You're saying Frank knew you and Teddi were alive. You're saying that Mary Bernadette, who has been with me every day of my life, that she *knew* you were alive." With every charge her voice rose. "Everyone knew everything but me."

"Yes."

"Even you. You knew Stephi and I had survived."

"Yes. In my heart I knew. Your aunt confirmed it." His eyes never left her. He never flinched.

Her heart felt leaden. Frozen for all time. She stared at him, not recognizing her husband in him at all. "God forgive you. I never will."

He let his head fall back against the cold stone. "So. You see for yourself. Even when his scheme fails, Frank wins." Rafe shrugged. He had steeled himself in all the long nights without her. He'd known there was no way to explain all this to Zoe in a way that she would forgive him. But that it came as no surprise to him upset her even more.

"Don't you even care?"

"On the contrary, *cara*," he answered, lifting his head, fixing her with his dark eyes. "I care. That is the one thing upon which you may depend."

But Zoe barely heard him. "How could he make my aunt, Mary Bernadette, who is sworn to God and who has dedicated her life to God, how could he make her lie to me? How could he make you *be* Paolo Bondi?"

"Simple," he answered her harshly. "The lives of Stephi and Teddi, even your life, Zoe, were always at stake. Always depended on my cooperation. And on the silence of your aunt—and she knew it."

"Then why would she send me to you?"

"Because, Zoe," he began, as if she were a child. "Don't you see that she had no choice? That it no longer mattered? Only the lives of our babies could have induced her to go along with Frank. The fact that Stephi will die anyway without Teddi, without her twin, is the only thing that could make Mary Bernadette defy him."

"Defy Frank?" Zoe breathed sharply. She understood, suddenly, exactly why her aunt had been so terribly upset at Emma Harding's suggestion that her search should begin among Rafe's relatives in Sicily. Stephi's illness had upset the seemingly infallible scheme. Whether by accident or design, Zoe was likely to discover that Rafe and Teddi had survived.

Mary Bernadette must have known. Stephi had an identical twin, a perfect match. A search was unnecessary. But to reveal that, to reunite the twins, was the same as defying Frank Clemenza.

From the moment Zoe had stepped onto a plane bound for Sicily, their lives had all been in great danger. Which was why, she understood in that instant, Mary Bernadette had not even wanted her to speak with Frank.

It all made a sudden, twisted sort of sense. Zoe shivered. Rafe sat carefully massaging his arm, watching her. Odd, she thought, how little light the flame put out, and how much it was possible to see, anyway. But the tiny flame could not dispel the cold seeping into her bones.

"Back in Turi's bar, how did you know I had mentioned Mary Bernadette to Cavallo?"

"Nicola told me." Rafe shivered as well, realizing for the first time how hungry he was. How hungry Zoe must be. How little fuel either of them had been running on for so many hours. They would have to leave this cave very soon, and not only to find food. But he needed to answer all of Zoe's questions so there would be no more delays. So she would help and not hinder his every move to get them to safety.

"Nicola Peretti is Frank's niece," he continued. "Grandniece, I think. She lived with baited breath for the moment she could report to Frank that any American had come to Vallazione. She was beside herself to inform me that there was not only an American woman in Turi's bar, but one whose aunt had sent her to Paolo Bondi. One who called herself Zoe Mastrangelo and would not be convinced to go away."

Zoe bit her lip. "Did you think I would not know you, Raphael? Your eyes? Your voice? Your hands? Did you think you could convince me that you were not my husband?"

He shook his head slowly back and forth. "No. But I was in fear for your life. I thought that if I denied you before God and all those witnesses, Frank would not find it necessary to enforce his threats."

She could only stare at him.

"I am sorry for the humiliation it caused you, Zoe, but not for the act itself."

She dried her tears. "What are we going to do, Rafe?"

"We are going to survive. Teddi will undergo the procedure you described, and Stephi will be made well."

He did not tell Zoe that when his daughters' welfare had been assured, Frank Clemenza's miserable life would not be worth the rectangle of earth required to bury him.

THE NEXT SEVENTEEN HOURS were the most grueling Zoe could remember since the night the *Persephone* had gone down. Once out of the cave, they crossed the rocky, uncertain landscape through a lemon grove to the farmhouse of an elderly priest. The cleric's sister Anna had been Rafe's own nanny more than thirty years before. With the deeply ingrained suspicion of a Sicilian *contadina*, Anna's granddaughter, a peasant woman, recognized trouble when she saw it and tried her best to make them go away.

Rafe threw himself on the mercy of the old priest. The old man agreed to hear Rafe's confession lest he died of his injuries before his sins could be heard and absolved.

The two men disappeared behind closed doors, and Zoe was left alone to deal with the narrow-faced, hostile woman. But when they departed, it was in the priest's old pickup truck, laden with a bottle of wine, fresh loaves of bread and a chunk of salt-cured meat. They had been given hot water to clean up, and Rafe was clad in a clean shirt that had belonged to the old man.

She didn't ask, afterward, whether Rafe confessed his sins or not. All that mattered was that the priest had helped them and sent them on their way with his blessings.

All night long Rafe drove south through the interior of the island, away from the coastal area of Marsala and Teddi, creating a trail that they hoped Cavallo would discern. Never doing anything terribly obvious, never leaving blatant clues, behaving as if they were afraid of something or someone. Cavallo was not stupid and they couldn't afford to do anything that would suggest a deliberate trail, but they needed to be convincingly on the road.

Hours later, Cavallo would be enraged to have tracked them only to find no one knew exactly how Teddi had arrived or departed.

At dawn they bought more petrol for the old pickup truck to begin traveling back north and west to Marsala. It had been nearly forty-eight hours since Zoe had last been with Stephi. Since Mary Bernadette had given her the name of Paolo Bondi. The call she placed from the gas station took twenty minutes to go through.

She asked for Stephi's room, expecting Mary Bernadette to answer. The operator patiently explained no calls were being taken in that room and no questions answered at the nursing station.

She asked to have her aunt paged. After yet another delay, the operator came back on the line. There had been no response to the page. She thought about asking for Emma Harding to be paged, but it was very late at night in Chicago and unlikely that Emma would be there. And Zoe had to consider whether calling Emma would endanger her in some way.

At last she gave up. The message she left with the operator for Mary Bernadette said only that her niece had called.

She hung up the old-fashioned telephone and pulled the shawl tighter around her. The sun had risen now, but it was still chilly. In the distance the ruins of some ancient stone temple stood silhouetted against the glare of the rising sun. A cock crowed and a donkey brayed nearby.

She had never felt so misplaced. So foreign. So out of touch and control.

She had sworn to do whatever was necessary for Stephi's sake, but she had never imagined herself running from threats she didn't understand from men she couldn't see or challenge or reason with. And she had never imagined that in coming here, she would be so thoroughly cut off from Stephi and everything that was familiar to her.

But she would go on doing what she had to do. It wasn't even as if she had any other choice but to pull her socks up and go on.

She climbed back into the truck and shook her head at Rafe's quizzical look. "No luck. I had to leave a message."

Rafe touched her cheek. "I am sorry, Zoe."

Shivering, Zoe battled back her tears. "Someone has ordered that no calls be put through to Stephi's room."

It didn't take a lot of imagination to guess who had issued such an order. Rafe pulled her close to him. Numbly, Zoe went. He pulled out and began to drive fast, avoiding the main roads wherever he could, in the direction of Marsala. After a while, Zoe fell asleep on his shoulder, but when they were nearing Marsala, she woke again.

"Where are we going?"

He touched her cheek with his thumb, then took his arm from around her. "I wish I knew."

"What does that mean?"

"I've never been there." He knew the name of his mother's paramour, but he didn't know where to find the villa of Giancarlo De Sica. The man was in textiles, his fortune made exporting a fine, supple leather from a special crossbreed of sheep on Sardine. His wealth bought and insured his privacy. But all was not lost, Rafe explained to her. His mother had spoken once of a man who would know where De Sica could be found. A certain bishop of the Trapani province.

He slowed as the truck gained on an old man leading a heavily laden donkey down the road. Rafe rolled down the window and asked for directions to the local bishop's residence. After a moment of gesturing and explanation, Rafe thanked the nearly toothless old man and drove on, rolling up the window.

"Why didn't you just ask for directions to De Sica's villa?" she asked.

"The old man is a peasant, *cara*. He wouldn't know. And if he did, he would probably lie."

"Why?"

Wincing at the occasional stab of pain in his shoulder, Rafe stretched his arm out again on the seat back behind her. "If you asked for directions in America, you would probably get them—depending, of course, on whom you

IT'S FUN!

IT'S FREE!

BIG BUCKS

HOW TO PLAY

It's so easy...grab a lucky coin, and go right to your BIG BUCKS game card. Scratch off silver squares in a STRAIGHT LINE (across, down, or diagonal) until 5 dollar signs are revealed. BINGO!...Doing this makes you eligible for a chance to win $1,000,000.00 in lifetime income ($33,333.33 each year for 30 years)! Also scratch all 4 corners to reveal the dollar signs. This entitles you to a chance to win the $50,000.00 Extra Bonus Prize! Void if more than 9 squares scratched off.

Your EXCLUSIVE PRIZE NUMBER is in the upper right corner of your game card. Return your game card and we'll activate your unique Sweepstakes Number, so it's important that your name and address section is completed correctly. This will permit us to identify you and match you with any cash prize rightfully yours! (SEE BACK OF BOOK FOR DETAILS.)

FREE BOOKS PLUS FREE GIFTS!

At the same time you play your BIG BUCKS game card for BIG CASH PRIZES...scratch the Lucky Charm to receive FOUR FREE

Harlequin Intrigue® novels, and a FREE GIFT, TOO! They're totally free, absolutely free with no obligation to buy anything!

These books have a cover price of $3.50 each. But THEY ARE TOTALLY FREE; even the shipping will be at our expense! The Harlequin Reader Service® is not like some book clubs. You don't have to make any minimum number of purchases–not even one!

The fact is, thousands of readers look forward to receiving four of the best new romance novels each month and they love our discount prices!

Of course you may play BIG BUCKS for cash prizes alone by not scratching off your Lucky Charm, but why not get everything that we are offering and that you are entitled to! You'll be glad you did.

asked and whether or not they knew. No one assumes that you will then go there and arrest the person or stick a knife in his gut or throw a bomb in his window.

"Here, my heart, when a stranger asks, those reasons are as likely as that he wishes merely to visit. And the old man would be held accountable for betraying the location. It is safer to say nothing, or to lie. And even safer not to know at all."

Zoe sighed. Safer, she thought, not to be in Sicily at all.

It was very early when they arrived, not yet seven o'clock in the morning. Still, Rafe banged on the door of the bishop's residence. Not willing to involve him by revealing their true identity, Rafe appealed to Eligio Dante, introducing Zoe as an American buyer of De Sica's textiles whom Giancarlo himself had invited to be a guest at his villa.

Zoe stood behind Rafe on the ancient stone steps of the bishop's quarters. A canopy of trailing vines shut out the intense blaze of the early morning sun, and in the small courtyard were lime trees and centuries-old vases planted with various herbs and flowers.

She understood almost none of Rafe's conversation with the bishop. The story, however, was that she had lost her way, her car had broken down, and Rafe had given her a lift.

Admitting to knowing De Sica, Dante was mildly amused by the story Rafe had invented. He offered—in English—to telephone Giancarlo De Sica and have him send a car for her.

Rafe dropped the pretense, the fabrication and his smile. He knew the bishop expected his offer to send them scurrying away like the charlatans they obviously were. "Please do. Mention the name of Teresa Mastrangelo."

The grizzled, burly man eyed them suspiciously. "Why is it that you believe I can help you?"

"I have heard you are Giancarlo's confessor," Rafe said.

Dante began to close the door. "You have been led astray. Giancarlo De Sica is not a religious man."

"But—"

"Regretfully, I cannot help you. Go away."

"Father, please!" Zoe cried, feeling time slipping fast away from her, putting out her arm to keep the door open.

"Signora," Rafe began in a warning voice.

"No, Rafe . . . no. We've tried this your way."

"Zoe, you do not know—"

She ignored his warning and turned to the priest. *"Per favore,* Father—"

He smiled sardonically. "I am bishop of Trapani province, madam, but I'm a native Californian. English will be fine."

Zoe nodded, reminded once again that nothing in Sicily was ever quite as it seemed. "My daughter's life has been threatened. My mother-in-law has escaped with her to Signor De Sica, thinking that he will take her out of Sicily. But my daughter is only five, Father, and I have not seen her since she was a baby. If you could tell me how to find Signor De Sica's villa before they are gone, I would be . . . I would be eternally grateful."

"I understand your problem." He widened the door a bit. His expression reflected his uncertainty, or an unwillingness to get involved in such affairs. "How old did you say your daughter is?"

"Five," Zoe answered. "A baby, really."

Eligio Dante cleared his throat. "De Sica's villa is at the end of a private road. You will not be allowed access."

"Maybe if you called him—"

He shook his head. "Despite my offer, I do not know the telephone number at the villa."

"We'll settle for directions," Rafe said.

Eligio sighed heavily and invited them inside while he drew a map. He explained that it was only because he was an American that he knew De Sica, who sometimes sought out Americans for social occasions but would never disclose his personal telephone number.

Rafe took the opportunity to question the bishop about landmarks and geographical features. The villa bordered on the sea, and to the best of Eligio's recollections, the beaches were private but unguarded.

Zoe thanked him and insisted on making a donation for his help.

"Thank you," he answered, accepting a handful of paper money, not quite smiling. "I'll take it for the soup kitchen in town. But if anyone asks, I never saw you, never talked to you, never even heard of you."

Rafe offered his hand to shake.

Eligio took it. "Rafe, Zoe," he said, defying his own statement that he had never heard of them. "I don't know what kind of trouble you are in, but go with God."

RAFE MADE ZOE PROMISE not to appeal to the guards on the De Sica estate as she had to the bishop. They had just been monumentally lucky that the man had turned out to be an American with the willingness to help them despite the fact that they were clearly dangerous to be associated with.

The uniformed men at the immense iron gate leading up to the villa of Giancarlo De Sica refused even to call their *padrone*.

"Can't you tell them your mother's name—"

Rafe signaled Zoe to hush, but no matter what question he asked, the young guard claimed to know nothing. More of the deeply ingrained suspicion.

Rafe began to back up the old pickup to the main road.

"Rafe, what did he say?"

He looked over to her. "This may or may not be the villa of Giancarlo De Sica. He is not in residence, he has no guests, he has had no guests for many weeks. He has never entertained a woman named Teresa Mastrangelo."

"Never?" Zoe gulped. "Does all of that mean your mother isn't here at all? Or maybe she tried to come here with Teddi but De Sica was out of the country?"

"She would never come here without checking first." Rafe shook his head. "What it comes down to is that the guards have been instructed to deny everything. De Sica is taking no chances. It means no one can get to Teddi."

"Including us."

"Yes. Including us." Far more prepared for that outcome than Zoe, Rafe had watched for a place in which to leave the battered old pickup truck as if it had run out of petrol.

Somewhere to begin trespassing.

Backing onto the main road, he turned, shifted and roared off in the direction they had come from. Slowing, perhaps three-quarters of a kilometer away, he pulled off the road into a copse of wild olive trees and dense scrub.

Excited and nervous at the prospect of seeing Teddi, Zoe was still frightened of trespassing to circumvent the guards. "I can't believe we have to do this. Isn't there anyone at your mother's house who would know De Sica's phone number?"

"No." Rafe took the key from the ignition and shoved it into his trouser pocket. "She lives alone. And about now, Cavallo has had time to figure out that we weren't in that car, and that we've been leading him on a wild-goose chase."

"But—"

"No buts. If we approach anyone in my family, on the phone or in person, they're as good as dead." He stopped, and reached to touch her hair, to pull it back so he could better see her face. "Zoe, I know this is all nearly impossible for you to believe. But if you want to see Teddi, you must simply trust me and do as I say."

Simply trust me. She stared at the olive tree branch scraping at the windshield. The sun had been up for hours now, and inside the pickup truck it was getting stiflingly hot. "Won't we be putting your mother and De Sica into danger by going there?"

"Possibly. But the guards have turned us away. And even if Cavallo knew we were here, he would think twice before tangling with De Sica. Anyway, my mother will be safely out of the country soon enough."

"*If* she has Teddi. *If* she's even here."

"She's here, Zoe. It's the only place she can be safe at all."

"What if Turi didn't find her? What if—"

"Zoe. *Cara.*" He stroked her cheek. "We have been twice blessed today. We cannot fail."

"You don't even believe that," Zoe accused him. "Don't patronize me, Rafe. I won't stand for it."

He smiled, and toyed with a lock of her hair. "Not every Sicilian husband would stand for your tongue, *cara mia.*" But seeing her wrenching fright, he grew sober.

"It's true, Zoe, that I don't believe the blessings of the two priests will keep us from harm. But I have to believe Turi did not fail, and that my mother has done what she promised to do if anything ever happened to me."

"So this…this plan was something you and your mother have spoken of before?"

"Yes. If something happened."

Still, to be so dependent on other people scared her. She gathered up her hair and twisted it into a braid, determined to get a grip on her emotions. "What happens if some underling thug of De Sica's guns us down on sight?"

Rafe smiled. "De Sica would have to be a thug himself to employ such lowlife. He is not a thug, *cara.* You'll see. Let's go."

Branches of the olive tree and the scrub beneath made it impossible to open her door. Zoe crawled out Rafe's side with Teddi's little bag of treasures.

Rafe took her hand and they set out across the stony field leading toward the beach. The harsh glare of the mid-morning sun made her feel sticky, but the chance of seeing Teddi again made her oblivious to the discomfort.

They crossed the harsh plateau with its weeds and cactus and stones and came finally to the edge of a cliff that dropped sharply off to the beach fronting the Mediterranean. Wispy clouds stacked high on one another.

The intense blue of the sea was reflected in the sky, and the heat haze blurred the line between the two. The place, the view, would have been breathtaking if it hadn't meant there was no way down to the beach.

"Now we know why Eligio didn't remember the beach being guarded," Rafe muttered. "We'll have to make our way from here south. The villa can't be too far."

"Maybe there are steps carved into the side of the cliff somewhere near the house?"

"I wouldn't count on it." Rafe took her hand and set off again. "The villa is likely built into the side of the cliff, with stairs going down from the house."

Zoe picked her way along beside Rafe. The breeze off the sea helped, but she could still feel her skin perspiring. "I keep wondering if I'll recognize her."

Rafe gave her a quizzical look.

Her lips weren't quite steady when she smiled. "Silly, I know."

"Not silly. Anxious, maybe." His hand tightened around hers, and she returned the pressure. He drew her attention. "Look, up there."

Shielding her eyes from the sun, she trained her gaze in the direction Rafe pointed. Between the branches of an almond tree growing wild, she spotted the tiled roof of the villa.

"Oh gosh. Teddi's...she's...oh, gosh. She's there, Rafe." Zoe felt incoherent with anticipation. Tongue-tied. "I know she's there. Can I hold her? I need to hold her. Can I do that? Can I hold her? I wouldn't take long, I promise—"

The sudden noise of a powerful engine cranking up in the distance cut her off.

"Oh, God," Zoe cried. "We're going to miss them."

Rafe swore. "It may not be as far off as it sounds." He tugged hard at her hand and lit out, running across the edge of the plateau as fast as he could manage with his ankle, which still challenged her to keep up through the patches of scrub and native wild grasses. "Hurry, *cara,* hurry!"

She ran with him, struggling for a second wind. The skirt of her dress clung to her thighs and flew behind her. The cliffside and the coastline curved suddenly inward, forming a natural cove. As Rafe had predicted, the villa was built into the side of the cliff, but there was no one in sight.

The helicopter sat poised to lift off. Zoe sank onto the ground in the weeds, searching desperately for signs of Teddi. The rotors began to turn, slowly at first, then too fast to see revolutions.

The whap-whapping sound of the helicopter blades slicing through the air seemed to grow and echo and multiply. Far below them at the level of the sea a gray-haired, well-built older man emerged from sliding glass doors followed by a woman dressed in white linen. Rafe's mother.

The man was carrying Teddi. Zoe's mouth went dry as dust.

He tossed Teddi into the air, then put her down. She danced excitedly around the deck. Thin and knobby-kneed and beautiful, she clapped and laughed and screamed for joy, though the sounds were drowned out by the helicopter.

Zoe's throat began to clog, remembering Teddi circling the wading pool on the *Persephone,* egging Stephi on to something even more flamboyant. Zoe had never seen her tiny daughter so exuberant and it tugged at her heart. For Stephi's sake, but also for Teddi's joy and fearlessness and vitality.

Watching Teddi from so far above, Zoe murmured, "She's beautiful, Rafe." Healthy and happy. He had done well raising her.

"How could she help it?" Rafe answered softly. "She is your daughter."

Teddi's long dark wavy hair was caught up in barrettes at each side, but her tresses danced in the turbulent air like the tiny skirt of her pink sundress. Her hair was longer than Stephi's, but from this distance, even Zoe could not have told them apart, except that Teddi's color was healthy and brown with the intense summer sun.

Stephi's was not.

Zoe cried out Teddi's name and began to wave, longing to reach out to her, to hold her just once. Was that too much to ask?

The man Zoe supposed was De Sica began to shepherd Teddi and Rafe's mother toward the waiting helicopter.

"No, wait!" Zoe cried, but De Sica helped Teresa Mastrangelo into the waiting helicopter, then lifted Teddi in to her. Zoe saw Teddi reaching out to her *nonna.* She had dreamed of Teddi reaching out to her in just that way. Of Teddi's sweet little arms closing around her neck. Much as Stephi would. Only Stephi hadn't the physical strength left to put much into a hug.

Zoe's fingers covered her mouth. Tears filled her eyes. "Damn it, it's not fair!" she cried. "All I wanted was to hold her once!"

The helicopter lifted a few feet off the ground, seemed to dip forward, hovered and then soared upward, turning for an instant toward them.

The moment seemed to Zoe both to freeze and be over in the space of a heartbeat. She and Rafe stood. They could be no more than fifty feet from the chopper. For an instant, she thought that Teddi must have seen them both frantically waving.

From behind her Rafe closed his arms around Zoe's shoulders. Maybe he expected her to crumble. The chopper turned sharply, cutting away from the cliffside. The whine of the turbo engine escalated with each increment of power. The brilliant white sun glinted off the body of the helicopter.

Teddi was gone.

She turned in the circle of his arms toward Rafe, and it was just as well that he had a hold of her, but not because she had come so heartbreakingly close to Teddi.

Behind him stood two men, their sidearms drawn and pointed.

Chapter Ten

"Rafe." He steadied her on her feet. "Behind you."

He turned, instinctively slow and easy, until he faced the gunmen. He kept his arms spread and visible. "Things just aren't getting any easier, are they, *cara?* Maybe if I pretend not to understand and we keep protesting we're innocent lost tourists—"

"How can you joke?" she whispered, too drained to feel truly afraid. "Rafe, these guys have guns! Are they going to kill us or are they the police?"

Rafe shrugged. "That's what I love about this country. Sometimes you can't tell the difference."

"Does that mean you don't know?"

Bursting into an angry stream of words, the older of the two, a tall, scrappy man with a fringe of curly gray hair, waved his gun in the air above his head.

Rafe took a deep breath and let it go, then gestured toward Zoe and answered him. Whatever he said caused the younger, heavier, more dangerous one to sneer and argue with his superior for a moment.

"What is he saying?"

"They're De Sica's men," Rafe answered. "He says we're a couple of fools, and we'll bring the carabinieri or low-life assassins or both, and why have we come here." He took his eyes off the guns for a second and glanced at her. "It sounds like he knows who we are but he can't believe we were so stupid as to come here. I explained that you had not seen your child in many years, so you came to see her. And we're on our way."

Zoe watched them with an eagle eye, as if there were anything she could do, anyway. The older of the two must have prevailed—both of them put away their guns, but neither one of them were pleased to be dealing with Rafe and her.

The older one jerked his head in the direction of the road, indicating that they should move that way and rattled off again at Rafe. The other man advanced on Zoe and started to give her a shove.

Before she knew what was happening Rafe stopped, pulled her behind him and confronted the man who had dared touch her. She didn't have to understand the language to get the gist of Rafe's warning. *Lay a hand on her and I'll kill you.*

She clutched her arms across her stomach. She couldn't believe he was getting into an argument with anyone possessing a gun.

"Rafe!"

"Shut up, Zoe."

She closed her mouth. She had been stupid. The last thing they needed was for it to look as if Rafe didn't even have her under control. In this country, that would be deadly. Rafe and the younger man stood glaring at each other until the older of De Sica's men ordered the younger one to break it off.

Never dropping his threatening look, Rafe took hold of Zoe's elbow and began walking toward where they had left the truck.

"Keep walking," Rafe ordered Zoe. "And don't ever do that again. Do you understand?"

"Yes."

"Now, what was it that you wanted to say?"

She tossed her head back. "He had a gun. I didn't think you should be threatening him—"

His hand clamped tighter on her elbow. "You didn't think at all."

For the benefit of De Sica's men he let his tone of voice convey his displeasure with her. "Young Tonio back there had to understand that if he touched you, he would have to come through me first, if you get my meaning."

Zoe shuddered. She had been truly stupid. If Rafe let the guy get away with shoving her around, Tonio would think he could do anything he wanted to her. "Are they going to let us leave?"

"No. They say we're to wait right here until De Sica returns and decides what to do with us."

"That's good, isn't it?" Zoe asked hopefully. "I mean, he helped your mother."

"That doesn't mean he'll help us," Rafe said. "He may already have done more than he would like." He frowned. "I can't tell if De Sica ordered them to bring us in or if they just happened to find us."

"Does it matter?" She stumbled over a half-buried stone in the field. Both their escorts reached for their guns, suspecting a trick. Rafe put out a hand to make sure she didn't fall and snapped at De Sica's guards, assuring them it was nothing.

"It matters," he said grimly.

"But—" she cast a quick glance over her shoulder at the two men behind them "—you don't think he'd detain us only to turn us over to Cavallo, do you?"

Rafe rolled his eyes at her eternal naïveté. "Not De Sica. But that's why it matters. If Cavallo has tracked us to the pickup and the word is out, unless De Sica somehow gave them specific instructions, these two could turn us over to Cavallo in a second. Especially if they thought there was something in it for them."

Zoe stepped over a dense patch of scrub. "So what do we do now?"

"Just keep quiet and do what you're told. Okay? Please?"

"Okay."

The pair of De Sica's men gestured for them to split up. Zoe was supposed to ride with Tonio in the jeep they had pulled up behind the truck, and Rafe with the older of the two. They wanted that truck out of sight.

She didn't know if that was a good sign or not. Either the pair was loyal to De Sica and trying to protect them, or else they didn't want anyone else spotting the truck and horning in on whatever reward might go to their captors. But she'd promised to keep her mouth shut, so she couldn't ask.

Rafe gave Tonio another warning glance for good measure then walked with her to the jeep.

She took a deep breath and, clinging to Teddi's pillow-case, climbed into the passenger seat, never looking in any direction but forward. Rafe followed in the pickup back to the gate, but there he was stopped. A heated discussion ensued, Rafe took his medical bag from the floor of the pickup, and one of the sentries got into the truck and roared off down the road.

Rafe and his guard walked down the road. She wanted to ask where they were taking the truck, but Rafe's expression warned her off.

Inside a door she assumed was a servant access, the older, leaner guard took them down flights of stairs that led below ground. He shut them in the dark cellar, locked the door and barred it for good measure.

"This isn't a particularly good sign, is it?" Her voice quavered, making her stab at humor a little pathetic. The dark didn't make it feel any better.

"Ah, Zoe." He reached unerringly for her in the dark and took her into his arms, holding her head to his chest.

Still clinging to Teddi's pillowcase of belongings, Zoe wrapped her arms around his waist. "You are coping," he said, "do you know that? You have always coped."

"Not very well." Without a glimmer of light, her other senses sharpened. Her awareness of his heart beating. The scent of him. The fruity smell of the cellar. "I'm so tired."

"I know." Burying his face in her hair for a moment, he inhaled. "I know." He pressed his lips to the top of her head, then let her go to make his way to the bare light bulb he'd seen hanging from the joists before they'd been shut away in the dark.

He switched the light on and the bulb cast a weak, silvery circle of light. The cellar was well ventilated and not old—an informal wine cellar doing double duty with the fresh vegetables and fruit that probably served the villa kitchen. Bottles of Sicilian wines made of the native grapes lined one wall, each one without a mote of dust on the bottle, and each tipped toward the corks. There were a few wheels of cheese and baskets of fruit and vegetables, a few jars of olives packed in oil.

"May as well make the best of this. Are you hungry?"

Zoe put down Teddi's things and shoved a tired hand through her masses of tangled hair, eyeing the cheese. "I bet I could eat that whole thing."

"Sorry. You're going to have to share, *cara*." He dug around a little while until he'd found a knife and a corkscrew. The scent of the cheese made Zoe's mouth water, and even the smell of the cork of the wine bottle made her feel light-headed.

He opened a jar of olives, then cut them both a hunk of the cheese. "Mind if we just share drinks from the bottle?"

"That would be fine." The cheese was very strong, and Zoe had to force herself to slow down. She'd eaten so little in so many days that even a few bites made her stomach cramp. The cellar was cool and quiet and offered at least the illusion of safety.

She took a small swallow of the wine and passed the bottle back to Rafe, savoring the incredibly fruity, crisp taste. If she could just have a shower and some fresh clothes . . . But she would settle for some assurance that Teddi and her *nonna* Teresa had gotten safely away.

"How long do you think it will be before your mother and Teddi get to Chicago?"

Rafe polished off his cheese and olives, then sat back and took another long pull of the prized wine. "I would bet De Sica got them out of here only in time to step right onto a flight to the States. With any luck, they'll be there in less than twenty-four hours." He offered her the wine bottle.

She shook her head. "I wish I—*we* could've been with her. And back with Stephi." No harm in asking, she thought. "Since Teddi's gone now, is there any reason why we can't go back? As soon as we get out of here, of course. I know we had to make it look like we had Teddi with us, but now we don't."

Rafe looked at her as if he wished he knew exactly how they were going to do that. He picked an apple from a barrel beside him, then started to peel it. "I don't have much of a plan, Zoe, if that's what you're asking. But it is true, there is no longer any reason to stay."

"Not much of a plan is better than nothing, isn't it?" she asked. "What are you thinking of?"

"There are probably fifty ways to leave the island. I—"

Zoe's hand flew to her lips. "Oh!"

"What is it?"

She shook her head. "Nothing. I was just reminded of an old song."

"What?"

" 'Fifty Ways to Leave Your Lover.' " He stared at her. "You know," she said. *"Slip out the back, Jack."*

His hands separated, the apple in one, the knife in the other.

She looked away. "It was just one of those nonsensical things that pop into your head. I didn't mean to think of it."

"Oh. Well. If you didn't mean to think of it." He sat back on the cool stone floor against the wall. "Fifty ways? I guess an explosion on a luxury yacht wasn't one of them, huh?"

She had no answer for that.

"I didn't think so. Too bad." He went back to peeling the apple. The knife blade squeaked cutting through the flesh of the fruit. His voice was low and harsh and very angry. "Maybe they'll want to rethink the lyrics."

"Rafe, stop it!"

He was suddenly angry. "What do you want from me, Zoe? Shall I just forget this apple and open a vein? Will that do it for you, Zoe? Answer me!"

"No." It took all her strength not to be frightened of him. Of his anger.

"No. Of course not. That would be over too quickly. Do you think you're the only one who has suffered?" He pitched the apple aside and flipped the knife by its tip at a wooden cask of oil. It stuck and quivered. "Oh, but I forgot. You don't want to hear about it."

"Rafe, that's not fair."

"Are you . . ." He cocked his jaw to the side and looked away from her. His voice cracked and strained. He had to start over twice. "Are you ever going to be able to get past this? Because if you're not, Zoe, we don't really need to worry about both of us getting out alive. Clemenza will welcome you home with open arms, and since he'll have won, maybe he'll even let me go back to being the shadow of my former self. I did what I had to do," he went on, "and if what I have to do now is let you take Teddi away from me, too, then fine. Just tell me."

"Damn you for saying that! You know I would never want that!"

"But you can't have it both ways, Zoe." He gave a bitter laugh. "I was going to say it would kill me to give up Teddi, but it won't. I won't be so lucky."

She couldn't stop the tears from welling in her eyes. A thousand lonely, endless nights had taken their toll on her.

She had never gotten past her anger at him for leaving her, and that was when she'd believed he had died. "Rafe, I have always loved you."

His eyes were filled with sadness. "Thanks for the reassurance."

"All I want to know is how you could let me go on believing you and Teddi were dead."

"Why did you ever believe it in the first place?"

"Because I saw that explosion and the blast and the fire eat you alive! I saw the yacht burn half the night and finally sink. I saw all that, Rafe, and yes, I believed you had died."

Rafe shook his head. "Stephi didn't believe it, did she?"

"She was only nineteen months old—"

"I didn't believe their lies, Zoe. Teddi didn't. Stephi didn't. You believed it."

"Because I'm naive, then! Because I don't understand a world where people blow other people up and where they tell lies even if the truth would be easier!" She shoved her hair back from her face. "You could have found a way. I would have run away with you. I would have taken our babies and gone to the ends of the earth with you. I would have—"

"So would I," he cut her off brutally. "But Clemenza didn't ask me to what hellhole I wanted to take my family into exile. He gave me an ultimatum, and every week for a year he took the trouble of sending me a picture he shot at a distance of you and Stephi. The message was loud and clear. *The camera could as easily be a gun.*"

She couldn't manage more than a panting little breath. Rafe got up and began to pace. It felt like there was nothing more to say to each other, which scared her more than his anger. "Rafe, you don't mean that . . . about the camera, literally. Do you?"

"Do you mean, did Clemenza ever actually say the words? No. He didn't have to. *Mio Dio,* Zoe, will you never wake up and smell the coffee? These were not portraits with charm and happy faces. They were surveillance photographs. And he wasn't sending them out of the goodness of his heart."

She had a sudden devastating image of herself and Stephi caught, frozen by the camera in some blithe, innocent moment when they might as easily have been the target in the cross hairs of a rifle. It was beyond her to believe that Frank could ever actually have done it, but even the threat pointed up her vulnerability. Her concept of the world as a safe place to be shattered.

Zoe turned numbly away.

"SISTER MARY BERNADETTE?"

"Yes?" she answered, turning from the window looking out of Stephi's isolation room.

"Just checking. Mr. Clemenza wanted to know if he would find you up here."

Mary Bernadette sighed. Her body ached from many sleepless hours spent watching over Stephi, and many more consumed with fear of what had become of Zoe.

It seemed that her precautions had backfired. She had hoped that Zoe would find her husband in the guise of Paolo Bondi and Stephi's little twin, Teddi, and return to Chicago before Clemenza knew she was gone. The longer he remained ignorant of Zoe's whereabouts, the better.

She should have known better. Somehow Clemenza had discovered that Zoe had gone to Sicily, and he knew why, which led Mary Bernadette to the conclusion that he had spoken to Emma Harding.

None of that mattered now, any more than it mattered that she had been able to look Frank in the eye and swear that she had not told Zoe that her husband and daughter were alive. At the time it had seemed vital to her. She had not broken her promise of silence to Frank—the promise she had made on pain of the lives of Zoe's children. But Mary Bernadette knew she should have told Zoe everything. Stephi would die, and soon, without a transfusion of her twin's white cells.

Twenty-twenty hindsight, she railed at herself.

She had taken the only mitigating steps she knew to take, advising Emma Harding and Joel Sebern that Stephi's identical twin, whom they had all thought dead, was alive. Both physicians were justifiably bewildered. Why hadn't Zoe known this? Mary Bernadette had told them flatly that the explanation would have to wait.

She felt in no condition to deal with Frank Clemenza. But then, what choice did she have?

None.

She would not speak with him in Stephi's room, however. He would get no closer to Stephi than the conference room down the hall unless it was over Mary Bernadette's dead body.

Fortunately, the child was sleeping, and she would not have to make excuses to her. She reached down to stroke Stephi's fevered brow. In the last several hours, an infection had taken hold despite the strict isolation and the best efforts of her doctors. It was the one thing they had all feared most—that Stephi would succumb to some infection or other before she could undergo a transplant of the cells that might have saved her.

Mary Bernadette said a silent blessing over Stephi, then turned and left the isolation room, discarding the gown that covered her habit and her paper mask. Already, Frank Clemenza was chatting amiably with the nurses.

How she despised him! Lord take her only remaining vanity, her Irish brogue, if he would also see fit to take Frank Clemenza from the face of the earth. But she was not accustomed to making deals with God, and she sentenced herself to penances far more severe than her confessor would dispense.

Frank spotted her as she drew near the nursing station. "Sister Mary Bernadette. What a saint you are. How is our little Stephi this morning?"

Saying nothing, mistrusting him so much that she believed him capable of diverting her long enough to have someone end Stephi's already fragile life, she asked one of the nurses she had known for years to go sit with Stephi in her absence.

She passed him only after she saw with her own eyes that the nurse had gone into Stephi's room. She walked into the conference room and tucked her hands from sight so he would not see her shaking in rage and fear of him.

She waited until he had closed the door. "What is it you want?"

He made himself comfortable, taking pleasure, she thought, in making her wait. "I understand that your niece left a message."

"Only that she had tried to reach me." Mary Bernadette smiled thinly. "Of course, that was after you assured me that she had already died a horrible death."

He shrugged. "It seems I was misinformed."

"Too bloody bad."

"Don't crow yet, old woman," he said, picking a piece of lint from his suit coat. "Her life is now numbered in hours."

"And that is at the Lord's discretion, not yours."

"Oh, it's the Lord you're counting on? Don't."

Mary Bernadette crossed herself. "Had you the powers of the Inquisition, I would still put my faith where it belongs." She looked at him pityingly, which she knew came as close to infuriating him as she could come. "You don't even know where she is, do you?"

"Don't let that be a comfort, Bernadette. You broke your vow of silence, and I assure you, she will pay for your weakness."

She felt suddenly panicky. "She has gone only because Stephi's life depends now upon her twin. Surely even you can see that it was impossible not to..." She trailed off, seeing the twist of Clemenza's lips. How foolish she had been to even think of appealing to his higher nature.

He had none.

"Your soul must be a vast, bleak wasteland. I pity you! What will finally be enough for you? Bishop Centi's fortune is yours. You have been rich beyond your wildest dreams for all these terrible years! I cannot imagine why you trouble yourself with the affairs of this hospital?"

He raised his brows. "Noblesse oblige, my dear woman. It is what the very rich have always done. Perhaps, Bernadette," he said, belittling her and her name, "I am not quite the heartless creature you assume, but a humanitarian and a leader. This hospital is a model of—"

"Spare me your self-important blather!"

"Spare me your pity, Bernadette," he commanded. "You will need it to reconcile your own miserable accounts in heaven."

"I have no fear—"

"But you should, old woman. None of them will escape alive, and their deaths will litter your conscience for the rest of your days."

HOURS PASSED. There were no windows. It was impossible for Zoe and Rafe to follow the progress of the day. Once they were allowed out long enough to use the bathroom facilities, but Zoe had spare time enough only to wash her face, rinse her mouth and to see that it was dark outside.

Her mind returned, again and again, countless times during the night, to images of clandestine photographs taken of her and Stephi. Unwary moments. Hundreds of them, when they had been at risk and she had taken her safety and Stephi's for granted.

Rafe had never had that luxury. She believed him, but she didn't understand. The silence between them stretched on and on.

They had been in the cellar twenty-seven hours when a loud thump at the top of the stairs indicated the door being unbarred, unlocked. She arose from her pile of rags and Rafe stood, turning toward the shaft of daylight pouring down the stairs, marred by the shadow of Giancarlo De Sica.

Dressed all in white, a short-sleeved polo shirt and slacks, he descended the stairs. Rafe took a deep breath.

De Sica came unsmiling upon Zoe, but he took her hand and kissed her wrist and finally turned to Rafe. He looked him up and down. "You must be Teresa's son." He spoke English, but in an Italian accent different from any Zoe had ever heard.

Rafe nodded. "Raphael Mastrangelo." He gestured with a tilt of his head toward Zoe, and introduced her as his wife.

"Giancarlo De Sica. I am relieved to see that our intruders are none other than little Teddi's parents." He stepped forward, a man as tall as Rafe but heavier with his years, with a full head of curling, graying hair. He put his hands on Rafe's shoulders.

Rafe returned the clasp.

"We learned by radio several moments into our flight that intruders had been picked up by my guards. Teresa had a feeling that it might have been you." De Sica turned back to Zoe. "You will wish to know, I have just heard from Teresa. She and your sweet daughter Theodora have arrived safely in Chicago. As we speak, they are almost certainly on their way to your hospital there."

Relief flooded into Zoe. They had made it. Unable to speak, she covered her lips for a moment. She turned to Rafe. "Will she know what to do?"

He nodded. "Turi will have told her to seek out Mary Bernadette as soon as they arrive."

"*Signore,* I will never be able to repay your kindness," she said simply. "Thank you so much."

Rafe bowed his head. "You have my undying gratitude as well," he added. "My mother is a very fortunate woman—"

De Sica waved a hand. "*Prego. Non c'e nulla.* I am the one of exceptional good fortune. But I must apologize for your treatment. There was some confusion in relaying my orders. I had no intention that you should be cast into the... how do you say, jail?"

Zoe smiled. Her relief was almost palpable. De Sica was extraordinarily charming. "Dungeon, do you mean, *signore?*"

"Giancarlo, please." A broad smile came over his face. "Dungeon. Yes. A hole in the ground, is that correct?" But he didn't wait for an answer. "I was delayed many hours in my return by repairs required on the helicopter, which I was forced to leave in Catania. I apologize. *Per favore.* Come with me now."

Zoe glanced at Rafe. He nodded. She turned to follow De Sica up the stairs, and Rafe came behind her, putting his hand on the small of her back. Giancarlo led them through the villa, through an enormous, gracious living area, to a wing with bedrooms.

At last he gestured for them to precede him into an expansive bedroom suite. "Here you will find everything you need to wash away the dust of your travels and rest. When you are feeling refreshed, Raphael and Zoe, come find me and we will speak together.'' He backed away and firmly closed the arched set of double doors.

Rafe heaved a big sigh and rolled his head to stretch his neck. Zoe turned slowly around, dismayed to find that she had felt safer in the windowless cellar.

Here, in a suite decorated with carved moldings inlaid in Italian marble, where the view was so spectacular, where she could actually use a sink with gold fixtures and a shower with two heads, here she felt a little less secure.

And hopelessly ungrateful—but there it was, this sudden perverse mistrust. Maybe it was only a symptom of losing her vaunted naïveté. Such wealth made men very, very powerful. And abusive of the power?

Men like Frank Clemenza.

She gave a soft sigh, noticing again that she had at last accepted what Rafe said of Clemenza as the truth. But accepting the truth only led inevitably back to the one question she would even ask Giancarlo De Sica if she had the chance.

Why are you doing this?

Frank had the money and the power to ruin her life with Rafe—and the lives of their babies—and he had used it. But why? Giancarlo De Sica had the money and the power in his hands to help them. But why would he?

Rafe had turned away and stripped off his shirt. There was a small amount of dried blood on the gauze covering his wound, but the burn scars on his back were what caught her attention.

She gave a small cry and her hand stretched helplessly toward him. He swung halfway around.

''What is it?''

''Your back...I...oh, Rafe.'' His beautiful, masculine muscled back was marred by hundreds of shiny white little islands of scar tissue. She felt herself pale and go sick to her stomach. ''You said your burns were not so bad.''

"I lied." He turned so she wouldn't be troubled by it anymore and stripped off his shoes and pants and lay back on the bed. "If you want to use the bathroom and bathe, do it. But hurry. De Sica doesn't mean to harbor us forever."

"Fine." She turned on her heel and went to the bathroom and locked the door. She meant to be angry, but the sequence of her actions made her flash for a moment on the suite aboard the *Persephone* when Rafe had flirted with her and she had flirted back and he'd come after her, threatening to knock the door down and embarrass her because Centi would hear them and the babies would awaken.

She caught sight of herself in the mirror, which didn't help. Her hair was impossibly tangled, and her eyes seemed dull and swollen. Her cheeks were dry and colorless, her lips chapped, her fingernails ragged, and a few remaining cactus spines festered in her hand. A stiff breeze would blow her over.

But just now Rafe had ordered her away as if he couldn't stand the sight of her another minute. The contrast between that afternoon aboard the yacht and now—wildly happy to angry, intimate to cold, playful to deadly earnest—made her feel a wave of hopelessness all over again.

Worse, she didn't have the emotional reserves to deal with memories clashing with the present.

She needed to be with her children now. Stephi *and* Teddi. And to see Stephi as healthy and vibrant as Teddi again.

She turned on both of the shower heads and stepped inside. The water was glorious, the shampoo richly scented, the soap smooth as glass, the clouds of steam luxurious. None of it could wash away the chasm of need that lay beneath her powerful maternal instincts. The need of a woman in love with a man to whom she had promised her life.

Rafe had lied about the severity of his burns to protect her from the horror of his experience. She finally understood that the scars were more than skin deep. That his physical impairments—the terrible burns he had suffered and the ankle that had not healed properly—were nothing to him compared to the emotional ruin of living under Frank Clemenza's threats to her and Stephi.

She thought that if he had loved her he would have found a way. She thought that she would never forgive him. He made her uncertain and confused about what there was to forgive.

He made her remember what she had kept hidden from herself. How deeply she had missed and still needed the unmatched affections of the man who had promised his life to her. Of her children's father.

Of a man who was scarred and angry, body and soul.

Chapter Eleven

Giancarlo De Sica awaited them in a covered courtyard overlooking the ocean. A plate of fruits and cheeses and sliced bread, its crust shiny with the finest olive oil, filled the table, along with glasses of iced Perrier and goblets of a richly colored wine.

Zoe had dressed in clothes the maid provided from Teresa's closet. The slacks hung loosely on her, but that was their fashion in any case, and the sleeveless raw linen blouse felt wonderfully cool.

Rafe had been given fresh clothing belonging to their host. Rafe had to cinch the waist of the slacks with a belt, but the sherry-colored silk shirt fit him well enough.

Though he had earlier waved off their gratitude, De Sica accepted Zoe's thanks for the use of Teresa's clothing. "She will be pleased to know that you wear them so beautifully."

"It's hard for me to believe she and I have never met," Zoe murmured. "She has already gone to enormous trouble, not only for Teddi, but for us."

"As have you, Don Giancarlo." Rafe downed the entire glass of wine. "I am deeply indebted to you."

Giancarlo nodded. His eyes, surrounded by deeply etched lines, flicked to each of them in turn, evaluating the sincerity of their words. He drew on his cigarette and made smoke rings in the air. Satisfied, he drew his chair closer to the table.

"I understand that one of your little daughters is very ill. And that it is important that you return to the United States as quickly as possible." He crushed out the cigarette, pushed away the plate of food and leaned on the table with both forearms.

"Nevertheless, your mother wished me to convey to you the message that there is a woman to whom you should speak before you leave Sicily." He paused, took out another unfiltered cigarette and held it between his fingers.

Rafe's brows drew sharply together. "Who?"

"Her name is Rosa Taviani. She is bilingual and exceptionally well versed in the finer things of life since leaving the employ of Frank Clemenza."

Rafe filled his glass. "Go on."

"Your mother indicated that this Taviani woman was the private-duty nurse provided to take care of you in the weeks following the explosion of the *Persephone*—in the employ of Frank Clemenza."

Rafe waited impatiently, knowing that De Sica would continue in his own good time.

Giancarlo sat back and lit the cigarette, then blew out the smoke. "Teresa has long been troubled by the lack of any reason for Clemenza's obsession with your lives. It is very un-Italian of her to believe there must be a logical reason for the actions of others. Still, she believes it possible that Taviani may be able to shed some light on the link between Clemenza, the explosion of the yacht and what later befell your family at his whim."

Rafe took a few olives and pieces of fruit to his plate. Zoe felt the tension edge up in her own body, and she knew by the pulsing of a tiny vein near his temple that this had caught his attention. There were a dozen things she could think of off the top of her head to ask of the woman who had taken care of Rafe—even if she had not been hired by Frank Clemenza.

"Please take no offense, Don Giancarlo," Rafe began, "but my children's health is a higher priority to me right now than to speak with a woman who may or may not know anything of use to me."

"To the health of your children," Giancarlo toasted, lifting his glass of rosé. Rafe matched him and echoed the sentiment. Giancarlo continued. "Nevertheless, I volunteered to bring the Taviani woman as a guest here to the villa to make her available to you."

Zoe paled. Something in the way he used the words *guest* and *available* made her cringe. Rafe cast her a warning look, which didn't escape De Sica.

"You are troubled, *cara* Zoe? You understand the nature of my offer to be no better than kidnapping?"

"Forgive me for saying so, but that is what it sounds like, Don Giancarlo."

He laughed uproariously at her. "You are a treasure beyond words! I have been told you are more stubbornly innocent of the ways of the world than is strictly healthy for you." He leaned toward her. "Kidnapping is a national pastime. It is meaningless, particularly since I ask only her foolish idle time as ransom."

Zoe opened her mouth, then shut it again. She didn't want to offend him, but she couldn't condone kidnapping, either. "I will cling to my innocence, Don Giancarlo, if it is all the same to you."

"If it is all the same to me?" He stared at her for what seemed an eternity, a game of chicken, a duel of eyes where whoever blinked first lost. He blinked quite deliberately, then laughed and clapped Rafe on the shoulder. "I like this woman!"

Rafe nodded and cuffed him back and the two of them postured with each other in Sicilian for a few moments. Probably discussing women as chattels, Zoe fumed.

But no matter how he interacted with other men, Rafe had never treated her in any way like property. He was newly shaven and bathed and breathtakingly handsome, and she could not take her eyes from him.

The conversation grew more serious. "Unfortunately, Teresa is a woman of high principles as well. She refused even to consider my offer, so I have done the next best thing."

"What is that?" Zoe asked softly.

"I have learned where Rosa Taviani may be found. She lives on the upper floor of a crumbling but still elegant palazzo in Palermo."

He turned to Rafe and spoke again in their shared language. Rafe's face darkened with anger, which didn't change over the course of several minutes. After several long exchanges Giancarlo excused himself from the table and left.

Zoe had waited patiently, but she was anxious to know what De Sica had said that so angered Rafe. "Was there some reason why I shouldn't hear what you were discussing with him?"

"No." But he lowered his gaze and toyed with the fruit on his plate. Something in his delay alarmed her. The way his brows came together, concentrating, dismissing. "We were speaking only of how our escape might be handled."

"There's more." She could feel it. "Rafe, I have a right to know—"

"He has heard rumors."

"Rumors." The word made her shudder. She was so tired of feeling frightened. "What has happened?"

"Nicola Peretti is dead."

"Oh, my God, no!"

Rafe grimaced. "There is more. Turi's truck has been torched and he is under what may politely be called 'house arrest.' If his brother were not in a position of power in the province, he would most certainly be dead."

"How can that be? I thought Cavallo would believe Turi had gone to the city only to pick up his usual order of liquor."

"That was what we hoped." Rafe shook his head and sighed, deeply concerned for his friend. "It doesn't matter how Cavallo found out. He did. Now all of the western provinces are alerted to be on the lookout for us."

"The police, you mean?"

"Yes, in addition to Clemenza's network of *sbirri*. Turi is to be held as an accomplice to the kidnapping for which we are charged—"

"Of our own child?" Zoe demanded incredulously.

"And," he said, nodding to her question, "the murder of Nicola Peretti."

"Officially?"

"Yes. Although communications are horrible. It may be a few days before all of Sicily is looking for us."

Zoe couldn't believe her ears. They had done nothing to warrant any criminal charges, but they were nevertheless the object of a manhunt based only on the word Frank Clemenza's puppet, Cavallo.

Had he murdered Nicola Peretti himself?

Death wasn't a consequence Zoe could understand. In America even the worst serial murderers could tie up their death sentences in appeals for years. And even then, at the eleventh hour, they could appeal for clemency.

But Frank's own blood relations were not immune. Nicola Peretti was almost certainly dead because Zoe had escaped her. Who would be next? Anyone who had helped them? The old priest who had given them the truck and his suspicious niece? Eligio Dante? Giancarlo De Sica?

For the first time she considered that Rafe had not exaggerated in the least the threat to their lives. If Frank could sanction the murder of his own niece, he had it within him to have killed them all without a trace of remorse had Rafe managed to let her know he was alive.

Curiously, though her eyes ached, they were dry. She met Rafe's gaze, and knew that he had seen the light beginning to dawn in her. Her naïveté burning away like a morning mist evaporating under the intense heat of the Sicilian sun. "I'm beginning to understand."

Rafe held her gaze for a long moment, then broke it off and shook his head wearily. "The irony is so thick I could choke on it."

"What?"

"I've wanted nothing more than that you understand. Somehow I had to make you see. But the truth is that I never wanted you to lose that innocence, Zoe."

He broke off and sighed heavily, unconsciously rubbing his shoulder. "You were untouched, *cara*. You believed in your tooth fairy and happily-ever-after endings. If I could take you back to a time before all this began, I would do it."

"Then, Raphael," she answered softly, "I would be no better off than Peter Pan, stuck in never-never land, never growing up."

A housemaid came to clear away their plates and replenish the wine carafe. She brought freshened ice water as well, garnished by slices of lemon, and took away the old glasses in which the hot Sicilian air had evaporated moisture almost before it appeared. But Zoe barely noticed the ministrations of De Sica's kitchen help.

She saw in a flash of bittersweet intuition that part of her attraction to Rafe had always been his machismo. His Latin virility. His two-fisted, arrogant, possessive, chest-beating willingness to get in the face of any man foolish enough to dare touch her.

If they had never run up against the machinations of Frank Clemenza, she might have basked in Rafe's intense love and his possessiveness to the end of her days. But their life had been corrupted, and she could never again look at the world in the same innocent, accepting, trustful way.

If there were impossible choices to be made like the one he had made to protect her life, and Stephi's and Teddi's, then she would take responsibility for them as well.

"Don't you think it's time I grew up, Raphael?"

He gave a small smile and the slow, dangerous blink that made her heart pound. "If you become any more a woman, Zoe, I will have to lock you away myself."

She had forgotten how quickly he could take her breath away and tie her tongue in knots. She had forgotten how intensely he affected her in the course of any day they shared. She cleared her throat. "Tell me the rest, Rafe, please. I should know what we are up against. We have put Signor De Sica in terrible danger as well, haven't we?"

Rafe nodded. "His guard drove the pickup truck as far as Sciacca to the south and east, intending to abandon it there, but he was pulled over and arrested. It will eventually cost De Sica hundreds of thousands of lire to get the man released. Meanwhile, the search is intensified in the southwestern provinces."

Zoe stared out at the tranquil sea and the cloudless cerulean blue sky. A bee buzzed nearby. The exotic, romantic scents and sights and sounds of the villa of Giancarlo De Sica were not so remote from the dangers Rafe described.

She drew a deep breath and sat back. "How are we going to escape, Raphael?" she asked, her voice barely above a whisper. "I need to be with Stephi and Teddi—"

"I know." He finished off his glass of wine and grimaced. "De Sica is now on the telephone, instructing one of his business agents to purchase tickets for us on every flight departing from western Europe to the States for the next three days."

"Wow." She saw instantly the wisdom of the strategy. It would be nearly impossible for Cavallo or even Clemenza to have every boarding gate at every airport covered in the search for them. "How ingenious."

"Yes."

"It must be costing De Sica a fortune," she mused. "Why is he willing to go to such lengths and expense for us?"

Rafe shrugged. "Before, it was an interesting diversion. He is, at heart, a decent man. It amused him to undermine Clemenza. Now, with his man detained in Sciacca and the trumped-up kidnap and murder charges against us, he is angry."

"A decent man," she echoed. "More than that, I think." She reached for the water pitcher to refill her glass, then took a long drink. "I still don't understand. We have to be able to get somewhere in order to use any of the airline tickets he is purchasing."

"De Sica believes that while the search is concentrated to the south, we will not be apprehended driving my mother's car to Palermo. Taviani is there, not to mention my travel documents. There is no way I could get on any international flight to the States without the proper documentation. Is your passport in your purse?"

"Yes." She hadn't needed a visa since she had planned to be in Sicily no more than a week, but she had not thought of the complication of Rafe's documents. "How is it possible that you still have your papers?"

"I don't. Not on me." Rafe polished off the last of the fruit on the platter. "But before we boarded the *Persephone* from Catania, remember, I placed all our travel documents in the hotel safe. With my death certificate, all my 'effects' were released by the Excelsior Hotel to my mother. She put them in a safety deposit box at a bank in Palermo where I kept my birth certificate and various investments and bonds."

"She had a key?" He nodded. "And you have a key now?"

"It is always in my medical bag, tucked beneath the bottom of the bag and the outer leather."

Zoe shook her head. "How extraordinarily lucky."

"Not lucky," he contradicted her. "Such plotting is instinctive to the Sicilian character, Zoe. Nothing is ever left to chance if it can be avoided. My bag is always with me, and in this way, so was any proof that Raphael Mastrangelo had ever existed."

He said all of this with a half smile, gently mocking his heritage. Zoe smiled as well, and thought it wasn't only for his machismo that she had fallen for him. But she was still focused on the mechanics of their escape. "What about from Palermo? We have to get to Rome or Paris or—"

"London," he said. "There are charter flights from Palermo to Luton in the U.K., tour group charters. We will be returning as if we had begun there, in the midst of English tourists. In that way our names are only on a private passenger manifest. Once we arrive at Luton we'll have to get to Heathrow, but I don't think it can be more than fifty kilometers. By this time tomorrow, we will be on our way."

Zoe sat stunned by the ingeniousness of the plan. Not only would they avoid the international airports on the Continent, but they would be able to fade into a crowd. And they would be in Britain—possibly on a flight to the States—before the other international flights De Sica had purchased were even scheduled to leave.

"There is one thing, Zoe. I think, and De Sica agrees, that you should call Stephi's doctors and arrange to have them begin the procedures to save her life without us."

"I don't—" She started to protest but he cut her off.

"Remember not to live in never-never land, *cara*," he admonished. "You must face the fact that once we leave this villa, anything could happen. We could be killed, Zoe. Both of us. Cavallo is not incompetent, and the carabinieri are not fools. Would you want the procedure delayed endlessly awaiting our arrival?"

"No. Of course not."

"Then let's go call them, Zoe. We must leave as soon as the sun goes down."

"What time is it?"

"A few minutes past 4:00 p.m. here. Nine in the morning in Chicago. Their offices should be open right now."

Zoe resigned herself to the call and pushed back her chair to get up.

Rafe followed. They went to place the call from the bedroom suites where they had showered. Zoe picked up the antique-style telephone and sat on the bed, surrounded by the trappings of Giancarlo De Sica's wealth. As she dialed, her fingers shook.

There was no reason to be so nervous. She knew that. But she had no way of knowing for certain whether Rafe's mother and Teddi had arrived at the hospital, or whether Mary Bernadette had acknowledged to her doctors that Stephi's twin was not dead, but very much alive and healthy.

She finished dialing the area code and number of Emma Harding's office, which was in the complex of professional offices next to Rose Memorial.

Rafe sat down beside her on the bed and Zoe took a deep breath as the line began to ring.

Emma's receptionist answered. Zoe had known Kate Bristol for several years.

"Kate, this is Zoe Mastrangelo. I'm calling overseas long distance. Is Emma in?"

"Zoe, my goodness!" Although the connection had gone through quickly enough, the quality was sketchy. "What a coincidence! Mr. Clemenza was just in, asking whether we had heard from you."

Zoe felt the blood rush from her head. "Did you say... Clemenza? Frank Clemenza?"

"I know." Kate giggled. "It's hard to believe the high and mighty was in our offices, but he was really very kind—and concerned about you. Have you found a cell donor yet for Stephi?''

"Yes." *Kate, he's not very kind,* Zoe thought. "But I have to speak to Emma right away."

"Zoe, I'm sorry, but Dr. Harding isn't in the office. She's off doing her monthly pro bono work at the downtown neighborhood clinics. Shall I try to get hold of her for you? Oh, but you're long distance—"

"No." Zoe swore softly under her breath, thinking what to do.

"What is it?" Rafe asked.

"Hold on, Katie, will you?" Zoe covered the phone and explained. "Stephi's pediatrician is gone for the morning. And Frank was in her office asking about us."

Rafe cursed and his features hardened.

"Katie, listen. I'd like to surprise Frank when I get back— "

"Why?"

Zoe bit her lip in frustration. "It's important, Katie, but I can't explain right now. Would you just not tell Frank?"

"If that's what you want," she answered doubtfully.

"I do, Katie. It's very important. When do you expect Dr. Harding? Two o'clock?" she repeated for Rafe's benefit.

"We'll call her from Palermo," he said, "unless you want to try the oncologist?"

She covered the phone again. "Should I?"

Rafe thought a moment. "Probably not. It's risky to call everyone involved. Clemenza has probably been there, too. Just tell this person we'll call back at 5:00 p.m., but if for some reason we can't, she should tell Harding that you may be delayed in Europe for several days and that you want her to go ahead with the procedure immediately."

Zoe nodded. "Katie, listen." She repeated the message nearly verbatim, then asked the receptionist to repeat it back to her, which she did.

"But Zoe, how can Dr. Harding proceed without a donor? Is there some problem?"

Zoe improvised. "The donor is already in the States, I think, but I've misplaced my passport and the consulate may take days to reissue."

"Bureaucrats," Katie clucked. "Can't get away from them. But I'll give Dr. Harding your messages if you don't connect later."

Zoe sighed gratefully. "Thanks, Katie. And remember, mum's the word?"

"Mum is definitely the word."

Zoe put the receiver back on the cradle hook and replaced the telephone on the table. She felt threatened and hemmed in and powerless to contain the imminent danger Clemenza represented. "He's everywhere, isn't he?"

Rafe said nothing, only stared at his hands. She knew it wasn't literally true, but he had to be moving in for the kill and all he had to do was choose the right place and time.

Thousands of miles from her, Stephi and Teddi's fate hinged on the ability of Mary Bernadette and Teresa Mastrangelo to keep them from harm's way.

They were ill-equipped for the likes of Frank Clemenza.

Chapter Twelve

Teresa Mastrangelo's car was a mauve-colored German import sports sedan, and its windows were tinted against the harsh, ubiquitous Sicilian sun. De Sica took Zoe in his arms and kissed her on both cheeks, then turned to Rafe and repeated the gesture of affection.

"Remember to give your too-logical mother my love."

Rafe nodded and thanked him one more time. "I remain in your debt, Don Giancarlo."

"There is no debt among men of honor. It has been my pleasure to assist you in these paltry ways."

His remark about Rafe's too-logical mother stuck with Zoe long after Rafe had driven away from the villa onto the autostrada leading north to Trapani and then east to Palermo. Teresa, Giancarlo had told them, had always been troubled by what she had called Clemenza's "obsession" with their lives. Giancarlo had called it Clemenza's whim.

But if it was overly demanding logic that insisted there must be a reason, something more than a whim, then Zoe was as guilty of it as Teresa Mastrangelo.

"Do you really believe Frank has done all of this for no reason?"

"No," he answered, breaking his silence of nearly all the twenty kilometers to Trapani. "And despite what Giancarlo said, neither does he. He was as convinced as my mother that it would be worth our while to track down Rosa Taviani.''

"I keep wondering what she knows. If she knows anything." Zoe watched the headlights of the oncoming traffic flickering on his profile. "You told me in the cave that only Frank knew why. But haven't you thought, in all this time, that you knew why? Ever any guesses?"

He took his eyes off the road to look at her for a minute. "I thought I knew why, once. But if I had to believe that, I would have gone insane, so I convinced myself it could never happen."

The tremor in his voice scared her. "What was it?"

"That Frank wanted you for himself."

Zoe felt for a moment as though every part of her body had suddenly shut down. She couldn't move or talk or breathe. On the surface of things, Rafe's fear would find a great deal of support.

She remembered the way Frank had looked at her on the yacht when Rafe was not there.

She remembered the way he had taken over and arranged her life afterward, from arranging her recuperation right up to purchasing the brownstone she lived in and deeding the house to her.

And she remembered the night he had proposed marriage to her, to offer her all the comforts and security and privileges that went with the fortune he had inherited from Centi.

She would never have married him for any reason, and in his heart, Rafe knew that, which must have been why he could convince himself that such a marriage would never take place.

She struggled with admitting any of it to Rafe. He had already suffered so much at the hands of Frank Clemenza. But though she knew it would only add fuel to the fire, she couldn't protect Rafe from the knowledge that Clemenza would gladly have taken his place in her life.

Rafe and her aunt Mary Bernadette had protected her from the truth, but the lies had exacted far too high a price from all of them. Stephi, most of all.

No, Zoe thought. The only weapon she had left to fight with was the truth, and she would keep none of it from Rafe.

"Frank did offer to marry me." She saw Rafe's jaw tighten. "I would never have done it, and I'm sure he knew that."

"But that didn't stop him from asking, did it?" Rafe asked, his voice murderously low.

"Nothing has stopped him, Rafe. But the point is, he didn't engineer that explosion because he was obsessed with me. Which still leaves us with zero for a reason."

Rafe was darkly quiet for another few minutes, staring hard, squinting against the lights of the oncoming traffic. At last he took a deep breath and let it go. "Okay. Let's start at the beginning. I don't think that he had any dark motives for bringing us onto the *Persephone.*"

Zoe nodded, searching her memories. "I agree. Everything up until that day was fine. I remember Frank asking again early that afternoon if we were enjoying ourselves. You and the babies had gone below to the stateroom for a nap."

"Which is when Frank spoke to you about Centi."

"Yes. And about the argument between them." She shifted sideways in the confines of her seat belt to face Rafe. "I remember him saying he hoped I hadn't been unduly troubled by the tension between him and Centi. That was also when he told me he'd been summoned to an important business meeting in New York. Representing Centi's business interests, he said."

"So he created an excuse to leave the *Persephone.*" Occupied for a moment with passing a car, Rafe moved back into his lane. "How would we know if he had actually been summoned somewhere or not?"

"We wouldn't have known—or had any reason to wonder, for that matter. He could have told us anything." She paused for a moment. "Do you think he had it in mind even then to blow up the yacht?"

Rafe nodded. "He had several hours to decide what to do. If Centi had threatened to cut him off, or donate everything he owned to Sacred Heart, or even the church—"

"Then killing Centi in the explosion would prevent him from doing anything foolish." Zoe shuddered. Frank had even admitted that Centi's judgment in his waning years had become more clouded with sentiment than Centi himself knew was wise. "But it doesn't make sense!"

"No part of it makes sense, Zoe."

"I know. But Frank was spending thousands of dollars to entertain us—to repay his debt of honor to you!" she protested. "You're saying that he was so desperate to get rid of Centi that it didn't matter to him that four innocent bystanders would die as well!"

"Look at it from Frank's viewpoint, Zoe." He rested both hands on the top of the steering wheel, then straightened his arms to stretch. "The death of innocent bystanders could only give greater credibility to the 'tragic accident' explanation. Who would seriously question the cause of Centi's death when the lives of others—especially tiny children—had also been lost?"

Zoe had no answer for that. A part of her wanted to reject Rafe's version of Frank's viewpoint flat out. People just didn't go around killing other people as easily as they would knock players off some board game.

Rafe looked over at her. "What are you thinking, *cara?*"

"That no one is that heartless. Not even Frank. I believe you, Rafe. I do. I just can't—"

"The problem you're having, Zoe," he interrupted gently, "is that this is all unimaginable to you. Trust me. It was not unimaginable to Frank. We don't know what happened between them, but he must have been very powerfully motivated—by something Centi had said or done or threatened—to get rid of him then and there no matter who else would be hurt."

"Or killed."

"Or killed," Rafe agreed.

"But don't you remember? I said Frank would never hurt Centi and you went off on this long, involved tangent. You said Frank wouldn't hurt Centi, but not for any reason that I thought. Remember?"

"Exactly, *cara*. So long as Frank had money of his own, he would feel a moral commitment to protect Centi's fortune and see to his comfort."

Zoe laughed without any humor. "After all of this it's hard to believe Frank ever felt a moral commitment to anything or anyone."

"I won't argue with that," Rafe responded. "But we know the disagreement had to do with Centi's estate. If you throw in the possibility of Centi's cutting Frank out of his will, Frank sees himself turned penniless overnight."

"So he concocts a plan to get rid of Centi along with four innocent bystanders to make the explosion a more believable disaster."

"That's one scenario." On the outskirts of Palermo, Rafe sat up. Driving in the city was a nightmare anytime, but after dark, it took a great deal more attention. "It doesn't explain how he behaved afterward." He looked startled. "Zoe, maybe that's it!"

He studied the surrounding buildings at an intersection and turned left toward the coast. "We didn't die, so instead of unfortunate victims, he had potential witnesses to what really happened."

A car leapt out in front of them from the curb. Rafe slammed on the brakes and the horn at the same time. He swore and muttered about a wreck being the last thing they needed, then asked, "Does that make sense?"

Zoe relaxed her grip on the door handle. "Yes. Except that I don't see why he needed to keep us apart."

Rafe pulled around the other car. "I don't know, either. In his scheme of things we were supposed to die in that explosion. He could only have decided afterward that it was vital to keep us apart. So he intercepted my mother's calls to you and sent your aunt to my bedside to deliver his ultimatum."

"But why?"

He shrugged. "Frank must have decided that only I was a danger to him, and that as long as he had you and Stephi under his control, he could be generous and let me live after all. But his original plan had to be concealing Centi's murder in the explosion—which could be blamed on the lightning."

"Rafe, maybe *that's* it," she suggested. "It was a real gamble to leave us on the yacht. He had to know there would be some slim possibility that we would survive. But if he was that anxious to be rid of Centi, maybe he didn't leave that part of it to chance." She thought a moment, fitting pieces. "You went after them. Did you ever actually see Centi?"

"Hold on." Again he studied the intersection, went through it and turned again at the next cross street. "No. I never saw him. When I got to Centi's stateroom, Teddi was alone. I thought he might have gone to see what had happened after the first blast."

Zoe shook her head. "I can't imagine Centi leaving Teddi alone, or why he would go anywhere without taking her."

"Maybe he thought she'd be safer where she was." He pulled suddenly into an alley. "Hell. I've missed it."

But it took only another minute to get back to the corner he'd wanted, and then he sidled to the curb, parked the car on the street and switched off the engine.

Zoe looked out her window. "Is this it? The palazzo where Taviani lives?"

"No. It's three blocks south of here," he answered, opening his door. "Stay put." He went around to open Zoe's door and take his doctor's bag from the back seat, then locked the car. "I think it's better if this car isn't parked right in front of Taviani's place."

"Will the police be looking for this car?"

"It's always a possibility. We can't be too careful, Zoe." He took her arm. "Come on."

They walked the three blocks with Rafe's arm draped possessively over her shoulders, attracting only the notice of the street urchins, and reached the entryway to Rosa Taviani's palazzo.

De Sica had said she occupied the entire second floor. Rafe thought it was possible that she took in renters for spare rooms, because the palazzo, although very old and in the midst of a squalid neighborhood, was in good repair, enormous and wildly expensive.

The ceiling was at least twenty feet high, supported by columns of marble. An elaborate curving staircase led up from the massive entryway to the second floor. Rafe explained whole families might live in apartments to either side. Zoe heard a burst of angry voices and slamming doors coming from behind one set of doors on the first floor.

They climbed the stairs. Only one door of the seven leading off the balcony had a peephole. Rafe stood to the side and had Zoe knock as a precaution against Rosa refusing to speak to him—if she even recognized him.

She opened the door to Zoe. Rafe stepped nearer, prepared to stick his foot in the door if she tried to slam it shut.

Dressed casually in jeans and a silk tank top, Rosa looked from one to the other without speaking, but it was clear from her expression that she recognized Rafe.

Pretty in an exotic way, she had high cheekbones and dramatic brows. But her hands, despite the care of her nails, which were long as talons and polished an almost black shade of red, belied her age and unlined complexion. Zoe thought she was probably nearing fifty.

She eyed his medical bag. "A house call, Signor Doctor. How wonderfully quaint."

"Rosa. It's been a long time," Rafe said in a voice and tone that implied they were old friends, but in English for Zoe's sake.

"The reports of your death were greatly exaggerated," she responded sarcastically in perfect English, following up with an outrageous Italian flirtation, stripping him with her eyes. "I preferred you nude."

Rafe gave a sardonic smile. He turned to Zoe and winked. "My wife, Zoe."

"A lucky woman." Rosa's features hardened, and she dropped the social amenities. She turned to Rafe. "What do you want?"

"To talk. That's all," Rafe answered.

Holding on to the door, she shrugged elaborately. "I would prefer not."

Rafe took a deep breath. "Please." He spoke softly to her in Italian, and whatever he said convinced her at least to allow them in.

She turned away, leaving the door open for them to enter or not as they chose. Coming to a sofa, she sat and plucked a cigarette from a pack on the end table.

Rafe sat in the opposite chair, and Zoe at the opposite end of the sofa. The room had the ambience of great wealth, but she noticed the worn, nearly frayed seams on the arm of the sofa.

"I suppose this is about Frank Clemenza," Rosa said, her words riding on a stream of smoke. "I must warn you, I value my life. Which means there is almost nothing I'll say to you."

"Nothing you say will leave this room, Rosa," Rafe promised her quietly.

Rosa snorted. "If I believed that I would be a fool." She narrowed her eyes against the smoke rising from her cigarette. "I am not a fool." She took another long drag then crushed out the cigarette. "Ask your questions. We will see."

Watching her, the way her features hardened, the way her lips tightened, the way she sat, Zoe wasn't hopeful.

"I want to know why Clemenza hired you to stay at my side around the clock, for starters."

She tossed her short hair. "I was bilingual, educated, private duty. He wanted to know everything at all times." She reached for another cigarette and lit it. "He was willing to pay for such extraordinary services."

"Did you know Clemenza before?" Rafe asked, watching her closely.

"Yes. We met at a ski resort in Austria."

"How is it that you speak English so well?"

"I was born in New York and returned to Naples with my mother at the age of twelve."

"Did Clemenza ever ask you to inject my IVs with a fatal dose of potassium?"

She drew again on the cigarette, considering. "It was always a possibility."

"Would you have done it?" Zoe asked.

Rosa turned to Zoe. "It would have been a shame, wouldn't it, to waste such a man? But yes. Alas." Resting her elbow on the arm of the sofa, she flicked her ashes into the half-full crystal ashtray. "In the dark, one man is much the same as another."

Rafe blinked. "Then you have not been with the right man," he said.

"But of course, that is not an offer, is it?" she returned, allowing her eyes to glance off Zoe.

"No. It's not."

Zoe could see his distaste for the woman in the shape of his lips, but she imagined Rosa Taviani only saw his humor.

Rafe questioned Rosa Taviani closely for nearly an hour. Had she known that he was not, in fact, dead? What were Clemenza's plans? How had she been paid? Had she been there when Sister Mary Bernadette arrived? But she had reported countless hours of information to Clemenza, and it was beginning to seem an impossible task to zero in on any connection between the explosion and Frank's later machinations.

Rafe finally got up in frustration at the lack of any meaningful answers and went to stand by the window overlooking the street squalor.

Zoe was left sitting with Rosa Taviani. She was tired as well, and her eyes burned from the haze of smoke. A part of her wanted to tear the woman's heart out for wasting their time while Stephi and Teddi were in such danger.

She hadn't realized how thin the veneer of her own civilized behavior was. Not at all convinced that the woman was being forthcoming, Zoe was not willing to give up.

"I have the feeling," she said, "that you are answering my husband's questions fully aware that nothing you are telling him is worth the time of day."

Rosa sighed dramatically and turned her head away. "Does it occur to you that I don't really care what you are feeling, *signora?*"

"You should, you know," Zoe responded carefully. "Let me tell you why. One of my small daughters is dying. The other has been hidden away from me with her father for well over three years. I am wanted for the murder of Nicola Peretti, who is Frank Clemenza's niece, and if I'm going to hang it may as well be for two lives as one.''

She paused long enough to snatch another as-yet-unlit cigarette from Rosa's hand and crush it in her own. Rafe had turned from the window and stood looking at her in surprise. She ignored him. ''Why did Frank hire you?''

Rosa stared at her, wondering, Zoe thought, if she were a greater threat than Clemenza would be if she answered. Her eyes had widened at Zoe's reference to the murder of Nicola Peretti. ''You have your share of moxie. I'll give you that. But surely Peretti's death is the perfect illustration of why I should not even have let you in my door.''

''Answer the question, Rosa,'' Zoe commanded. ''Why, exactly, did Frank hire you?''

Rosa sat thinking for a moment, never taking her eyes from Zoe. ''You said your daughter was hidden away from you with her father. Frank Clemenza did this,'' she stated, seeking only confirmation of what she had so quickly put together.

''Yes. In addition to destroying the yacht and murdering his cousin.''

Rosa sat forward and her eyes glittered hard as diamonds. Any allegiance to Frank Clemenza evaporated the moment she understood what he had done. ''To a child he did this.'' She shook her head. ''He hired me because he wanted to know what your husband remembered about the . . . accident.''

''The explosion, you mean,'' Zoe corrected her. ''Did you know that he had caused it?''

''Yes,'' she snapped. ''Somehow he made the yacht go boom.''

Zoe went very still. Despite Rosa's biting sarcasm, here was proof, not only of Rafe's judgment, but that Frank was responsible for what had happened on the yacht. ''Do you know why?''

"His filthy rich cousin Bishop Vincenti Rosario was aboard, wasn't he?" she asked, as if the answer were so obvious that a slow-witted child could guess.

Zoe saw Rafe from the corner of her eye motioning for her to continue. "Did Frank believe my husband would remember something incriminating him?"

Rosa combed her fingers through her hair. She might despise what he had done, but her fear of Clemenza's retribution remained. "I can't tell you what he thought. But what did he have to fear? Nothing could ever be proven. The evidence went down with the good bishop."

That was true, Zoe thought. There would be nothing left of physical evidence. "He was afraid of something, Rosa."

"All I know is what he told me," she answered scornfully.

"What was it, Rosa?" Rafe asked from behind her, his voice low and terribly dangerous. He returned to his seat, but everything about his posture warned that he was running very low on patience.

"I tell you, I don't know! The only thing that ever got a rise out of him was that, early on, when you were stoned out of your mind on pain medications, you rambled on and on about some Bible. I had the impression it belonged to the dead bishop."

Exchanging glances with Zoe, Rafe straightened in his chair, his tension multiplied a hundred times. "What about it?"

Rosa shrugged. "You were too incoherent to tell anything more."

"Did Frank settle for that answer, Rosa?" Zoe asked.

"From me?" She shrugged. "Yes. But that is when he sent for the nun from America. Sister Mary Bernadette, I believe?"

Chapter Thirteen

Rafe sat back and scraped a hand through his hair, then rose from his chair. "Zoe. Let's get out of here."

She got up but Rosa remained seated and gave him a quizzical look. "Does that mean you're done with me?"

"Yes."

Still sitting, she asked, "Where will you go? I assume the carabinieri are after you."

He picked up his medical bag and looked down at her. "I think it would be better for both of us if you don't know. That in fact, we never came here at all."

Rafe stared at her, assessing whether she would deny that she'd ever seen them or get on the phone to the police the minute the two of them were out the door.

She returned his hard look. "I would be a fool to turn you in. Clemenza is a user and a murderer, and I want no more notice from him than if I were an ignorant peasant villager."

She turned away from them as if they did not exist. Rafe took Zoe's hand and they left, closing the door behind them. Zoe waited until they had hit the street to question Rafe.

"Rafe, what is it about Centi's Bible? I don't understand."

He put his hand at the nape of her neck and spoke in low tones, guiding her in a different direction than they had come. "Don't walk so fast, *cara*." Understanding that they should not appear to be going anywhere very fast, she slowed her pace. "That's better."

"Where are we going?"

"To the first rooms we find for rent."

"What time is it?"

He checked his watch, knowing she was interested only in making sure they called Emma Harding on time. "Half an hour till we call the States."

Zoe shivered. The night air was still sweltering, but the street they were on was dark and ominous-feeling, and without Rafe, nowhere she'd have been caught dead alone. She'd never have taken a room so arbitrarily, either. Just picking one from a sign on a door. But this was Rafe's territory. He knew it. And almost anything would be better than the floor of a cave.

"About Centi's Bible?" she asked again.

Rafe scanned around them for signs of any trouble, then shook his head. "I don't know, but if that's what made Frank nervous, then—" he shrugged "—there must be something to it."

"Did you see it when you went to find Teddi and Centi? The two of them had gone below so Teddi could play with his Bible. Remember?"

"Yes. Teddi was wearing Centi's rosary beads—like a necklace. She must have had his Bible in her hands." He paused at the street corner and took advantage of a car passing through the intersection to glance around. The area was not lit well, nor was there much traffic. And pedestrians were almost expected to hold up cars. He started out into the intersection, his hand still gently cupping her nape.

"I remember thinking the Bible would be safe in Teddi's hands. I didn't think she'd let go of it. But then I never saw Centi." He nearly stopped walking with a sudden memory.

She urged him on, both to walk and tell her.

"Zoe, when I'd given up on finding Centi I went tearing up the stairs. Teddi was really afraid by then. Screaming. She dropped the Bible. I happened to catch it, and I remember thinking I was going to have to bail out, that we'd lost the Bible in the sea and Teddi would be heartbroken. I stuck it down the back of her diaper and after that I never thought about it again."

"Do you think it was still on Teddi when you were rescued?"

He tried to keep watching for trouble and focus on the memory at once. "I don't know. I think she still had his rosary beads around her neck.... I remember her putting them in her mouth.... I don't know about the Bible."

Something caught his eye, jerking him out of the memories. He looked back behind them on the street, then took Zoe's hand and began to walk diagonally across to the other side of the street. A door verging nearly on the street itself had a Rooms for Rent sign. Pensione.

Rafe banged on the door. Standing behind him, Zoe looked at the outside of the place he had chosen. It had the same sort of exterior as the palazzo where Rosa lived, though if there had ever been such a grand entrance it had long since been converted to living space. Several small wrought-iron balconies hung out above her.

A tall, thin woman came to the door in a nightdress and hair net. Rafe turned on his flattering, low intimate tones just to ask the old woman for a room. She was probably seventy, regal despite her nightclothes, and looked to be a northern European expatriate.

As usual, Rafe's innate, sincere charm turned the trick. The old woman flirted shamelessly as if Zoe were not even there. The room they were given was exquisite, and the only one in the palazzo with a telephone.

There was a luxurious double brass bed, a coverlet made of hand-crocheted lace, which was repeated at the windows. A crystal decanter of marsala sat on a silver tray, surrounded by dainty aperitif glasses. Next to that was an antique chair covered in very old, rich dark green velvet.

Zoe sighed gratefully as Rafe coaxed the little woman out, promising to take some of her fruits and marzipan in the morning. Best of all, Zoe thought, was the claw-footed bathtub.

"Did you know about this place?" Zoe asked, letting herself fall onto the feather bed.

"No. But the architecture gave it away as an old palazzo. The woman is an old duchess whose fortune was squandered twenty years ago. She rents out rooms for the sake of keeping hold of this place."

Rafe kicked off his shoes and fell back onto the bed as well, making its springs squeak.

Both of them lay there a moment in silence, staring up at the ceiling with its heavy layer of cracked and decaying plaster, neither of them missing the significance of being on one bed together for the first time in almost four years.

Or of the fact that their first time of coming together in the cavern had ended with her wish that it never happen again.

Or that the feelings between them, the fierce attraction between them and the deep well of shared experience had not disappeared because of her angry words.

But they must still call Emma Harding before anything else. Beside her, Rafe took Zoe's hand. She squeezed his fingers. He returned the pressure.

"Do you think I should put in the call for Emma?" she asked.

He rolled toward her and cuffed her gently on the chin. "I think you should go wash your face and have a sip of the duchess's fine, aged marsala, and *then* put through your call."

"In that order."

"No other."

She rolled toward him. A few feet separated them. "I had forgotten how bossy you are."

His gaze roamed her face. "I had forgotten how beautiful you are." He swallowed. Her tongue wetted her lips. Her eyelids fell closed as desire shot through her. He scooped his hand beneath her neck and drew her nearer to him. He lifted his head and rolled still further toward her, his eyes focused on her lips. She felt the warmth of his breath, heard her own heart begin to pound. Heat radiated from his body and desire from his eyes. Hovering above her, savoring the anticipation, he lowered his head by small increments toward her.

She had never feared or wanted a kiss so much in her life.

He touched his lips to hers. His eyes fell closed, and she closed hers. He caressed her lips lightly, angling this way and that, letting his tongue trace the shape of her lips and the tiny crevices within. At last he sealed his lips to hers and deepened the kiss. He told her in a language more ancient and eloquent than words, *Ti voglio*. I want you.

There was a bittersweetness to their kiss. A glow. A sorrow. A quality of remembrance and regret, a taste of promise and hope. Zoe touched his cheek, tracked his whiskers, followed the swirls her fingers knew so intimately and had never forgotten. He drew back only to look into her eyes, to measure her acceptance, to bathe his consciousness in the sweet languor he had evoked in her.

Again his eyelids fell shut. She loved the shape of his eyes, his thick, black-as-night lashes, the heavy, masculine shape of his brows. But when he renewed the kiss she let her eyes fall closed to feel again the soft, consuming power of his lips. He let the kiss fade, ending what had only just begun, but their breaths still mingled, and the sound from deep within him resonated in her.

Rafe let all the sensations course through him, then swallowed a taste he had savored as much as he had craved it. "Go make your call, Zoe."

She let her thumb stroke once more down the pattern of his whiskers. There was so much unrequited need in her that it was hard to move, hard to separate from him, but the call couldn't wait. She needed to know how Stephi was, touch base with Emma, and be reassured that elsewhere things were not so desperately dangerous. To be reminded of things more familiar to her. And to know that Teresa and Teddi had arrived safely.

She sat up and got off the bed, then went to wash her face and dry it with linens more elegant than the tatters would suggest.

Rafe opened the crystal decanter and poured them both an aperitif of marsala. Gratefully, she accepted the delicately fluted little glass. Sipping the wine, she picked up the receiver from the hook, dialed for an operator and asked for long distance collect.

Emma immediately accepted charges. "Zoe, my God, is that you?"

Zoe was so thankful to hear Emma's voice that tears sprang to her eyes. Even the connection was good. "Emma, yes. It's me. Have you—"

"Zoe, listen. I don't know what's going on, but let me fill you in at this end. Stephi has spiked a fever in the last thirty-six hours. We think we have it under control, but—"

Zoe felt the threat of a fever like a hot poker in her heart. "Emma, is she dying?"

"No, Zoe. She isn't dying. Please don't worry about that." Emma's tone implied there were other things to worry about. "Mary Bernadette is always there, and her *nonna*—Teresa Mastrangelo. Zoe, is she your mother-in-law?"

"Yes."

"Well, she's here, with a child she says is Stephi's twin."

"She is, Emma. Teddi is Stephi's twin. I know this is complicated, but we want you to go ahead with the apheresis and—"

"I don't doubt what you're saying, Zoe. This child is so like Stephi it's uncanny—even for an identical twin. Teresa Mastrangelo says she is Stephi's twin, and Mary Bernadette does as well. But there's a problem."

Zoe felt herself tensing with fear. "Frank Clemenza."

"Well, yes," she answered. "But he has a case, Zoe. The child's papers say she is Evangelina Morelli. Your mother-in-law explained to me that there was no time to get a consular certificate documenting Teddi's status as an American citizen. In order to get this child—your Teddi—into the States, she had to use the passport of—" she hesitated, thinking "—Rafe's sister's child? His niece?"

"Yes, but she *is* Teddi."

"But on her cousin's passport she is in the country illegally, Zoe. Frank has called the Immigration and Naturalization Service."

"Oh, my God, no!" Zoe looked to Rafe, who was sitting on the end of the bed facing her.

"Not to have her deported, he says, but only to clear up the child's identity. But, effectively, it stops us from proceeding."

Zoe swallowed the lump of fear in her throat. "Hold for a minute, Emma." Zoe told Rafe about the passport issue, and Frank's call to the authorities.

Rafe cursed and stood. "I'll kill him," he swore. "Damn him to hell!"

Feeling the same emotions, Zoe took a deep breath. "Emma, listen—you can stall them. You can take the tests and prove they are identical twins. Tell them Teddi's grandmother must have picked up the wrong passport. Tell them—"

"Zoe, listen. Mary Bernadette is doing all of that, and she still pulls a lot of weight around here. She's even got Brad MacPherson, the head of the hospital's public relations, working up a human interest story on Stephi and Teddi and the big, bad bureaucracy—which isn't endearing him to Clemenza, I can tell you that."

Zoe shook her head. "Emma, isn't there any way around it?"

"Even if there were, Zoe, Frank has the bases covered. Rose Memorial Medical Center will not perform the procedure at this time. Frank has already indicated that though it breaks his heart, he will have to disallow any action until a permit is signed for both children by the parents."

Hopelessness and anger and resentment seethed in Zoe, and yet none of her emotions yielded her anything to say. She had needed the reassurance of normalcy, but even in the hospital named for Centi, Frank would let her child die, ostensibly over technicalities. What was there to say to such evil?

Seething inside, she still felt numb as she recounted for Rafe the measure of Frank Clemenza's retaliation.

Rafe forced himself to stay in control when in truth he wanted to tear up the earth. "Zoe, this will all work out, I promise you. Tell your friend to pull Teddi's birth certificate and get a correct ID. She is an American citizen, and no matter what papers she came in under, proof of Teddi's identity will clear up her citizenship status."

Zoe repeated all this, then added, "We will be in Chicago within thirty-six hours, Emma. Can you be ready to move the minute we walk in the door?"

"Your message said you had misplaced your passport—"

"We'll be there, Emma. Please be ready to go."

"Then it's true. Rafe is also alive."

"Yes. He's here with me now."

"Zoe, are you okay?" Emma asked. "Are you in trouble? Frank is so angry beneath the veneer of civility. Mary Bernadette is opposing him. I don't understand any of this."

"I don't, either, Emma. Not really. Please give Stephi a hug for me. Tell her I love her very much. And Teddi."

"Oh, Zoe, you should see them together. It's like . . ." Words failed her. "It's magical. Stephi is so excited. I think Teddi's being here is better than the battery of antibiotics she's gotten. She has just lit up believing you found her papa and he is coming home."

Zoe reached out to hold Rafe's hand. These were the first words of any encouragement she had heard in countless hours. "Emma, thank you. I could never tell you what hearing that means to me."

To her it meant, though every rational argument flew in the face of it, that Frank would not win this desperate clandestine battle. That maybe the forces of good in the universe could still overcome the darkness and evil Frank had come to represent in her mind.

"We'll be there, Emma. Rafe and I. We'll be there."

"I'll be ready."

Zoe hung up, breaking the connection.

"*Cara, bellissima,* you have the most poignant expression on your face."

Zoe caught her lower lip between her teeth to contain her smile. "Emma was just telling me how magical it has been to see Teddi and Stephi together. How Teddi's being there has made Stephi so excited and happy. She says it's even better than the antibiotics."

Rafe nodded. Zoe could see that he was profoundly touched, even speechless. Staggered by the resilience of a child's spirit.

After a few moments he asked, "What did she say about Clemenza?"

Zoe thought. "She said he claims to have gone to the INS only to straighten out the mixed-up identities—but the hospital is precluded from going on because of that." She repeated Emma's estimation of Frank's anger, which was inexplicable to her.

Rafe nodded. His eyes gleamed. "Frank has lost his nerve, Zoe. Again and again we have escaped him, all of us. Remember his powerful superstitions? Soon he will believe it is the hand of God himself protecting us. He is impotent with his rage. If he is resorting to immigration violations, he is running scared."

Zoe gave a half smile. "I remember thinking Mary Bernadette and your mother would be no match for Frank."

"Except as he dares threaten our precious *piccoline*. No man is the match of a woman protecting her children, or her children's children."

Zoe took a deep breath. It was all far from over and far too soon to let down her guard. But a part of her felt the truth of Frank's superstitious nature shriveling into paranoia.

Rafe still sat on the end of the bed. "Zoe, do you have a picture of Stephi?"

"Of course! Hand me my purse."

He retrieved the bag. She took out a pile of pictures from an envelope. Pictures she had selected to bring, thinking that the photos would help convince whatever relatives of Rafe's that she could find to help Stephi by being tested.

Rafe spent long seconds with each one, smiling, touching Stephi's face. *Tesoro,* he murmured. Treasure, his pet name for Stephi. She suddenly understood why he had asked—to replace the memories of surveillance photos.

She swallowed the bitter taste even the thought of such pictures gave her.

He handed the photos back to her. "To have them together again..." He shook his head. *"Stelline mie."* Little stars, Stephi and Teddi. Stars in the heavens of his and Zoe's own private firmament. His smile transformed his face. He looked at Zoe. "And you are as vital as the sun to me, *amore mio*. Come with me to bathe."

He stood and drew her to her feet, then let go of her hand. So suddenly the moment was upon her when she must make the decision. To be his wife again, or not.

She had lashed out at him and swore she never wanted what had happened in the cave to happen between them again. He would not touch her again in any intimate way, not more than the kiss they had shared required.

He had never seduced any woman over her stated objections, had never needed to do so, and Zoe knew he would not start with her, no matter that she was his wife.

He had extended the invitation to bathe with him, but she must make the overture. This was not an idle decision to be taken, *yes* today and *no* tomorrow. What he required of her was both recanting her rejection and a commitment to be intimate again.

The choice was hers.

"Yes. I will come bathe with you." She took the hand he offered and went willingly with him to the claw-footed tub. To her mind as much as to her heart, there was no decision to be made.

He was her husband, and the father of her little girls. And though there remained so many places that hurt between them, she would love him as ceaselessly as she was permitted time on this earth.

He let her go and stripped out of the shirt De Sica had given him. She admired him frankly, stunned by the power of his visual impact on her, the masculine tufts of black hair beneath his arms, surrounded by heavy muscle; the breadth of his chest; the definition of his pectorals; the hard ridges of abdominal muscle. The deep dimple of his navel was surrounded with whorls of hair. Even her stitches to his shoulder, intact and healing, made him appear more ruggedly male.

"Your turn, *amore mio.*"

Her breath rushed out of her. Her lips were dry as old bones. She licked them. His eyes filled with hunger old as humanity. She crossed her arms and stripped the linen blouse slowly over her head. The caramel-colored camisole must go as well to be fair.

His eyes narrowed, almost in pain. Again she crossed her arms before her and caught up the lace hem and removed the camisole all in one deliberate, instinctively lithe, sinuous move and she was naked from the waist up.

Rafe's breath caught in his throat. Memory had failed him. The supple line of her neck, the feminine curve of her shoulders, the perfection of her breasts drawn taut, smaller now than he remembered because for so many months they had been swollen to nurse not one infant but two. The image made him as reverent of her as he was desirous.

Her nipples had darkened then as well; now they were much the color of his own lips against her porcelain flesh. He bowed his head almost in prayer. He had been without Zoe, without a woman at all for so long, such pleasure must be taken in small measures.

He stripped out of his slacks and shorts. Aroused, reverent, wanting to honor her body with his.

Reflexively Zoe gasped. At the strength of him, at the power and the grace and the lack of false modesty bordering on arrogance—the conviction that he could please her like no other man who had ever lived. From the front she would never have guessed at the damage reflected in the scars on his back and buttocks. Every sweeping line of him made her long to hold him and be held. To be part of him.

She lowered and stepped out of her slacks and panties as well, and held out a hand to him. Together, wordlessly, they stepped into the water and together sank into it.

He turned her so that she faced away from him, leaned back and pulled her to him. The water was clear and came up to her neck. Steam still rose from its surface. Zoe gave a moan of restful pleasure.

"Come to me, Zoe," he urged her. "Come to me." He lifted her so that she sat in his naked lap, her legs resting on top of his. His chest molded to her back, his arousal to her spine, his teeth to one shoulder, one large hand to her thigh and the other to her breast.

"Zoe, beauty, *tesoro. Ti amo.*" I love you.

She had never felt her spirit so touched or her body so engulfed, so…possessed. She let her head fall back to rest on his shoulder. Powerful feminine urges racked her body— urges to rock her hips, to take him inside her, to put her lips to his skin and her hands to cup him—but he made her be still.

Beneath the surface of the water he stroked her breast, in circles against her tender peak with his palm, tugging with his fingers, scraping her with his knuckles and the back of his hand, scraping with his wrist. Over and over again, slowly at first, then more quickly, and harder, until she knew nothing else but that she would go mad with the intense pleasure, the arching climax he coaxed from her with nothing more than his hand caressing her breast.

She cried out. She cried his name. She cried because though she had peaked, the yearning deep inside her had only grown hotter and more urgent.

"We have only begun," he whispered harshly into her ear. With his other hand he touched her most intimate place, and she knew he would repeat the pattern of stroking and caressing. He brought her to a climax again, and yet again, until she would have no more without him. Slickened with the warm water, she turned and straddled him and took him into her and indulged all her instinctive, feminine answers.

When she was done he knew her arrogance as well, for she had pleased him like no other, and he gave her everything he had to give.

"WHAT DO YOU THINK became of Centi?" she asked. Though they were both physically and emotionally drained, neither of them could sleep.

"Almost anything could have happened."

"But what do *you* think?"

He rolled his head on the bed to look at her in the moonlight. "I think you were right, Zoe. He would not willingly have left Teddi alone—which means someone took him away by force. After that...who knows? Either he was knocked over the head and locked up somewhere and left to go down with the ship, or he was forced over the side."

Zoe sighed. "I have sometimes found myself thinking Centi is still alive. What if Frank staged the whole thing? He only had to make it look as if Centi had died so that he would inherit."

Rafe looked at her. "Tell me about it—about the times when you've thought Centi was alive."

"I can't think of any specific times—"

"Don't think. Tell me."

"Okay." She let her mind roam. "Odd times. When I would get a phone call, sometimes I thought it would be him. Or...something would come up that I wanted to tell him."

"Zoe," he said, puzzled by her examples, "you were never that close to Centi. It would be surprising if we heard from him twice a year."

"I know." She shifted, turning on her side to face him. His fingers threaded in her hair. "I don't think that in all the years I was growing up that I could have seen him more than half a dozen times, either. But...what were you thinking? That he *is* alive?"

"I doubt it very much, Zoe. How could it have happened? How could Frank have kept someone of Centi's stature hidden away from the world for so long?"

She shivered. "I read a novel once where the heroine was committed to a mental institution. Theoretically, it's possible. I've even heard of people who get committed for just doing their job—like collecting the quarters from a pay telephone."

"For a small time, maybe." Rafe idly rubbed his jaw. "It is just Machiavellian enough to appeal to Frank."

"Suppose the captain nabbed Centi and put him in the speedboat. Or even the seaplane Frank was on. Isn't that possible?" She kicked aside the sheet and sat up in the bed. "It would explain why Teddi was left alone, why she still had his Bible and rosary.... It would have been the perfect answer to Frank's moral dilemma. He would not have had to harm a hair on Centi's head to make it appear as though he had died."

Zoe was improvising the scenario off the top of her head, but Rafe was beginning to see the possibilities. "It would also explain why my memory of the Bible alarmed him. Centi had to have been murdered or snatched. Otherwise he would have the Bible and rosary with him."

She wondered if he knew how closely his words echoed De Sica's, that kidnapping was a national pastime.

He lay silent for a while. "Is it a feeling you have, *amore?* An intuition that Centi is alive?"

"I have never thought of it like that. Why?"

He shrugged. "I don't think people trust their own intuition enough. But what you're telling me doesn't sound like an intuitive feeling in you that Centi had somehow survived."

"Even if it were, my record in the intuition department is pretty shaky, Rafe."

She had to swallow, but even then her voice seemed to her as untrustworthy as her instincts. "You told me that

Teddi thought Stephi and I were lost. Stephi didn't know what to believe, but she sure never accepted that you and Teddi were in heaven and not coming back.''

Rafe cleared his throat as well. ''What did you do?''

''I talked to a child psychologist. Peter Lewiston is his name. He said it was likely a twin phenomenon for Stephi to feel so strongly that the other half of her was still there—somewhere. Still alive, anyway.'' Zoe swiped at a tear escaping her eye. ''Which was all understandable. Except *I* knew you were dead. Stephi's emotions must have been similar to the emotions of people who have physically lost a limb but swear they can still feel sensations.''

He stroked her hair. ''Zoe.'' His voice was low. Strained. ''You were doing the best you could.''

''Was I?'' She gave a half-anguished, half-angry sigh. ''I'm the one who lied to her all those years. Lewiston—all of her doctors, really—thinks that Stephi's disease is her emotional, last-ditch effort to make me let her papa come back.''

Rafe shook his head, not in denial of the opinion, but because the likelihood of it sliced into him. ''You were not keeping me from her, Zoe.''

''No. But she believed I was.''

Wordlessly, Rafe gathered Zoe into his arms and they lay together, each of them undone by sorrow that cut soul-deep.

THEY WERE UP at the first light of day. They accepted the duchess's pastries, drank a cappuccino and walked the four kilometers to the bank by eight-thirty, when it opened. The bank guard nodded affably enough, but in his hands was the morning issue of *Il Giornale di Sicilia*. Zoe felt her stomach turn sickeningly.

On its front page were plastered their photos, and the headline translated roughly into Manhunt Continues.

Chapter Fourteen

"Say nothing and keep walking, *cara,*" Rafe warned softly, steering her through the bank. Near the back, two armed guards protected the entrance to the vault containing all safety deposit boxes. Security cameras followed their every move. Rafe handed his medical bag to Zoe and took from his pocket the key he had retrieved from the lining. He wore sunglasses; Zoe had none.

He exchanged a few words with the bank employee. The conversation was brief and businesslike and led to his entry into the vault. Zoe sat outside the vault in a chair, trying to seem invisible to the eyes of the cameras.

A telephone rang. Her stomach pitched again. A guard snatched up the receiver and listened a moment. His gaze fell on her—she couldn't tell whether by chance or on purpose. She willed herself to appear bored and vaguely annoyed at the wait. He frowned as if trying to recall whether he had ever seen her before, or where. Her tension edged up. He hung up the telephone and cast her one more suspicious glance. The two guards muttered together and laughed.

Rafe returned through the vault door carrying a bulging manila envelope. The guards straightened. Rafe jerked his head, and she joined him. They walked out of the bank into the intense, bright light of the Sicilian sun, turned left and kept walking.

Three blocks went by before Rafe spoke. "Like clockwork, *amore*," he said. "Candy from a baby." But he was well aware that they had strolled in and out of the lion's den.

"Rafe, they knew. The way that guard looked at me—"

"Forget it, Zoe. You must behave boldly. They can smell fear." He didn't have to tell her what the consequences would be. But when they returned the four kilometers and rounded the corner two blocks from where they had left his mother's car, a shaft of pure fear shot through him as well.

There were carabinieri everywhere and at least three police vehicles blocking their car. Dozens of other police were in the process of creating a police cordon for three hundred meters in all directions.

"Oh, my God," Zoe whispered.

Rafe's breath locked in his throat. He held Zoe's hand tighter. His instinctive reaction was to turn around and walk away with her, but he couldn't bring himself to turn his back to the cops.

"What are we going to do?"

He swallowed hard on the cold fear. Their pictures were in newspapers everywhere. What were the chances that even one of the uniformed carabinieri could fail to recognize them? "Come with me. We are ignorant tourists. Act the part."

Still holding her hand, he stepped into the street and stood before the nearest uniform. "Say, what's happening?" he asked in English.

"Yes, officer," Zoe added, sounding breathless. "Is there some trouble? Do you speak American?"

The cop looked at them as if he couldn't believe two such brainless people could walk the face of the earth. He gestured rudely toward the other side of the cordon and barked at them in rapid, angry bursts of Italian.

Zoe was going to throw up. She knew it. She couldn't imagine an outcome much worse than being slammed into some foreign prison where they could throw away the key and forget about you. But she clung to Rafe's arm and looked up at him determined to play her role. "What is he saying, dear?"

Rafe began to back away, taking her with him, making stupid American apologetic noises in the middle of which he answered her. "To get our imbecile American butts out of here. Can't we see we're interfering in police business? Think we should follow his advice?"

The cop yelled at them again to get out, and directed the cops stretching the cordon behind them to let the cretin Americans through.

They walked past the cops, behaving like tourists disgruntled with their treatment, but by the time they had crossed the street and gone a block, Zoe was shaking with the aftereffects of the adrenaline coursing through her. "Can we go home now?"

Rafe laughed softly and pulled her into the shadows of a crevice between tenement buildings. He held her close for a moment, then kissed her hard. "Let's go home."

THE BRITISH TOUR GROUP that De Sica had arranged for them to join gathered in the lobby of the Centrale near Quattro Canti old quarter at ten o'clock. The bus to shuttle the package-tour patrons to the airport had arrived and the driver was calling for them to board the bus.

Breathless from keeping a dogged pace on foot to the old quarter, feeling sticky and overheated from the sweltering heat of the city, Zoe and Rafe agreed they should be among the first few to board. Rafe went to the desk and asked for an envelope in the name of Giancarlo De Sica.

Inside were the promised return tickets issued by the tour group.

Outside, the distinctive alternating tones of half a dozen police sirens wailed by. Several members of the tour group stood gawking at the curiosity-seekers in the wake of the police cars. Grimly, Rafe took up a newspaper folded to conceal their photos, and offered the tickets to the driver. He boarded the bus with Zoe fifth in line.

At the airport, lines of cars were being systematically stopped, emptied and searched. Rafe said nothing, only took her hand and focused on the story printed in the morning paper. Sick with fear, Zoe watched a grim-faced, swarthy little man board their bus at the checkpoint.

A brash elderly woman three seats in front of them stood up to ask what all the excitement was about. She read spy novels, she said, and this seemed just like a scene from one of them. Double-o-seven, wasn't it, dearie? The security guard snapped at her in English to sit down and shut up. He was so angry by the time she huffed and made the decision to comply that he snarled obscenely, accompanied by an equally vulgar gesture, and ignored the entire balance of the tour group.

Shaking his head, Rafe let out the breath he'd been holding. "It could as easily have gone the other way."

Zoe was still quaking inside. "What do you mean?"

"He could have jerked every one of us off the bus." He didn't need to go through what would have happened had they been caught there at the checkpoint.

Rafe drew a deep breath and returned to reading the newspaper. Turning pages to get to the end of the article, he swore softly.

"What is it?"

He finished. His expression hardened. "They've taken Turi into custody, which means he's in Cavallo's jail cell."

"Oh, no!" Zoe shook her head. "Is there anything we can do for him?"

Rafe shrugged. There wasn't, and Zoe saw that the consequences of their escape made Rafe angry and sick at heart. He folded the paper and stuck it in the pocket in the back of the seat in front of them.

After they had passed the checkpoint, he took from the manila envelope the thick package he had not recognized among the contents of his safety deposit box.

Zoe straightened in the seat next to him. "What is that?"

"I don't know. Something of my mother's, maybe. It looks like a stationery box." The package was tied tightly with string, and its contents did not shift or rattle around inside. Rafe forced one double strand of the string off one corner, then slid the cross-strands off the box.

The bus came to a stop again at the designated Pilgrim Air gate. The group of mostly British travelers was asked to wait a moment in the air-conditioned bus.

Zoe took the scraps of string. Rafe opened the box, then pulled away layers of tissue. At the bottom lay Centi's rosary and leather-bound Bible.

Zoe stared at them. "Oh, my God."

Rafe picked up the strand of onyx beads. The cross was carved from rosewood, which had become slightly warped. The finish was also damaged. "When the hospital in Messina released Teddi to my mother, they must have given her these as well."

Zoe picked up the small Bible, which would fit in most any pocket. It was damaged as well. The leather binding was stiff and twisted from having been waterlogged. Most of the pages had stuck together and dried in thick clumps. She doubted they could ever be restored.

She felt unexpectedly muddled over Centi's dearest possessions. Maybe it was because they provided a certain emotional metaphor for the damage that had befallen their little family. Maybe because the Bible and rosary were tangible reminders of the bishop himself.

Or maybe, Zoe thought, because their existence outside of Centi's hands confirmed Rafe's memories and proved even his nightmare suspicions. Centi had not gone willingly to his fate.

"I wish it were true that he is still alive."

He stroked her cheek. His face was very near to hers. She saw the doubt in his eyes, the sorrow in the lines surrounding them. "I know. Centi was a very special man."

Rafe gave her the rosary when the tour group leader returned to suggest that they all now leave the bus and use the facilities. Zoe wrapped it around the Bible as she had sometimes seen Centi do, bundled them carefully in the tissue paper and put them in her purse.

They boarded the Pilgrim Air flight bound for Luton. The tour group manifest guaranteeing the appropriate passports of all passengers was turned routinely over to the airport official. The attendants went through their routines. The plane taxied, awaited controller permission, lifted off and flew out of Sicily at 11:37 a.m., central European time—as was its routine.

But nothing about their escape from Sicily felt routine to Zoe. Tears of sheer relief crept down her cheeks. They were on their way home to Stephi and Teddi. Next to her, Rafe was already snoring softly. For a few hours in the air, they would be completely safe.

Luton was safe, and Heathrow was safe, and for another eleven hours or so they slept off and on.

Chicago wasn't so safe.

"ALL RIGHT, ZOE. Rafe. Here's what we're facing," John Salinger, attorney-at-law, began. "There is some question of your involvement in the murder of Nicola Peretti in..." he paused to consult his associate, a young woman named Barbara Jelniker.

The firm of Jakes, Salinger, Bennett and Hopwell was considered to be premier in Chicago. John Salinger was not only the firm's top gun, but a man who owed the successful reattachment of his hand, cut off in an automobile accident, to the surgical prowess of Dr. Raphael Mastrangelo.

"Vallazione," Barbara Jelniker provided.

"In Vallazione, Palermo province, Sicily," Salinger continued. "The U.S. embassy has been advised that the charges will be forthcoming. Zoe, you are an American citizen, and Rafe, as I understand this now, last left America in the status of a permanent resident alien, married to a U.S. citizen. Is that right?"

"That's right, John," Zoe snapped, pacing the conference room in the Chicago offices of the Justice Department, "but isn't the point to stall this travesty long enough for us to—"

"Zoe," Rafe said, interrupting her gently, "let John finish. He understands the urgency, I am sure."

Within three minutes of the time Rafe and Zoe had presented their passports at O'Hare, an assortment of Justice Department officials, as well as representatives of the FBI and the INS, descended with the full force of the U.S. government.

Zoe and Rafe were taken into custody. They had been in Chicago for some twenty hours, and though Zoe had spoken briefly to Mary Bernadette, they had not been allowed to go to the hospital.

"I do understand," John said. "I have kids of my own. Believe me, I understand. Here's the thing. The conditions of extradition and deportation have to be covered in treaties between governments. There are serious questions as to whether or not any treaties now in force cover the specific conditions in your case. Sicily is an autonomous region, and its police are organized separate from the Italian forces. It is not even clear whether you are being charged or only wanted for questioning in the death of Miss Peretti."

"That's because they can't keep their lies straight!" Zoe said.

"That may very well be. But the long and short of it is, deportation and/or extradition hearings are not an immediate concern for either of you. At 6:00 a.m. this morning I spoke to Federal District Court Judge Harold Watkins and explained your situation with Stephi and Teddi. Watkins is inclined to set you free on your own recognizance pending anything definite—which may never develop at all. He is consulting with the Justice gurus in Washington, D.C., but he promised me an answer by noon."

Rafe checked his watch. "That's forty minutes from now."

"Yes. Now, as to Teddi's status. The testing done by Immunological Associates proves that she is, in fact, the identical twin of Stephi. They are both dual nationals, recognized in international law here in the States by jus soli, right of birth, and in Italy by jus sanguinis, right of blood or descent."

"So even though Teddi has lived in Sicily for the past three and a half years, there is no question of her remaining here?" Zoe asked.

"None at all. Your mother, Rafe, may face charges for having brought Teddi into the U.S. under papers not her own—but I doubt it. I—" he broke off when the telephone rang. "This may be Judge Watkins now." Salinger answered the call, listened for a few moments, then hung up and smiled. "You're free as birds." He smiled sardonically. "So far today you've foiled the cops on one side of the Atlantic and befuddled the international treaty gurus on the other. Any further tricks up your sleeves?"

FRANK CLEMENZA was unnerved.

Never in his far-ranging experience had he been witness to so many freakish failures. Time and again Mastrangelo and Zoe had slipped through the cracks. He might have expected his useless niece to lose them, but Cavallo was deadly, without pity or morals, and his greed knew no bounds. It spooked Frank to know that Mastrangelo had managed to escape Cavallo even once.

He couldn't understand it. There could be no explanation for it other than that the pair of them led charmed lives. Protected. Bullet-proof. The darlings of guardian angels.

God himself didn't want them to die.

Frank recognized these thoughts were superstitious, unreasoning fear on his part. He knew, but when his trusted aide, Carlin Santini, had thrown that in his face yet again, in a fit of rage bordering on apoplexy, Frank had fired him, point-blank. The impertinence of the man, the disrespect, the I-told-you-so's had finally been too much.

Now Frank had no one to rail at but himself.

In his mind he recounted the failures of everyone from his niece right on up to and including the security forces, farces he sneered to himself, at the airport.

Mastrangelo and Zoe had not only escaped their imminent deaths time and again, they had boarded one international flight after another and landed free as birds at O'Hare. Or nearly so.

He had just heard that the bleeding hearts in the Justice Department had set them free as well.

He stared at the muted television set, at images of a gum commercial with nubile young identical twins prancing around in bikinis. That they were twins infuriated him anew.

The local news returned to the air. He upped the volume. The news anchor made some introductory comments meant to warm the heart. That galled Frank. The picture cut away to a clip of Mastrangelo and Zoe exiting the federal building accompanied by their lawyers, and that galled Frank.

The on-the-scene reporter asked if they had seen their little girls yet, and what they were going to do next. A dozen other reporters shouted equally banal questions. Rafe stopped to reply.

He yammered on about how very grateful they were to be back in the States, how much they appreciated the incredible support of the community, and then begged ever-so-endearingly off from answering any further questions as they hadn't yet seen their daughters.

Frank switched off the television and dropped despondently into his chair. So many conflicting emotions roiled in his heart. He had once admired Raphael Mastrangelo, then feared him, and finally controlled him.

But here he was, back again, apparently unscathed.

Frank was both very rich and very powerful. He conducted the affairs of Rose Memorial with an impeccable demeanor and a savvy, insightful understanding of the ever-shifting demands of hospital administration. And he did it all out of the goodness of his heart.

All this, with a start in life in a dusty little Sicilian village still clinging to the old ways like a dying man clings to life.

But neither his awesome wealth nor his power protected Frank from feeling sick with fear of Mastrangelo and what he knew. If it hadn't been for that Bible...

Nothing seemed to matter. Not the wealth, which was so vast no man could spend it all. Not the power, either, which like Goliath, was defeated at a stone's throw. He had spared their lives once already, but they were thankless. Not even his own life seemed to matter.

Sometimes, of late, he had forgotten what it was that held the power to destroy his life of rare privilege and true service. Then it would all come back, visceral memories of that morning. The shock. The outrage. Centi's shaking hand, scrawling spidery abominations in his Bible.

Zoe Mastrangelo's very existence offended Frank. He despised her all the more because he was and had always been attracted to her and she had rejected him.

He placed one last call to Sicily. Cavallo might yet redeem himself.

But in the end, to get over these irrational fears that Zoe and Mastrangelo would not be made to die, Frank would have to take care of them himself. He should never have depended upon others.

He had forgotten, but now he remembered. In Italy there were no choirs, only soloists.

Chapter Fifteen

Brad MacPherson, publicity director of Rose Memorial Medical Center, was in the difficult position of trying to convince the press to leave off their pursuit of Zoe and Rafe at the hospital entrance. He allowed them to take their photographs and videotapes as far as the old Sacred Heart entrance. A number of them wrapped their stories there.

The minute the cameras and reporters had gone, Zoe turned to Brad and introduced Rafe. "Brad, we were concerned that Frank would stop us from entering the hospital."

"Or try to stop us," Rafe said.

Brad walked with them. "I don't know what to think. Up until now, I've never had a quarrel with what he does, but he's been totally unpredictable for the last week. This morning he told me he wouldn't be able to be on hand personally to welcome you." He shrugged. "Go figure. He asked me to convey his apologies—I do think he really regretted having had to delay the procedure for your daughters."

Zoe exchanged glances with Rafe. Neither one of them believed Frank regretted anything he'd done.

"Listen," Brad said, "I'll leave you here. I'm sure you'd like a private reunion with Stephi and Teddi. I hope the procedure goes well. I'll check back with you tomorrow."

"Thanks, Brad." Zoe took a deep breath, feeling more threatened than ever by Frank's behavior. After Brad had gone she turned to Rafe. "Frank is just toying with us, isn't he? He'll let us have this, and then he'll find some way to jerk it all away from us again."

"He won't succeed, *cara,* I promise you that." He stroked her hair and smiled. "Let's go see our little girls."

Holding tight to Teddi's pillowcase of treasures, Zoe took Rafe to the set of old elevators on the east wing. They got off on the seventh floor and turned down the hall. Outside of Stephi's isolation room, Mary Bernadette sat reading to Teddi, who sat in her lap.

"Oh, Rafe. Help me remember this." Her hand closed into a fist, holding Rafe's sleeve. She was suddenly nervous; all her senses heightened. She wanted to burn this moment into her memory.

Her leather flats made thudding noises on the carpeted floor. Late afternoon sunshine poured into the tall modern windows. A few nurses and a ward secretary sat chatting at the nursing station. A couple of interns. A social worker. People Zoe knew, who recognized her. One who even recognized Rafe.

But Zoe's attention was fixed on Teddi. One of the nurses called a greeting. Teddi's small body came alert at the sound of Zoe's name. She twisted in Mary Bernadette's lap, saw her papa coming, saw Zoe and shrieked in excitement. "Mammina! Papa!"

"Teddi." Zoe sank to her knees to be on a level with Teddi when she flew into her arms. She cradled Teddi close for a moment, touching her hair, gathering in her scent, feeling the wiry little body mold to her, clinging to her neck. "Teddi, my sweet Teddi."

There seemed too much to absorb, too many details to memorize, too many feelings—relief and joy, the sensation of her heart mending—competing in her heart. Teddi. Dear Lord.

Teddi pulled back and began to jabber excitedly in Italian. Zoe showed her the pillowcase, and when Teddi saw the things inside, her music box and her crocheted lamb and the shell, her eyes lit up even more. Clapping her hands, she turned to jump into Rafe's waiting arms.

"Ah, Teddi, my precious *coccolina*."

Her legs around Rafe's waist, Teddi stiffened and leaned back and scolded. "English, Papa!"

"*Coccolina?*" he said, and Teddi nodded eagerly.

"*Coccolina…coccolina…*" He pretended to think for a minute. "Ah! Snuggle bunny…no! Better—Teddi bear!"

"Teddi *bear!*" she repeated, bright-eyed and incredulous. She rattled on a moment in Italian again.

Rafe interpreted for Zoe. "She says Stephi has a teddy bear, and now she has two teddy bears."

Zoe's heart squeezed tight at the hug Teddi gave her papa, at the kisses flying between them and the chattering back and forth. Teddi adored her papa, and for a moment Zoe felt a stab of jealousy. But Teddi reached out for her from Rafe's arms, and she joined into their hug.

Mary Bernadette had risen and come to them. "Zoe, child."

Zoe turned in time to see her aunt daubing a rare tear away. "Oh, Auntie." She clung to Mary Bernadette a moment, inhaling her familiar scent. Zoe couldn't even think now about Mary Bernadette's part in letting her believe Rafe and Teddi had died. Too many feelings assailed her with her aunt as well that would need time and forgiveness to heal, but she was the one who had sent Zoe to Paolo Bondi. "Mary B., I've missed you."

"All the pain and grief, Zoe. I am so sorry."

"It's over and done now. Come with me to see Stephi."

Mary Bernadette stepped back a bit. "The poor mite's seen enough of me to last awhile. You go along."

Rafe put Teddi down. She ran ahead to Stephi's door and pulled the paper masks from a box for each of them. They were the sort that had small elastic bands sewn in that stretched from the mask to hook behind each ear. "Like this, Mammina," she said when it looked to her as if Zoe didn't know what to do with it.

"*Grazie,* Teddi," she replied solemnly, struggling to keep her tears at bay.

"Welcome," Teddi announced. "You were not lost," she said earnestly.

Zoe crouched beside Teddi and the stand of isolation room supplies. "That's right. Mommy and Stephi weren't lost, but we didn't know where to find you and Papa."

Teddi's beautiful dark eyes searched Zoe's over their masks. For an instant she seemed ready to cry, but she didn't. She patted Zoe's cheek between the elastic bands. "So sad, Mammina?"

Zoe shook her head. "No more, *piccina.* Little one. These are happy tears."

"Happytears," she repeated as if the two words were one. "Stephi needs happytears."

"Yes." Zoe looked up at Rafe, who seemed in a daydream watching her with Teddi. "Is Papa ready to go give Stephi happytears?"

He nodded, not trusting his own voice, and hooked his mask from one ear to the other with one hand.

Teddi gave them each an adult-sized gown, then slipped into a miniature one herself and turned around holding up her hair for Zoe to tie it. Zoe looked from Teddi's dear, thin little neck to Rafe. Even when the newness of being together again wore off, she would still be crazy about this child.

Teddi pushed through the door to Stephi's room. Stephi lay in the bed, sound asleep. Teresa Mastrangelo sat to one side of the bed. She stood as they walked in. Zoe acknowledged the mother-in-law she had never met with a smile beneath her mask. Teresa nodded, the expression in her eyes one of greeting and relief.

Zoe turned back to Rafe, but Stephi had already consumed his attention. He stood very still, staring at her, watching her sleep. She was surrounded by posters and balloons and pinups, and trappings not so innocent — IVs and monitors and boxes of disposable gloves.

Teddi tugged at Rafe's isolation gown. He bent low for her to whisper in his ear.

He nodded. "It will be okay if you wake her." She took his hand and drew him close to Stephi's bed. Zoe went to the other side. Rafe glanced at his mother and nodded, then turned to focus on Stephi.

Her pallor hadn't improved at all, but the last time Zoe had seen her, Stephi's little brow had been creased in pain and worry even in her sleep. Now her brow was free of worry, and she was sleeping peacefully. Emma hadn't exaggerated the good it had done Stephi to have Teddi here.

Teddi whispered through the bars of the bed rails. "Stephi? Stephi?"

She stretched and yawned and rubbed her eyes, then turned toward Teddi's voice. "Teddi!" she said softly.

Smiling broadly, Teddi pointed to Rafe. "Look! See? Papa is here!"

Stephi's eyes darted above and behind her twin to Rafe. Her eyes shut and opened, growing wider and wider. Her tiny lips pursed tight and her eyes grew bright. Stephi wasn't trusting herself to believe that her Papa was truly back with her. She rolled her head the other way, instinctively seeking Zoe and reassurances.

"Mama?" Stephi searched Zoe's eyes.

Zoe nodded. "It's true, Stephikins."

Rafe spoke softly to her. "Ciao, tesoro mio. You are so beautiful." More than Teddi's words, more than Zoe's reassurances, Stephi trusted his voice. The anxiety that momentarily clouded her face vanished. She smiled brilliantly at Zoe and then at Rafe, and then she stretched out her arms for him. "Papa."

He lifted her into his arms. Her bare little legs went around his waist and her arms circled his neck. She tucked her head at his neck.

Holding his precious, sick little child with one arm, adjusting the IV lines coming from beneath her collarbone with his other hand, Rafe looked to Zoe, and both their eyes filled. The moment was too full, too alive, rife with emotion. Heavy and unbearably light and a gift too precious and overdue. He buried his head next to Stephi's and just clung to her, stroking her hair, murmuring endearments, crooning reassurances.

Silent little tears soaked through Rafe's shirt, and he was undone. He sat in the rocking chair with Stephi, and spoke gently to Teddi, who instinctively held back, waiting, sharing her papa. She slipped around the bed and took Zoe's hand.

Teddi worried desperately, speaking half in Italian, half in English, that this was against the rules. Mustn't-breathe-on-Stephi, mustn't-tire-Stephi kind of rules.

Her *nonna* Teresa answered. For Papa, this once, the rules could be bent just a little.

THE COLLECTION of Teddi's white cells began at ten o'clock the next morning.

Zoe helped the floor nurse move another pediatric bed into Stephi's room for Teddi. The apheresis technician arrived with the instrument, which was nearly the size of a portable X-ray machine.

Yards of tubing had been fitted into monitors and pumps. Apheresis was like any blood donation, the technician explained, except that once in the machine, the anticoagulated blood cells entered a centrifuge spinning at nearly a thousand RPM.

The white cells Stephi needed to fight infections would separate from all the others and float over a sort of dam to be collected in a specialized sterile bag. All the rest of the blood would be returned to Teddi.

"I spent several hours with Stephi and Teddi a couple of days ago," the technician explained to Zoe, "showing them pictures of some other kids that we've done the procedure with. Teddi even came down for an hour and watched a grown-up donor in the process."

"So you're sure she'll have no trouble with this?" Zoe asked.

"The worst part is being still. You can't move around a lot with needles in your arms, but she'll be fine."

Meanwhile, Teddi was poring over the notebook of photos with Rafe, explaining everything she knew. She would have one big needle in each arm, one to take out the blood and one to put it back. "Stephi has much needles but not bigger," she assured him with some importance.

"*Many* needles, Teddi bear."

"Many," she repeated solemnly. "Not bigger."

Teddi went on to explain that she would have to be pretty still for a *long* time—four or five hours—but that was okay because she'd already practiced. "Cake!"

"You mean it's a piece of cake," Stephi added helpfully.

Zoe and Rafe stood back, talking with Emma and Joel. "How soon will we know if Stephi's bone marrow has begun to manufacture the cells on its own?" Rafe asked Sebern.

"We call it engrafting, as if it were a regular organ transplant. We'll do a blood count every day. I'd say we could be looking at a week to ten days. When we know, we'll take her off the antibiotics and see how she does.

With a twin's cells," he added, "we're virtually assured of success. And Stephi's own emotional status is so much more positive."

The technician prepped Teddi's skin on the inside of both arms with an anesthetic cream, and when the needles were put in she didn't feel them. Stephi watched everything closely from her bed, and both their eyes grew big as saucers when Teddi's blood began to go through the tubing.

When the collection was done by three, Sebern began transfusing the cells to Stephi through the IVs already in place. Emma Harding brought in balloons and streamers and kazoos. Mary Bernadette and Rafe's mother came in and everyone sang Happy Birthday to mark the beginning of Stephi's new and healthy life.

But waiting outside the door of Stephi's room were two agents of the FBI, prepared to act on the warrant filed in Sicily for the arrest of Dr. Raphael Mastrangelo, aka Dr. Paolo Bondi, for the murder of Nicola Peretti.

"ZOE, THE DIFFERENCE now is that formal charges have been filed against Rafe," John Salinger explained over the phone. "The existing treaties clearly apply, and the U.S. is obliged to honor the demand. The extradition hearing is a formality. All I can do at this point is to delay it as long as possible."

"Which is forty-eight hours from nine o'clock this morning." Pacing the VIP suite Brad MacPherson had provided Rafe's mother, Zoe combed her hair back with her fingers, working hard at staying in control of her anger. Even before the procedure had begun to restore Stephi's immune cells with Teddi's, their father's extradition had been carved in stone.

Zoe supposed she should be grateful that the FBI agents had waited to take Rafe into custody until the transfusion was done, but Rafe had had to tell Stephi and Teddi that

he must go away for a few weeks. She'd drawn on her last
reserves, staying with her little girls until they both fell
asleep. But the strain of keeping alive some hope in them
that Rafe would be back just in time for Stephi to come
home had stripped her patience.

She had thirty-six hours before the extradition hearing.
It would be a matter of only a few hours before Rafe was
flown out of the country and delivered into Cavallo's
hands.

She forced herself to sit down and take a deep breath.
"John, do you know why I'm not being charged?"

"They aren't required to explain why you were of interest before, and not now, Zoe. But what they have on Rafe
now—which they apparently didn't have before—is an eye-
witness to the murder."

"That's impossible, John! I left Nicola Peretti drunk on
her kitchen floor. Rafe never saw her after that. We left
Vallazione in the middle of the night, and—"

"Zoe, listen to me. All that will be important to Rafe's
defense, but until the trial, it's irrelevant. Rafe wanted me
to tell you that the witness is a man named Turi Difalco."

She nearly dropped the phone. Her heart plummeted. It
was a lie that Rafe had killed Nicola and a lie that Turi had
witnessed the murder. He hadn't even been in Vallazione.
He'd been driving Teddi to her grandmother. By helping
Rafe get Teddi out of Vallazione, Turi had crossed Frank
Clemenza, and he would pay for it.

Cavallo had Turi dead to rights.

He could either testify against Rafe with whatever lies
Cavallo put in his mouth, or die. Or maybe, Zoe thought
bitterly, Cavallo would let Turi live and pick off his children one by one instead.

Chapter Sixteen

"Zoe? You've been silent a long time. Want to tell me about it?" Salinger asked.

"No." She thought to ask him to stick by the phone because the next call he got would be because she'd been charged with murder. She didn't think he'd appreciate the black humor.

Frank Clemenza could deal with her next.

She found him chairing an evening session of the board of directors of Rose Memorial Medical Center. The room was paneled, carpeted and furnished to the heights of boardroom luxury. She knew Frank's philosophy was that a board composed of Chicago's elite, serving in the hospital on a volunteer capacity, deserved nothing less.

She walked in on the meeting through the door at the far end of the room. Dressed in gray linen slacks and a silk knit top, she was inappropriately clad for the gathering. Whichever member had been speaking stopped, and one by one the board members turned to look at her. It took Frank the longest to notice her. Or perhaps it was deliberate.

He stood and took a deep breath, already pulling off a world-class act. He would never have expected her to confront him here, and she knew it.

"Zoe." He looked around the table. "Ladies and gentlemen, for those of you who may not recognize her, may I introduce Zoe Mastrangelo, head of our medical records department here at Rose Memorial, and the niece of Sister Mary Bernadette."

She never took her eyes off him. Inside she was shaking with rage. "I want you to call off your hit men, Frank."

"Zoe, my dear, this is most inappropriate. We are in the midst of important hospital business. I really must insist that you—"

"Oh, of course," she interrupted him in a scathing tone of voice. "The business of the hospital renamed in memory of Bishop Rosario," she said, looking around at the confused expressions of board members. "What will you do if it turns out Centi isn't dead after all?"

Frank drew a shallow breath, blinked, looked down at his fingers planted on the conference table and shook his head. "Please, Mr. Pierson. If you wish to continue without me, I'll be but a moment. Otherwise you might all take a small break and help yourselves to the bar and dessert tray."

He turned and walked away from the table toward the end of the room where Zoe stood. He passed by her and didn't stop until he had reached his offices.

Zoe followed and closed the door behind her. He poured himself a shot of Scotch, downed it and turned back to her. "Now, suppose you tell me what it is that you want."

"It's very simple, Frank. I want the murder charges and extradition warrants against Rafe dropped. Now. Tonight."

"Tonight."

"Yes. And while you're at it, see to it that Turi Difalco is released and lives to be a very old man."

Frank snorted a laugh and massaged the bridge of his nose. "While it is true that I have a great deal of influence, my dear, even I cannot command the police forces of a foreign nation to drop such serious charges as these."

God, how she hated him, Zoe thought. The plush beige carpet and furnishings in his office would support entire villages in Sicily. He could buy and sell the carabinieri with his pocket change. She stared at him.

"You can, and you will."

"What makes you think so?" He frowned at her as if he couldn't fathom her behavior. "You come in here making hysterical demands, hinting that Centi is not dead. Is this sane?" He put down the shot glass very deliberately. His expression was carefully neutral, but his nostrils flared and his eyes flicked at her in disdain. "Do I look suddenly helpless to you? Suddenly forgiving? Suddenly ignorant? What is it, Zoe, that makes you believe so foolishly that you may even speak to me in such a manner?"

Her fear of him spilled over into her anger, like lava into an already seething caldron. "You kill people. You know what that says to me, that you resort to such violence? That you are a coward. Your act in these surroundings is remarkable, but in your heart you're like a mistreated animal, lashing out at whatever interferes with you."

He brought his hands together three times in loud, derisive claps. "Please, go on. Your harangue is most eloquent, if a bit inflammatory. Is there a point to be made? Because otherwise I haven't the time to indulge your futile flailing about."

Her chin went up. He wouldn't steamroll her. She wouldn't let him. "You know Rafe didn't kill Nicola Peretti."

"Nevertheless, Paolo Bondi, otherwise known as Raphael Mastrangelo, will wind up before a firing squad."

She swallowed, regarding him with contempt. "Make the call, Frank."

"Or what? You'll make a fool of yourself running around insisting that Centi is not dead?" He snorted.

"Forgive me if I am unable to make much of a display of consternation." He turned around and poured himself another drink.

Sipping on it this time, he went to his desk. "Get out, Zoe."

He must have thought she was done. Defeated. But she'd only been waiting for his full attention. She drew a deep breath and played her trump card. "I have Centi's Bible."

His eyes narrowed. He poured down the rest of his drink and turned in the high-backed leather executive chair to look out over the dark courtyard lit by a few old-fashioned gas lanterns. He sat there for a long while. She watched his reflection in the glass. By his silence she knew that she had struck a nerve with her gamble.

"What an intriguing twist," he remarked at last, still staring out. "I suppose I have your little Teddi to thank for that."

Zoe felt a tremor of fear pass over her. He knew her well enough not to bother worrying whether she might be lying. He knew she wasn't. She would never have expected Frank to remember that it was Teddi who had been so taken by Centi's Bible, either. But she knew Frank was baiting her. She would give away nothing.

He turned toward her in his chair. "What do you intend to do with this small artifact of Centi's life?" he asked, as if it had no more than sentimental interest, but with a strained quality she would have missed had she known him less well.

Her silence had unnerved him. She knew it. But unless his wariness meant that Centi was alive, she had no idea what Frank feared, what the Bible meant to him or exactly how to use her narrow advantage. If she guessed wrong, everything was lost.

She must convince Frank that she was being intentionally vague, and not ignorantly so. "I thought I might just hold it over your head for the next thirty years or so. The Bible will be in a safety deposit box. It will never see the light of day again—so long as you leave us alone. So long as nothing ever happens to any of us, including Turi Difalco.''

''Blackmail?'' He tented his fingers over his abdomen and laughed unpleasantly. ''A woman after my own heart.''

''We're nothing alike.'' His comparison made her skin crawl. She sat down in the leather club chair opposite him. ''Make the call, Frank.''

''That's all?'' he asked, perhaps reconsidering any likeness between them. Turning in his chair, he looked at her in continuing astonishment. ''With Centi's Bible in your possession you ask no ransom? No hush money? No trusts for the higher education of your lovely children? How forward-looking is that? Can it be true,'' he asked mockingly, ''that you are so selfishly motivated? Is Raphael really that good?''

''A father is worth more to my little girls than all the money you...acquired with Centi's estate.''

''Is that so.'' His eyes burned into her. She felt somehow ambushed. He clarified her perception. ''Coming from you, the misbegotten child of a woman too shamed ever to speak of her illicit coupling, I do believe I understand.''

Zoe stared at him for a moment, then at her hands, unable to prevent the stain of color spreading upward from her neck. Despite Mary Bernadette's care, in her heart Zoe had always been tormented by her mother's tight-lipped refusals to admit Zoe even had a father.

People were cruel. Children were cruel. Her mother's silence only invited mean-spirited speculation, which Zoe hadn't understood till long after her mother died.

Frank's cruel reminder dredged up all the guileless pain, all the hot, unreasoning, childlike feelings of worthlessness and panic. Of course she wanted nothing more than to spare her little girls those wretched experiences. Of course she wanted back the man whose love dispelled such memories in her like a bonfire banishes the cold and dark.

She wanted nothing more than to tell Frank Clemenza to go straight to hell. That they would be better off taking their chances with the likes of Cavallo than Frank.

She didn't believe it. If Rafe were deported and handed back over to Cavallo, he would ultimately face a firing squad. She knew that as certainly as she knew that her only choice was to deal with Frank, and everything depended upon how she handled him now.

"You understand me perfectly. Get Rafe exonerated and Turi Difalco released. Leave us in peace, Frank. That's all I want."

"Dear Zoe, even the sight of you offends me, and your threats to reveal that Centi is alive bore me." Still he stared at her. "Am I to take it on faith that you will honor your word? That Centi's Bible will never turn up again?"

Zoe swallowed hard on the lump of cold fear. Was he admitting to her now that Centi was still alive? Or only taunting her? His cruelty knew no boundaries. She couldn't ask, because then he would know that she had no idea what it meant to Frank that she had Centi's Bible.

"I have no doubt you could still devise some retribution, Frank, if I cheated you. But I would never take such a chance, I assure you."

He gave a wintry smile. Frank was many things, but never slow-witted, and she saw that her promises of trustworthiness spoke volumes on her doubt of his integrity.

Her stomach twisted in foreboding of his power, but she could see no way other than to hold Centi's Bible over his head as a means of salvaging Rafe's life and Turi's freedom.

Frank rose from his chair and went to pour himself another shot of liquor. He pulled at the knot in his tie to loosen it, regarding her with contempt in his dark eyes. He gestured dismissively. "I am weary of this charade. The end is long past due. I will agree to your terms. In return, you will leave Rose Memorial forever, and you will never again so much as whisper Centi's name. Are we in agreement?"

Feeling chilled to the marrow by his response, Zoe struggled against the show of weakness her visible shivering would be. "Yes."

"Fine." He put down the shot glass and freshened his mouth on a sprig of mint taken from the wet bar refrigerator. "I've a meeting to conclude." He spat out the mint. "After that I will make the necessary calls. I leave the hospital at ten in the morning for Cleveland. When I return on the day after tomorrow, I will expect to hear that you have made plans to leave Chicago within ten days, thereby ending our association forever.

"Don't think of betraying me, Zoe," he warned. "Or by comparison to me, Cavallo will seem like a saint."

He paused at the door and turned, his face taken up in a pleasant smile that made her skin crawl. "Good night, Zoe."

RAFE'S RELEASE HAD TAKEN an astonishingly short time to accomplish. So short, in fact, as to be suspect at every level. The State Department and the people at Justice were understandably mystified at the on-again, off-again demands for his immediate extradition. According to Salinger, to whom Zoe had spoken a few hours ago, even when warned that the U.S. would not consider any future reversals, the warrants were dropped. In addition, Turi Difalco was not only released, he was allowed to telephone Rafe and confirm his freedom.

In the twin's hospital room—less than twenty-four hours after Zoe had confronted Frank—she and Rafe sat talking quietly with Mary Bernadette and Teresa. The little girls had both fallen asleep by 8:00 p.m. None but Zoe had sensed Rafe's tension.

Her aunt had waited with Zoe nearby Stephi and Teddi most of the day, and they had taken the small moments to speak of Mary Bernadette's role in keeping Rafe and Teddi's existence secret. And of Zoe's troubled childhood and the terrible secrets that went back even further.

"I believe it was to spare you, Zoe," Mary Bernadette had said of her sister's refusal even on her deathbed to impart the name of Zoe's father. "Better that you never knew your father at all than to know and be rejected by him as she was."

All her life, Zoe realized in the course of that conversation, people had done things and kept the terrible silences to spare her, but the secrets had only left her emotionally defenseless and ignorant. Still, Zoe had told herself, Mary Bernadette was getting old. She'd done the best for her sister's child that she knew how to do, even when it became a matter of lying to her niece to protect them all.

Rafe had come in then, having been driven to the hospital by John Salinger after his release. They had all feared for the course of Stephi's recovery if her papa was snatched out of her life again, as it appeared he would be. But the fear was at least temporarily suppressed as he endured the overwhelming outpour of Stephi and Teddi's relief in another bittersweet reunion.

Spending the past few hours together playing Chutes and Ladders and Candyland and half a dozen versions of Mario saving the Princess, Zoe's heart sank. Rafe didn't look at her often, and when he did let their eyes meet, she knew he suspected she had cut some foolish deal with Frank.

She wanted to tell him how Frank had taunted her, speaking as if Centi were still alive, and that in the hours since then, she had begun to believe Frank had meant exactly what he said. *Your threats to reveal Centi is alive bore me.*

But they had spent every moment since Rafe's release with Stephi and Teddi, and Zoe hadn't had the chance.

At last the little girls fell asleep. Rafe stood, took her by the hand and excused them both to his mother and Mary Bernadette.

In silence they went out of doors, heading toward the old building where VIP suites were maintained by the hospital. Rafe would not step foot in the brownstone Frank had bought Zoe. Shadows deepened as the last rays of sun disappeared from the autumn evening. The scent of flowers from planters at intervals along the walk still hung in the moist, warm air.

He stuffed his hands into his pockets and asked what she had done to secure his release. She told him what deal she had offered, and what terms Frank had given. He opened the lobby door for her but said nothing. Her nerves already frayed to the point of no return, she stabbed at the elevator button and lashed out at him.

"For heaven's sake, Rafe, did you expect me to sit idly by and watch you be deported?" His face was a mask of relentless control, and she felt suddenly afraid. "My God, you're actually going to condemn me again for believing Frank would make them set you free, aren't you?"

"You never learn, Zoe. You keep falling into the trap of thinking he has even one moral fiber in his body." The elevator doors slid apart, but she stood rooted to the floor. "Get on, Zoe," he said grimly, taking her by the elbow.

She jerked away from him and stepped onto the elevator without his aid. "I am not the helpless, simpering woman you obviously believe me to be," she snapped in the hushed elevator. "And you can't see past your arrogant, macho nose to see that there was no other way. I am not so stupid as to believe Frank has suddenly turned into an honorable man."

"That may be true, *cara*," he answered, escorting her quickly down the hall after the elevator doors opened again on their floor. "But you took a monumentally stupid risk. He might have killed you then and there, or any time since. The same thing you did could have been accomplished through John Salinger."

He rammed the key in the door and shoved it open. He waited until she had crossed the threshold, then followed and closed the door. He pinned her against the door with his body. "What were you thinking to confront him alone?"

"Silly me," she hissed angrily, "hoping to save your ungrateful neck." He was right about the attorney, of course, but she was fed up with feeling so out of control of her own destiny, with *being* helpless. "Whatever danger there might have been in my scheme, Frank didn't strangle me, then or since."

His hands planted on the door at the level of her ears, he turned his head, then shoved off and turned away from her. "So long as Frank Clemenza is alive, our lives are all endangered." Rafe's voice was cold with the calculated, deliberate intent to remove the threat of Frank Clemenza from their lives himself.

A stabbing pang of fear ripped through her. "You can't mean to kill him."

He turned to look at her with a blazing intensity. "Don't think you can dissuade me, Zoe. He has come too close too many times." His eyes were filled with hatred, his heart with puzzlement at her inability to understand this most basic part of his character. "What kind of man stands impotently by while his wife and children are slaughtered?"

Tears filled Zoe's eyes, and she raged at his macho thinking. "What kind of man would willingly face the gas chamber, abandoning his wife and children? I will never forgive you!"

"So you have said, for my many unforgivable acts." His handsome, compelling Latin features hardened; she knew that he hurt unspeakably. "Frank must nevertheless die before he can take your lives."

"We could go to the police," she said, struggling to keep her reason. "We could tell them everything and they would have to take him in."

He shook his head sadly. "With his wealth and power and the reputation he has carefully cultivated in this city, we would be taken for wild-eyed fanatics, and he would not even be required to offer an explanation for our frivolous charges."

"But they're not frivolous, Rafe. Centi is alive!"

"Zoe..." His throat clenched. "I know you want to believe that, but—"

"It's not only what I want to believe. Frank practically threw it in my face. He's so incredibly arrogant that he has probably kept Centi prisoner all these years right in the mansion he purchased with Centi's fortune."

He shook his head and let go of her. Turning away, pacing, he rubbed his chest as if his heart hurt for her foolishness in clinging to the futile hope that Centi was not long dead. "Zoe, *cara,* why do you believe this? Frank Clemenza is a liar. A monster. He has kept us apart by the most vile lies for so long—why do you believe him now?"

She had no answer. None but that if Centi were alive, he would be the proof of Frank's inhuman crimes and there would be no need of the revenge Rafe promised. Revenge that would take him from her more surely than Frank's pitiless lies.

Slowly Rafe shook his head. "It is true that I am a hopeless romantic, Zoe," he said, powerful emotions leaking into the tremor in his voice, "but it is far better that I go to whatever grim fate awaits me without your forgiveness than that you and Stephi and Teddi die at the whim of Frank Clemenza."

"If you love me, then stay with me," she cried desperately, abandoning reason. "You find a way! You *find* a way, damn you!"

His throat convulsed. "There is no way, *amore mio,* but that Frank Clemenza die before he kills you."

Every part of her ached. Her heart, her eyes, her throat, her womb. He meant what he said, and he would act on his words to protect his family with his dying breath. She might pretend to hate him, never to find it in herself to forgive him, but he was unerringly the man she had married and would love to the end of time because of those things.

"Come to me, Zoe. *Ti amo.* Let me give your heart reason to find forgiveness before it is too late."

She went willingly to him, and he gathered her into his arms. He held her close and kissed her fiercely, then swept her into his embrace and carried her to the double bed covered in a rich quilt. Slowly, as if memorizing every part of her, every small blemish, every feminine curve, he undressed her, and she undressed him.

His kisses deeper, his emotions never more committed to the act of making love to her, his arousal never more powerful, he spoke to her in a thousand ways the depth of his love. His hand swept over her breast to her belly, till he covered her and his fingers opened and caressed and stroked her to a frenzy of desire. He was poised above her. She reached for him and arched her hips and he drove his sex into her, thrusting them both beyond the mindless quest for union to the place where eternity seemed here and present and theirs.

Zoe wept, because Rafe's incredible passion rode higher than ever before on the crest of his certainty that they would likely never again be together in this way.

But though he would not be denied the only course he could take to save the lives of his beloved and their precious little girls, Rafe had never refused Zoe anything. In the silent, dark hours near dawn, he agreed to go with her. To see, in Frank Clemenza's absence, if he had this once told the truth.

To see if Vincenti Rosario was alive.

Chapter Seventeen

"Centi *is* alive."

In the early morning light, Zoe sat in her peignoir at the old-fashioned window seat.

Rafe turned in the bed and raised himself up on one elbow. "Did he say to you in so many words, 'Centi is alive'?"

"No." She stared out the window at the shadows of flowers cast on the ground by the lanterns. "Right after he said that the sight of me offends him, he said that my threats to reveal that Centi *is alive* bore him. Why wouldn't he say *was* alive?"

Rafe cleared his throat. "Zoe, it's putting too much faith in a few words to jump to the conclusion that he literally meant Centi is alive."

"I don't think so," she disagreed, frowning. "I think he meant to say exactly that. He was taunting me, Rafe. I know it. And I still think he is so incredibly arrogant that he has probably kept Centi prisoner right in the mansion that he purchased with Centi's fortune."

Rafe could not dispute the level of Frank Clemenza's egotism, but to keep Centi under his own roof?

"It fits. Frank could see to Centi's every need and still be totally in control. Think of it. Frank inherited at least sixty million dollars on the presumption that Centi was killed in that explosion.''

"And a legal decree, which is not handed out like a flier on a street corner,'' he reminded her.

Zoe got up and began to pace the bedroom, growing more convinced that she was right.

"Rafe, if Centi is alive, Frank cannot afford the slightest possibility that someone, somewhere, would recognize him, or that Centi might actually manage to convince some caretaker that he is Bishop Vincenti Rosario.''

Rafe drew a deep breath. "You may be right, Zoe. But if I were in Frank's place, I would have stuck Centi on some property in Timbuktu where his caretakers couldn't even speak his language.''

She would not be dissuaded. "Frank is in Cleveland tonight and for most of tomorrow. I'm going to his house to find out. Will you come with me or not?''

He agreed after several more moments of discussing the issue. Not, Zoe thought, because he necessarily believed that Centi was alive, but in anticipation that he would soon have to leave her to make sure Clemenza did not survive long enough to exact his final revenge.

THE HOUSE IN WHICH FRANK lived owed its grandeur as much to the sweeping expanse of the landscaping in front and the private beach on Lake Michigan at the back as to the architecture. The drive itself was a full half mile long, and the trees arching over it were in full fall color.

Autumn leaves. This would be the autumn of Stephi's recovery, and the season would be still more established in Zoe's heart.

Rafe parked the rented Taurus. Too pent-up to wait, Zoe got out on her own, climbed the brick steps to the entry and rang the door chimes.

The housekeeper answered almost immediately, but the moment she recognized Zoe a look of wariness took hold in her eyes.

"Maisie, may we come in?" Zoe asked. "It's very important."

The woman stiffened and folded her arms. "No. Not while the Mister is not here. I don't want any trouble."

"I know. I promise you, we don't want any trouble, either."

"Then what do you want?"

"To look around, Maisie," Rafe said, and introduced himself. He offered her his hand. Haltingly she took it. He held her hand in both of his and forced her eye contact. "I think you know why."

Zoe shot Rafe a startled glance. Did he expect the housekeeper to admit straight out that Centi was alive? That he had been kept prisoner in this mausoleum of a house?

"I've got no idea what you're talking about."

"Your houseguest, Maisie," Rafe answered. "We would like to speak with Bishop Rosario."

"Rosario? A bishop...?" She blinked oddly, then stared at Rafe. "Of the church?"

"Yes. Rosario," Zoe repeated. "A bishop of the church."

"There is no one here like that."

"Then like what?" Rafe asked, his voice low, but she refused to answer. He switched tactics. "Maisie, listen to me. I know what it is like to live in the fear of Mr. Clemenza. I'm sure he hired you because you can keep your mouth shut. But if Bishop Rosario is alive and in this house, and if he is here against his will, you could go to jail just because you knew about it."

She swallowed and her hands fluttered in anxiety before she folded them together. She managed not to look into the eyes of either Rafe or Zoe. "There's a man here. One of the poor creatures, great and small, as the Mister says, that he takes care of. Like . . . the fish," she finished weakly. "Mister keeps an aquarium."

Like the fish? Zoe went very still inside. *One of the poor creatures?* Frank was depraved. It must be true. Centi was here. Alive.

It had been one thing to suspect that Centi was alive. To believe that Frank could have held him captive here, hidden away from the world. It was another thing altogether to be staring into the stubborn face of a woman who had doubtlessly served Centi's meals day in and day out for all these years without ever knowing who it was she was caring for.

"I want to see him. Now," she said, shoving past the housekeeper. "Where is he?"

Maisie stepped back. Rafe followed and shut the door behind him. The housekeeper said nothing.

"We'll find him, Maisie," Rafe said gently. "It would be simpler if you told us where."

She swallowed. "Up the stairs. All the way up. You hear me," she added. "All I ever did was what I was told."

But Zoe had already turned on her heel and begun running up the steps of the broad, winding staircase, its cherrywood handrail decorated in brass and marble. Rafe followed. She began throwing open doors along the length of the second-story hallway, but Rafe found the staircase leading up to the third floor behind a door at the end of the hall.

"Zoe, here."

She stepped back, closed the door and walked to the end of the hall. Behind him she saw a straight, narrow staircase leading up.

She felt suddenly afraid of what they might find. "I can't believe he is really up there." She had argued the possibility, but the stark reality of it dazed her. "Rafe, this is too awful. What if he's bedridden or crippled or suffering—"

"Then he needs our help all the more, *cara.*"

"This is too easy. Frank would not be so careless. Why wouldn't he have guards on Centi? Or at least at the door? Someone more formidable than an old housekeeper. Maybe we should call the police, or an ambulance—"

He caught her around the shoulders and touched a finger to her lips. "I took the precaution of making sure that Frank is in fact in Cleveland." Rafe touched her hair, stroked her cheek, looked into her eyes. He had thought of those things as well. His survival skills were so well honed he could have predicted the trap. "His pilot is registered at the hotel and has checked in, and Frank has checked into his usual suite. Let's just see first. If Centi is here, we'll have reason to call the police."

Her lips trembled. She pursed them tight and nodded, then took a deep breath and started up the dark stairs. A narrow strip of daylight shone beneath the door. At the landing she knocked softly. There was no response. She turned to Rafe.

"Open the door, Zoe."

She turned back and opened the door a crack. "Centi?" she called softly, but still there was no answer. Just past the door she saw the arm of an easy chair. "Centi?"

Impatient with herself, Zoe tossed her head and went through the door. Standing, bent with age, leaning on a cane, staring out the window, was Centi, still unaware of their presence.

"Centi."

Dressed simply in black slacks and a white shirt, he turned. His hair was snow-white, full and perfectly barbered, his eyes fiercely dark and bright in the pallor of his face.

He seemed not to recognize her. She took one step and then another and crossed the room that she thought in the back of her mind was a prison cell of exceptional caliber.

The floor was maple hardwood, covered in part by a Persian carpet. The ceiling rose to twenty feet, and the walls were lined with built-in bookshelves filled with a collector's appreciation. A large bed and treadmill dominated the far end of the forty-foot room.

"Centi, it's Zoe... and Rafe."

The morning sunlight poured in behind him, and Centi bowed his head. When he gathered the strength to look up again, his dark eyes were bright with tears. He breathed deeply and shuddered. "Zoe. And Rafe."

She smiled through tears of her own. "Yes, Centi. Zoe and Rafe. Are you well? Are you okay?"

He gave a sharp sigh and bowed his head again. "I think, now that you have come, I shall be fine. But I wish a hug, if you please."

She closed the remaining few feet between them and went into Centi's arms. Even though bent with his advanced age, he was still a head taller than she. His cane fell to the floor as he closed his arms around her, and he let his chin rest on her head. He spoke softly in Italian, words that sounded to Zoe like a blessing.

He felt stronger in her arms than his appearance would suggest, and when he released her and summoned Rafe, he managed without the cane. The two of them exchanged a hug as well.

"Come. Let us sit awhile and talk." Rafe retrieved Centi's cane, and he headed slowly toward the easy chair. Zoe moved the only other chair in the room over the carpet and placed it facing Centi. Rafe sat cross-legged on the floor beside her.

Centi's eyes feasted on them both. "It is more than these old eyes can bear to see you both. I have no visitors, you know." A sad smile collided with his overpowering emotions.

A smile that unsettled her. "Centi, come away from here with us. If you can't manage the stairs, Rafe could carry you, I'm sure. And—"

He held up his hand. "I have been content, Zoe. Truly, I cannot imagine spending my days and nights anywhere else now."

"But you've been a prisoner here, Centi! It is lovely, but it is a prison. Did Frank keep you drugged? Somehow sedated so you could not pick up a telephone—"

"For a little while," he answered. "A month, maybe two. No more than that." By his tone, he seemed to be defending Frank.

"How could that be? Are you saying that he had no need of sedatives after he brought you to this place?"

"Yes. Precisely that. This is the prison of my own choosing," he answered gently.

She didn't believe him. "Maybe it feels familiar now, like an old shoe, you know, but surely you—"

"I swear to you, child, that it is so."

"Centi, no—" she began, but Rafe interrupted her.

"Centi," he said, "I understand. The same could be said of my exile in Vallazione. I chose to stay, as you have chosen to stay here. Tell me if there is a difference."

Centi's chin began to quiver.

Rafe pressed his point. "A choice such as you and I have made is no choice at all if there is only the alternative of your loved ones suffering or dying."

Centi turned his head to the window and stared out at the expanse of lawn backed by the still larger blue expanse of Lake Michigan. It seemed to calm his nerves.

"I see that there is much we need to discuss. Perhaps, *cara* Zoe, you would pick up the telephone by my bed and have Maisie prepare us a tray of fruit and pastries. Perhaps a cup of cappuccino."

"Of course, Centi." She rose from the chair and did as he had bid her. The telephone was not for outside calls, but rang only, she supposed, within Maisie's hearing. She picked up the phone on the third ring, and agreed to prepare the tray.

When Zoe took her place again beside Rafe, Centi smiled in the deeply spiritual way that she had remembered from long ago.

"Help me to understand. What happened to you, Centi?" she asked. "How did this all happen to you? To us?"

He stared into her eyes for a terribly long time, then closed his own. "I made so many grievous errors in my life that it is difficult to think where to start."

She felt a frisson of apprehension prowl up her spine. "Centi, this is not about anything you have done. Frank is the one who orchestrated this horrible charade. Frank is the one who—"

Again he held up a hand to silence her. "We are speaking now of my transgressions, which are many. To live out my days in a place no better than a fancy cage is little enough penance."

"I'm sorry, Centi," she protested fiercely, "but we are talking about far more than your transgressions, whatever they might have been. What did my babies ever do to deserve what happened to them? What did Rafe or I ever do that Frank should destroy our lives? What did you ever do that this," she gestured to include the length and breadth of the attic room "—is too little penance?"

Centi's expression hardened, and he spoke as if recounting his sins in the confessional. "For thirty years I used the wealth I had inherited to control Frank. I became a priest, and in an indecently short time, a bishop. I betrayed my vows over and over again in many ways. Never taking a stand, never completely committing, never strong enough to choose between my vocation in God and whatever else I wanted."

"By that fateful day aboard the *Persephone,*" he went on, "the repercussions of my lifelong offenses had become clear to me, and I was considering the ways I could begin to mend them. I confided in Frank my intention to alter my will."

Centi paused and closed his eyes again, as if to go on required more energy than he had left in him.

Rafe drew the conclusion. "In order not to lose what he must have considered is rightful inheritance, Frank made his move. He would make it appear that you died in the explosion. Zoe and I assumed that in Frank's mind, our deaths would only make the explosion more credible as an accident. More tragic."

The old man sighed heavily. "If only it were that simple."

"What does that mean, Centi?" Zoe cried softly.

But he only gave a bittersweet smile and fell into reminiscences. "I remember I had taken your precious little Teddi below, to my stateroom...." He trailed off as if trying to recapture fading memories, and just then the sound of a dumbwaiter whooshed nearby and a bell rang.

"That will be our small repast," Centi said. "The door—do you see it there, Zoe, in the bookcase?"

She spotted the dumbwaiter door concealed in the woodwork. Retrieving the tray, she exchanged glances with Rafe, thinking that perhaps Centi's recollections may not be a digression, but a beginning to the answer to her question.

"I remember," Rafe encouraged him after they had each taken a small plate of pastries and fruit and poured the cappuccino. "Zoe had objected, but you were determined that Teddi be allowed to play with your small Bible. 'Suffer the little children, Zoe,' you said.''

Centi blinked and nodded, smiling tenderly. "Yes. Teddi put my rosary around her neck." He frowned. "The next thing was that I was overpowered...there, in my stateroom, by the captain of the yacht. Raymond? No. Raoul...I suppose I was tossed aboard the seaplane that Frank had ordered out of Catania. I was transported by private jet back to the United States."

"Then there must have been someone who saw you alive, who knew you hadn't died in the explosion," Zoe said.

"Truly, I do not know how Frank managed to keep secret that I had not died in the explosion. All I know is that he was successful."

Zoe bit her lip in concentration. "Centi, I can accept that Frank felt threatened by what you said to him that morning. I can even buy that he would sacrifice us to make the whole scheme work. What I can't see is why he forced Rafe into the decision to let me believe that he and Teddi had died."

"There is a flaw in your reasoning, Zoe. But to keep you separated was paramount to the success of his plan," Centi said simply. "He knew that you, Raphael, had certain memories of my Bible. He feared those memories most of all, and he knew that an enforced separation from Zoe and Stephi would distract you for a very long time from the truth."

Zoe began to sense that in all their speculation, she and Rafe had not begun to plumb the depths and complexity of Frank's motivations.

"Centi, it would have been so simple to let Rafe die in that hospital—or even to inject some fatal drug into his IVs. Why would Frank let Rafe live, even under another identity, if he feared whatever secret was locked in Rafe's memories?''

Centi finished a morsel of fruit, and his hand wavered near his eyes. Zoe knew that he was tiring.

"Listen closely. I could have escaped this incarceration, I am certain. I could have thrown myself out the window, or attracted the attention of a gardener or appealed to Maisie. I am not an inarticulate man, and I understand the human heart. Maisie could not have refused to help me to escape had I put my mind to convincing her.

"I knew this to be true," he concluded, "that with patience and timing, I could have made good an escape. Frank understood it as well. So I was able to say to him, 'Spare the lives of Zoe and Raphael and their small daughters, and I will promise never to attempt an escape or to reveal my identity, even so much as to Maisie.' It is because of this agreement between us that you are alive today."

"Except, my dear cousin," came the voice of Frank Clemenza from the doorway, "that *Zoe and Raphael and their small daughters* are not precisely the words you used."

Centi raised his head. Rafe shot up from the floor like lightning. Zoe's flesh crawled with goose bumps. Frank came out of the shadow of the landing, and in his hand was a wicked-looking gun, fitted with a silencer, pointed more or less at her.

"I will kill you," Rafe uttered, his voice filled with deadly, unspent rage, his hands curled into fists.

"You aren't capable of it," Frank spat contemptuously. "Now, sit down before our most beloved Zoe takes a bullet in the gut." He came closer and waited until Rafe had complied under the threat.

"You are fool enough to walk in here and reassure your lovely misbegotten bitch of a wife that I had indeed gone to Cleveland," he continued. He snorted and sat on the back of Centi's easy chair, the gun aimed always at Zoe. "In fact, I had simply to bait the trap with the suggestion that my esteemed cousin was yet alive, send a double in my place to Cleveland and wait for you to come looking. Too easy, indeed."

Rafe said nothing, though none of them could miss the fierce, murderous rage roiling in him. Zoe stared at him. "You can't hope to get away with this, Frank."

"Don't bore me with your ignorant warnings, Zoe," he answered. "Should all else fail, you will die, and I will retire to a life of wealth and ease in Rio de Janeiro and take Maisie along with me. You will notice there is not even one of my trusted bodyguards on the premises. If Cavallo can be fooled by the likes of you, what hope is there, really? *Chi gioca solo gioca bene.* I play alone, now, for keeps and to win."

His hate-filled gaze shifted to Centi. "Please, Centi, continue. I am curious to see how much more you can tell before the truth is at last revealed. It is owed, I think, before you all die."

Zoe felt cold to her marrow. Centi looked deathly pale, and Rafe murderously flushed. "What is he talking about, Centi?"

"Yes, what are we talking about?" Frank echoed. "Return to the flaw in little Zoe's reasoning, why don't you?"

Centi bowed his head a moment, then drew a deep, resigned breath and met her gaze. "Your assumption that your deaths would merely lend authenticity to the accident is correct only so far as it goes. I would often speak to Frank of decisions I had already taken as if I were consulting him. So, when I told him that I had decided to alter my will, he assumed that I had already done so. I had not. Which meant that you did not have to die."

"Centi, please," Zoe begged. "What are you talking about?"

He left off telling the story, glanced at Frank, then turned back. "You were to be my heirs."

She felt suddenly very threatened and her stomach lurched sickeningly. She reached for Rafe's shoulder to steady her. "Why, Centi? Why would you name us your heirs?"

"Tell her, old man," Frank commanded. "You will die this time, but not before you have confronted your nasty little secret. *Tell her why!*"

Centi looked at his liver-spotted hands. "Because *bellissima mia*. Zoe. You are my daughter."

Zoe shook her head, though the truth of it jangled in her head. "That's not possible."

"Oh, but it is." Frank sneered. "You see, the deal Centi posed to me was to spare the life not 'of Zoe and her children,' but the lives of his daughter and grandchildren." Frank waited for that to sink in. "If you have not yet hidden the Bible away, Zoe, now would be an appropriate time to return it to Centi."

Numbed beyond thinking independently of Frank's hard-edged suggestion, Zoe reached for her purse and brought out Centi's tissue-wrapped treasures. She handed the old man the tiny, damaged Bible wrapped in his rosary beads.

He stared at them for a moment as if he had thought never to see them again. His fingers shook. He plucked at the pages inside, separating them carelessly until he came to the one he searched for.

He gave the small Bible back to Zoe, open to that page. There he had written Zoe's name after his, and Teddi's and Stephi's below that. The ink had run, but not so much that his account of the generations was not perfectly clear.

The book fell from her hands. Rafe picked it up and stared at the spidery, handwritten acknowledgement of Centi's daughter and her daughters. This was what Frank had feared. Proof enough to contest his inheritance of Centi's fortune, even after Frank knew the will had not been changed.

"Your mother, Zoe," Frank taunted, "was little more than a whore, perhaps worse, and you are the illegitimate, misbegotten spawn of a philandering bishop."

"Shut your filthy mouth, Frank," Rafe snarled, the violence in his voice cracking Frank's composure, though he was the one with the gun.

Zoe's eyes filled with tears and her throat swelled. There were a hundred questions hurtling through her mind, and as many accusations, but she could get none of them past her throat.

Centi's eyes glimmered as well. "Your aunt Mary Bernadette and I once traveled together to an international hospital administration conference. We spent hours speaking of her favorite preoccupation—the road not taken, the twists and turns our lives take. I never suspected I was nearly at such a fork in my own path.

"After the conference I went away with a woman I had met there. It simply happened—apart from everything else I had ever done or been or dreamed." Centi's eyes focused away from everything in the room, back into the mists of his memory, and a light shone in his face. "I had broken my vow of celibacy, but I felt blessed by my acts of love with this woman."

Zoe remembered, suddenly, how on the yacht Frank had said to her, *see how he watches you and Rafe together... you have made him remember again the sacrifices he has made in his life.*

Centi drew a deep breath. "We left that small hotel in the Berkshires never expecting to see each other again, but we were wrong. We had conceived a child."

Centi lifted his chin. His head trembled in emotion. "A time, a moment of transformation waited upon me, but I believed I was too important, too essential to my vocation. I was called to be more than I had been, to be a husband and father to the child I had planted in her."

He stared at Zoe. His eyes filled with tears and his chin quivered. She felt suddenly afraid to listen to him anymore, but she was frozen. Her hand closed tightly on Rafe's shoulder.

"I was afraid," Centi said, wiping away tears that flowed into the corners of his mouth. "When the time came to step forth and acknowledge that I had been with this woman whose soul was tied in eternity to mine, I denied her. Ever after, she denied me. I knew that in my lifetime I would never look into my child's face and be recognized or loved as a father. The woman, Zoe, was your dear mother."

A maelstrom of emotions took hold inside her. Centi . . . beloved Centi was her father? But the wonder clashed horribly with the loss, the anguish, the absence of a father in her life. And everything her tiny children had suffered stemmed from this—the rejection and lies of Bishop Vincenti Rosario and his eleventh-hour attempt to put it all to rights by bequeathing his great fortune to her.

She swiped the tears from her cheeks with the back of her hand. She had loved him so long it seemed impossible that she could so despise him in the space of a heartbeat. "I never understood why I had no father. I never understood why my mother couldn't smile. But she must finally have died of a broken heart, and you have caused me and my children untold heartache."

Her words rained down on Centi's head like hailstones, but she couldn't stop. Centi bore her recriminations as one who had grown skilled at recognizing the depth of his own human failings.

"I would never have taken your inheritance," she went stonily on. "You might as well have given it to Frank straight out. He, at least, cares about your...your money." Her voice made even the word a vile thing.

"Well, well, well. Maybe there is still some accommodation we can reach," Frank suggested. But before the words were fully out of his mouth, Rafe lunged at him, roaring his anger, taking him wholly off guard.

"Accommodation!" He belted the gun from Frank's hand and jerked him hard from the back of Centi's chair, throwing him up against the bookcase by his throat. "You bastard! You stole *years* of our lives, and you dare speak of *accommodation?*"

"Yes!" Frank's face contorted with hatred and raw fear as Rafe's fist choked his windpipe. "You make me sick, you sanctimonious, ingrate cretin! I spared your miserable lives."

"You spared yourself the fear of your immortal soul burning to ashes in hell." Still holding Frank by the throat he pulled back and slammed him against the bookcase again. "I'll give you *accommodation,* Frank. Choose how you are to die, and then make your peace with your Maker."

"Rafe, stop it!" Zoe cried, springing from her chair.

"Stay out of this, Zoe," he warned her, renewing his choke hold on Frank.

"No! I will not stay out of this. We have a chance now! If you kill him, everything is lost!"

Rafe stared into the frenzied face of the bastard he had sworn a thousand times to kill. Pure, unadulterated rage filled him and adrenaline poured into his blood at a fearsome rate.

The toll of Frank Clemenza's corruptions could never be counted. He had stolen more than years from them all. He had stolen Stephi's health, Teddi's mother, Zoe's ability to trust Rafe and Rafe's own pittance of faith in humanity.

But Zoe was right. To kill him would cost Rafe more than Frank had already exacted. But there was no power on earth, not even Zoe's threat, that could make him let Clemenza go without a single scratch.

Rafe jerked the miserable man forward again, turned and landed a punch at Frank's gut that was packed with all his rage. Frank sprawled, doubled over and shrieking, to the floor, but Rafe bent to grab him up again and deliver more killing blows.

"Rafe, you stupid macho idiot!" Zoe cried out. "Please. *Please* stop. Centi is alive. The police will come now. They'll see the fraud of his death and the money Frank stole...." She stopped and took a deep breath. "Please," she begged. "Don't kill him. Stay with me. Stay with *us*."

Rafe stood over Clemenza, his fists still clenched, breathing hard to rid himself of the terrible, murderous energy. He wanted Clemenza to get up, to have an excuse to deck him once more, but that wasn't going to happen. But now, hearing Zoe's reasoning, he knew that what had seemed utterly impossible, that there was another way, was true. He saw that there was a chance. That Clemenza would be made to pay and put away in prison.

He turned to look at Zoe. He would have more chances to make love to her. They might have more babies. In time, Zoe might even reconcile the love he knew she felt for Centi with the fact that he was the father who had never acknowledged her existence.

But before he might indulge a single prayer that he had a future with her, with Stephi and Teddi, he must deliver Clemenza into the hands of real justice.

He gave a curt nod, turned from her and dragged Frank to his feet, then down the stairs to phone the police. Her heart thudding painfully, Zoe exchanged a long, agonized look with her father, and then followed Rafe down the stairs.

The police came in short order. The explanations went on for more than an hour. Rafe never let go of Zoe's hand once the officers arrived and took control of Frank Clemenza, who snarled imprecations and threats until his attorney arrived and advised him to shut the hell up.

After the police, with Clemenza in tow, had piled into their cars and turned off the flashing lights and driven in a caravan back out the half-mile drive, Rafe let go of Zoe's hand and walked a few steps from her.

He turned back to her, hands stuck in his pockets. "Zoe, *amore mio,*" he said in a low, menacing voice, his head cocked at the upstairs prison. "What was it you called me up there?"

Her precious pointed chin shot up and her hands went to her hips. "I said you are a stupid macho idiot."

"That's what I thought you said." He smiled, then looked down, and the smile faded because his heart was filled to overflowing with emotions more complex, more powerful, more consuming, than *I love you* or *ti amo* could possibly express.

"Zoe, my heart, if I promise to give up the stupid idiot part, would it be all right with you if I kept the rest?"

"Raphael, my love," she said with tears welling in her eyes, "macho does not come without the stupid idiot part. I am afraid that you must keep it all."

He gave her the slow, intimate blink that inevitably made her pulse skitter.

She smiled through her tears. "Somehow, I promise you, I will endure it."

Epilogue

On the twenty-third of September in the following year, on the seventh anniversary of his parents' marriage, Andrew Rosario Mastrangelo was baptized in the Sacred Heart Sanctuary in the midst of Rose Memorial Medical Center.

His grandfather Vincenti, due to his advanced age, his record of service and years of suffering, had been allowed to quietly retire. This day he was given special dispensation to perform the baptismal sacrament for Andrew.

Many people were there who knew how precious and unlikely a child this was, whose parents had once thought they would never see each other again. People such as his great-aunt Mary Bernadette, and his grandmother Teresa Vitale Mastrangelo De Sica and her husband, Don Giancarlo.

There were people there who knew his adoring older sisters, who knew how desperately sick Stephi had been, who had taken care of her and knew how supremely healthy she was now thanks to his other sister Teddi. People like Emma Harding and Joel Sebern and Peter Lewiston.

And then there was Turi Difalco, whose wife Grazielle and their seven children occupied one entire pew of the Sacred Heart Sanctuary. Turi stood as Andrew's godfather.

Frank Clemenza, however, was not at the baptismal ceremony. He was doing time in a maximum security prison—and "time" was to be the rest of his natural life—for fraud, intent to defraud, conspiracy, murder, first-degree attempted murder, first-degree assault. . . .

Centi finished the blessing and handed Andrew back to his father. Zoe kissed her own father's cheek and thanked him. The three of them walked out of the sanctuary together.

"Centi, have you decided to come live with us," Zoe asked, "now that the house is nearly completed? We have saved the attic especially for you."

Centi stopped and turned to pinch her cheek, but he could not keep the smile from his voice or his eyes. "How do you tolerate this woman's wicked tongue, Raphael?"

Looking lady-killer macho and devastatingly handsome in his black morning tuxedo, Rafe looked into Zoe's eyes. "Very well, Centi. Very well indeed."

MILLION DOLLAR SWEEPSTAKES (III)

No purchase necessary. To enter, follow the directions published. Method of entry may vary. For eligibility, entries must be received no later than March 31, 1996. No liability is assumed for printing errors, lost, late or misdirected entries. Odds of winning are determined by the number of eligible entries distributed and received. Prizewinners will be determined no later than June 30, 1996.

Sweepstakes open to residents of the U.S. (except Puerto Rico), Canada, Europe and Taiwan who are 18 years of age or older. All applicable laws and regulations apply. Sweepstakes offer void wherever prohibited by law. Values of all prizes are in U.S. currency. This sweepstakes is presented by Torstar Corp., its subsidiaries and affiliates, in conjunction with book, merchandise and/or product offerings. For a copy of the Official Rules send a self-addressed, stamped envelope (WA residents need not affix return postage) to: MILLION DOLLAR SWEEPSTAKES (III) Rules, P.O. Box 4573, Blair, NE 68009, USA.

EXTRA BONUS PRIZE DRAWING

No purchase necessary. The Extra Bonus Prize will be awarded in a random drawing to be conducted no later than 5/30/96 from among all entries received. To qualify, entries must be received by 3/31/96 and comply with published directions. Drawing open to residents of the U.S. (except Puerto Rico), Canada, Europe and Taiwan who are 18 years of age or older. All applicable laws and regulations apply; offer void wherever prohibited by law. Odds of winning are dependent upon number of eligible entries received. Prize is valued in U.S. currency. The offer is presented by Torstar Corp., its subsidiaries and affiliates in conjunction with book, merchandise and/or product offering. For a copy of the Official Rules governing this sweepstakes, send a self-addressed, stamped envelope (WA residents need not affix return postage) to: Extra Bonus Prize Drawing Rules, P.O. Box 4590, Blair, NE 68009, USA.

SWP-H395

Into a world where danger lurks around
every corner, and there's a fine line between trust
and betrayal, comes a tall, dark and handsome man.

Intuition draws you to him...but instinct keeps you
away. Is he really one of those...

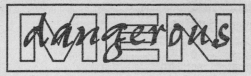

Don't miss even one of the twelve sexy but secretive
men, coming to you one per month in 1995.

In May, look for
#321 TRUST WITH YOUR LIFE
by M.L. Gamble

**Take a walk on the wild side...with our
"DANGEROUS MEN"!**

HARLEQUIN®
INTRIGUE®

**HARLEQUIN INTRIGUE AUTHOR KELSEY ROBERTS
SERVES UP A DOUBLE DOSE OF DANGER AND DESIRE
IN THE EXCITING NEW MINISERIES:**

THE ROSE TATTOO

At the Rose Tattoo, Southern Specialties are served with a
Side Order of Suspense:

On the Menu for June

Dylan Tanner—tall, dark and delectable
Shelby Hunnicott—sweet and sassy
Sizzling Suspense—saucy red herrings with a twist

On the Menu for July

J. D. Porter—hot and spicy
Tory Conway—sinfully rich
Southern Fried Secrets—succulent and juicy

On the Menu for August

Wes Porter—subtly scrumptious
Destiny Talbott—tart and tangy
Mouth-Watering Mystery—deceptively delicious

Look for Harlequin Intrigue's response to your
hearty appetite for suspense: THE ROSE TATTOO,
coming in June, July and August.

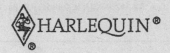

HARLEQUIN®

Don't miss these Harlequin favorites by some of our most
distinguished authors!
And now, you can receive a discount by ordering two or more titles!

HT #25607	PLAIN JANE'S MAN by Kristine Rolofson	$2.99 U.S./$3.50 CAN. ☐
HT #25616	THE BOUNTY HUNTER by Vicki Lewis Thompson	$2.99 U.S./$3.50 CAN. ☐
HP #11674	THE CRUELLEST LIE by Susan Napier	$2.99 U.S./$3.50 CAN. ☐
HP #11699	ISLAND ENCHANTMENT by Robyn Donald	$2.99 U.S./$3.50 CAN. ☐
HR #03268	THE BAD PENNY by Susan Fox	$2.99 ☐
HR #03303	BABY MAKES THREE by Emma Goldrick	$2.99 ☐
HS #70570	REUNITED by Evelyn A. Crowe	$3.50 ☐
HS #70611	ALESSANDRA & THE ARCHANGEL by Judith Arnold	$3.50 U.S./$3.99 CAN. ☐
HI #22291	CRIMSON NIGHTMARE by Patricia Rosemoor	$2.99 U.S./$3.50 CAN. ☐
HAR #16549	THE WEDDING GAMBLE by Muriel Jensen	$3.50 U.S./$3.99 CAN. ☐
HAR #16558	QUINN'S WAY by Rebecca Flanders	$3.50 U.S./$3.99 CAN. ☐
HH #28802	COUNTERFEIT LAIRD by Erin Yorke	$3.99 ☐
HH #28824	A WARRIOR'S WAY by Margaret Moore	$3.99 U.S./$4.50 CAN. ☐

(limited quantities available on certain titles)

	AMOUNT	$
DEDUCT:	**10% DISCOUNT FOR 2+ BOOKS**	$
ADD:	**POSTAGE & HANDLING**	$
	($1.00 for one book, 50¢ for each additional)	
	APPLICABLE TAXES*	$_____
	TOTAL PAYABLE	$_____
	(check or money order—please do not send cash)	

To order, complete this form and send it, along with a check or money order for the
total above, payable to Harlequin Books, to: **In the U.S.:** 3010 Walden Avenue,
P.O. Box 9047, Buffalo, NY 14269-9047; **In Canada:** P.O. Box 613, Fort Erie, Ontario,
L2A 5X3.

Name: _____

Address: _____ City: _____

State/Prov.: _____ Zip/Postal Code: _____

*New York residents remit applicable sales taxes.
Canadian residents remit applicable GST and provincial taxes.

HBACK-AJ2